Hell's Dodo

Hell's Dodo

Waves of Darkness

Book 5

Tamara A. Lowery

Steele Rose Publishing

Hell's Dodo

By

Tamara A. Lowery

Table of Contents

In Memoriam

Charles Edward "Charlie" Bland

1966-2015

Beloved Cousin and the "little brother" my husband never had. You will always be in our hearts and enjoy a permanent spot on Viktor's crew. Fair seas, Mr. Bland

Acknowledgments

I would like to thank Kenneth Sutton for allowing me to use his name in a semi red shirting, actually more of a Tuckerization, since I don't kill him in this book. He was one of the runners up in the red shirt contest I ran during Chattacon in 2014. His name has been applied to an unfortunate pirate who has a close call with death.

I would also like to thank one of my coworkers, Wesley Taylor, for allowing me to red shirt him. He kept pestering me good-naturedly to put him in one of my books. [insert evil maniacal laughter here] He has now learned to be careful what he wishes for to the point my original publisher and editor had me cut most of the scene. It has been fully restored for this 2nd edition.

$\mathcal{A}$uthor's Forward and Warning

Each book in the Waves of Darkness series has contained a prologue section titled "Once Upon a Tide...." The purpose of this is to impart backstory about the primary character and/or some of the secondary characters and to set up some of the dynamics of their relationships and interactions. I try to make sure some element in the main story ties in with the prologue, even if I put it at the tail end of the story, as I did in Blood Curse (book 1).

Because of an idea suggested by one of my favorite BookTubers, Petrik Leo, I started including synopses of the previous books in the series at the end of each book to help readers refresh their memories of the story so far. I titled this segment "Here Be Spoilers." I started doing this in book 3, Silent Fathoms. I also wish to let readers who keep up with such things know that the official word count of Hell's Dodo minus all the fore and after matter is 76,727.

My warning is to those of you, my readers, who may have trigger issues concerning domestic violence. If you have been following the series from the beginning, you know that I am unafraid to tackle unsavory subjects. I do not endorse ANY violence, domestic or otherwise, but I do not deny its existence, either. Sometimes, to make a character believable, an author has to place them in stressful, dangerous, and unpleasant situations. I do not write this series for children and innocents.

Please keep in mind that my pirates are not nice people. Vampires are serial killers by definition.

That being said, if you do have trigger issues with domestic violence, I advise you to skip the prologue of this book. It contains an incident from one of the character's childhood that is heartbreaking.

Thank you for reading.

Once Upon a Tide...

"You whore!"

The words struck the woman almost as forcefully as her husband's open palm. She stumbled to the floor from the blow, stunned more by the accusation.

"I have been nothing but faithful to you, Nolan. How can you call me that?" she protested.

He raised his hand again, causing her to wince. The two young boys cowering in the corner ran to their mother. The younger one buried his face in her shoulder. The older one hugged her from the other side, glaring up at his father.

"You're a liar and a harlot," Nolan spat at her. "I've seen how that rogue, Tucker, comes sniffing around here when I'm off on my business. I have more eyes than just the two in my head, Beulah, and I'm no fool."

Her own temper flared. "I never said you were, Nolan; but you are acting like one if you think I'd ever have anything to do with that low creature. The way he looks at me makes my skin crawl."

He backhanded her, splitting her lip. "A pretty lie, that. I confronted the bastard. Not only did he admit having you, he told me how you've been bedding men from the docks for years."

"That's not true! Mr. Tucker is a liar! He should never have said those things about Mama!" the older boy yelled.

Nolan jabbed a warning finger at his son. "Shut it, Britt. Get away from that whore and get your things. Now, boy!"

"You can't take my sons!" Beulah cried.

The scorn and hatred on his face made her flinch. "I am only taking my son, slut. You can keep your little bastard there." He pointed his chin at the younger boy. "I know Britt's mine. You were at least virgin when we wed. As for that one, how do I know he's mine or not? He could be anyone's."

"You are Jimmy's father, Nolan. I swear I have never been with another man. I don't know what evil has poisoned you against me, but please don't take it out on the children." Her voice shook with emotion.

"Be silent!" He struck her again, this time hard enough to knock her against the wall. Her head caught the corner of a shelf, and she crumpled like a rag doll, blood pouring from her scalp.

Both boys screamed for their mother.

Nolan reached down and grasped Britt by the arm, yanking him away from his mother and brother. When Jimmy reached for Britt, their father shoved him back. He stumbled and landed on his mother, who didn't respond.

Within the hour, father and eldest son were packed and out of the modest house.

Two days later, Joseph Tucker came to call on Beulah Westin. He knew that Nolan was gone, probably for good this time, and he prepared to play the part of comforter to the heartbroken woman. He knew his lies drove her husband away, but he had a fresh set of lies to feed her which should convince her of his innocence in the matter.

When she didn't answer the door, he eased it open and went in. "Mrs. Westin?"

He got no response. A foul odor filled the house, and he heard a whimper from the next room. What he saw when he entered sickened him.

Beulah lay on the floor, a congealed, blackened puddle of blood around her head, swollen and blown by flies. Her younger son, Jimmy, sat next to her, swatting at the flies.

The child looked pale and gaunt, almost on the verge of collapsing. Tucker must have made some noise. The boy looked up with lost and haunted eyes.

"Mr. Tucker? Can you help? Mama won't get up. I think she's sick. I'm hungry."

"Dear God, what have I done?" he thought.

"Mr. Tucker?" the boy asked again.

The only answer he got was the sight of the man running from the room to retch.

Chapter 1

Belladonna paused as she passed Mr. Grimm's cabin. The sound of retching caught her attention as she made her way toward the weather deck; not a customary sound to emanate from the first mate's cabin.

A short time later, Brianna Belmont emerged carrying a full chamber pot and looking a little green around the gills. She stopped short when she noticed the siren standing there.

"Oh, *bonjour*."

"From the look on your face, I would say it is not such a good day," Belle commented.

Brianna shook her head. "*Non,* this *mal de mer* plagues me in the mornings now."

The siren sniffed the air around the woman; then she smiled wryly. "You are not seasick. You are pregnant. Does Mr. Grimm know?"

"Pregnant?" What looked like panic began to shine in her eyes. "How?"

"The usual way, I imagine; and I take it by your reaction that he does not know. You need to tell him. I would also suggest you pay a visit to Dr. Coffin, even though I don't think much of these human healers."

Tamara A. Lowery

Brianna seemed to still be in shock. She set the chamber pot down next to the bulkhead. When she straightened back up, her face grew pasty and her eyes went glassy the only warning the siren had that the woman was about to faint.

Belle just managed to catch her before she could collapse to the deck. It was one of those times she was grateful she wasn't human. Easily lifting the unconscious woman, she carried her back into the cabin and laid her on the bed.

As she made sure Brianna was comfortable, she reached out along the mental link she shared with the captain, Viktor Brandewyne. *"Captain, let Mr. Grimm know he needs to come check on his woman. Send Dr. Coffin down, as well."*

Hezekiah Grimm and Matthew Coffin arrived at about the same time. Belladonna wiped Brianna's face with a damp cloth. Before either man could ask any questions, the woman awoke and clutched the siren's wrist.

"Is the *bebe* all right?"

"Baby?" Grimm echoed, stunned.

Belle nodded. "Yes."

Grimm knelt beside the bed and took the rag from the siren. "I knew you hadn't been feeling well the past few mornings, Brie. I had no idea. I thought it was just the food not agreeing with you."

"That may be all it is, Mr. Grimm," the doctor said. "Nausea is not exclusive to pregnancy."

Hell's Dodo

Belle stood and leaned against the bulkhead. She knew the woman was pregnant, but she also knew Dr. Coffin was not about to take her word for it.

He proceeded to ask Brianna, "Do you remember when your last monthly course was?"

"Doctor!" Grimm protested such a personal and blunt question.

"It is a necessary question, Mr. Grimm, I assure you. Unless something is wrong with either mother or child, it is usual for her moon blood to cease until after delivery."

Brianna rested one hand on her belly and grasped Grimm's hand in her other. "It is so hard to keep track of time on this ship," she replied, "but I think it has been over a couple of months. I just didn't pay it much mind."

"Have you been craving unusual foods?"

"*Non*; lately the very thought of food sickens me."

"That will change before long," Belle spoke up. "They are going to be hungry."

"They?" Brianna questioned. Simultaneously, Grimm asked, "How many children is she carrying?"

Coffin protested, "We still don't know if she really is pregnant, Belladonna. The evidence is purely circumstantial."

The siren fixed him with an emotionless stare, making him back up a pace nervously. "Keep in mind, Dr. Coffin, that I am not human. I have senses you could barely comprehend. Her scent tells me she is pregnant. The human female body undergoes unmistakable changes to harbor new life."

"Very well," he ceded.

"Belle," Grimm drew her attention. "You said, 'they.' How many?"

"*Mademoiselle* Belmont is carrying twins, Mr. Grimm: one male, one female," she answered.

Brianna adapted quickly to the news. She seemed happy but also nervous and uncertain. "What magic did you use to divine that, *Mademoiselle* Belle?"

The siren smiled. "No magic. As a sea creature, I am able to use sound to 'see' things. There are small sensory organs at the corners of my eyes, too small for you to see, but much more sensitive than human ears. Just as I can scream at levels that can destroy a human mind, I can emit sounds too low or too high for a human to hear. Underwater, it allows me to locate prey by the echoes. In your case, it enables me to 'see' into your womb. There are two infants forming. The variation in your scent tells me you carry both male and female."

Coffin sounded intrigued. "So, it is a natural ability. You are a fascinating creature, my dear. Perhaps we can talk sometime about internal anatomy. I always thought I could be a better doctor if I could just understand better the inner workings of my patients."

"An interesting proposal, Doctor. I will think about it, but for now, I need to hunt." She dismissed herself.

Hell's Dodo

After giving general advice to avoid anything strenuous and to eschew restrictive garments, Dr. Coffin excused himself, as well.

Grimm sat and gazed silently at Brianna. He felt surprise at how much the news affected him. Lord knew he had countless bastards floating around out there. He'd had more women than he cared to count.

Somehow, things felt different this time. He truly cared for Brianna. If he were completely honest with himself, he believed he loved her; and now she bore his twin children.

The scrutiny became too much for her. "What is it, Hezekiah?"

"I need to get you off this ship."

She misunderstood his purpose. "Oh, so now that I am with child, you will just dump me in the first port we come to? I thought I meant something to you." Her tone carried hurt and anger. It caught him off guard.

"What? No! No, Brianna, I'm not trying to get rid of you. I would never put you off the ship in just any old port," he protested.

"Then what is it?"

"This isn't a good environment for you in your condition," he proceeded cautiously. He didn't want to upset her. "You need to be in a safe port, where you can have fresh food, good shelter during storms, and access to a midwife I would trust not to eat our children."

"Oh." He knew she understood that last statement was not a joke. She'd witnessed the siren taking a victim a couple of times. "What port did you have in mind?"

Grimm went in search of the captain. He would have to get the go ahead from Viktor for what he had in mind.

He found Captain Brandewyne in his cabin going over charts and old log books from captured prizes. This practice often provided a fair guide to predicting the best shipping lanes to haunt for fat prizes. The days of the Spanish treasure ships were long past, but there was still a thriving trade culture one could turn a decent profit on.

Vik looked up at Grimm's knock. "Come in, Hezekiah; everything well with your woman?"

"Yes and no. We're less than a week south of it; what say we put in at Savannah?"

The first mate now held his captain's undivided attention. His face made plain that he wondered why Grimm had the sudden urge to visit Viktor's home port. "You have a particular reason for wanting to go there? It can't be for supplies. We've plenty of stores aboard."

"Brianna is with child. I need to find a safe place for her. Savannah is a friendly port for both of us," he explained.

"I'll be honest. I'm surprised you've kept her around this long. Usually, you discard them wherever, once you've finished with them," Vik observed. "What is different about this one, Hezekiah? I seem to recall you were very slow to bed her after claiming her."

Grimm might've easily taken offense at his captain's comments had they not accurately described his usual behavior with women. He sighed and realized he needed to be honest with himself as well as with his captain.

"I love her. I don't know why. Maybe I'm getting old."

"Nonsense, man; you don't look a day over ninety," Vik joked. Grimm couldn't help but laugh.

"Thank ye," he smirked. "Seriously, though, I haven't had the urge to go wenching in port since I claimed her. I really don't want to put her ashore, where I can't watch over her, but it would be best for all concerned that I do."

Viktor nodded in agreement with his friend's judgment. "Aye, I see why you chose Savannah. It is a safe port for her." A sudden thought seemed to strike him, for he continued, "but not under the name of Belmont. Percival Worthing, that bastard who bought her as a 'bride,' does quite a bit of business there. Her surname would definitely draw his attention."

"Are you suggesting what I think, Vik?"

The vampire he called captain just looked at him.

"You are. I can see it in your face." He ran a hand through his hair, rubbing at his scalp. With a wry half-smile, he said, "I guess I did this to myself. We'll have to make sure the preacher keeps his mouth shut. She'll *want* a preacher, too."

"Aye, I imagine she will, Hezekiah; but aren't you forgetting something?"

"What?"

"You have to ask her first."

"Bugger."

"Aye." Vik laughed.

Chapter 2

Briana felt great relief at hearing Grimm's proposal. His willingness to share his name with her and their children gave her a sense of security she hadn't realized was missing. He really wasn't trying to get rid of her after using her. He was promising to come back for her and protect her.

When they got to Savannah, she had to settle for an Episcopalian minister. The port city seemed welcoming to just about every sect and denomination *except* Catholic. She thought it just as well. A priest probably would have made it a drawn out process with confession and penance for having carnal relations outside of wedlock. The fact that Hezekiah Grimm was not Catholic would have proven a blockade, as well; then there would have been the lack of parental blessing to contend with.

Looking at it from that perspective, she was glad that the wedding was simple, quick, and private.

For his part, Grimm didn't see fit to let her know how dangerous it would have been for her to keep her maiden name. He didn't want her to think that was the only reason he was marrying her.

As a wedding gift, he gave her a gold necklace set with five emeralds. The largest stone, set in the center, was as large as his thumbnail. Four smaller stones flanked it, two to either side. She thought it too extravagant.

"Keep it, even if you don't wear it, love," he told her, closing her hand over it. "I have no idea how long it will be before we return to this port. If necessary, you can remove the stones and melt the gold down to a small ingot to sell them. Margery, at the Black Flag, will be able to help you sell it. She can see to it you aren't cheated."

"Thank you, Hezekiah. I hope that I do not need to do that, though," she said. "It seems such a lovely thing. I would hate to destroy it."

His gave her a wry smile. "I know. I think that's why I never got around to selling it, myself."

Viktor joined them outside the church. He noticed the necklace but refrained from teasing his first mate about it. Grimm felt gratitude for that. When they first acquired it, his response to his captain's teasing about gifting it to some wench had been that he never paid, they paid him. He hated to think what his bride would think of that joke.

"The minister assured me he will not talk to anyone about this marriage," the vampire told him. "He understands the need for privacy and has no desire to endanger the innocent."

Hell's Dodo

Grimm frowned worried that Brianna would guess the true reason behind the precaution. "Are you sure your powers will work on a man of the cloth?"

Viktor shrugged. "They are as human as the next man. However, it was unnecessary to go to that length. He brought the subject up."

"Oh?" This came as unexpected news.

"Aye," Viktor confirmed. "Apparently, he used to be one of the Brethren. He knows your reputation quite well, Hezekiah, so his concern is twofold. If word got out that you have a wife and children, they could become targets of hunters thinking to use them against you."

"I hadn't thought of that, Hezekiah," Brianna said fearfully. "I never meant to put you in such a position."

"I put myself in this position, love," he reassured her. "It's your safety I worry about. I've been taking care of myself for years. Most pirates never make it past their twenty-fifth birthday. I'm already forty-one."

"What was the reverend's other concern, Captain Brandewyne?" she asked.

"That if word got out and something happened, we would know who to blame."

She looked back and forth between the two pirates. It gave her a feeling of gratitude and a touch of fear that they would not hesitate to avenge her, even if it meant going up against a man of God. She resolved to take every precaution to avoid putting her husband or his captain in a position to have to do so.

"Have you thought of where to house her, Hezekiah?" Viktor broached a subject the first mate had not yet mentioned.

"I was thinking of buying a small place."

Vik shook his head. "Maybe later, after the children come, but I think she'd be better off close to a good midwife. Would you be willing to come with me to see if Mother Celie will take her in?"

The relief shone on Grimm's face. He'd hoped for this, but he hadn't wanted to impose on his friend. Old Celie had delivered Viktor. She'd raised him as her own after his mother died in childbirth. He hoped Brianna would not meet a similar fate bearing his children.

"Do you think she will?"

Viktor shrugged. "Won't know until we ask."

Celie sat by the cook fire in front of her tabby shack waiting for them. She smiled warmly at Brianna to give the young woman a sense of welcome and security.

"I've been expecting you for some time now, *Madame* Grimm."

On impulse, Brianna walked over and hugged the old woman. This earned bemused smiles from the pirates.

Hell's Dodo

Celie's smile brightened and her eyebrows rose as if something had surprised her. She held the other woman at arm's length and looked at her with a knowing eye. "You are expecting twins," she beamed.

"So I have been told," Brianna confirmed. "How did you know?"

"Old Mother Celie knows things," the old woman said with a wink. She turned her attention to the two pirates. "You were wise to bring her here, Hezekiah Grimm. I will see to it she is kept safe and that she and the children are well cared for."

She peered harder at him and beckoned him forward. "Come here where I can see you better."

He obeyed even though he seemed puzzled by the sudden scrutiny. When she sniffed the air around him, he looked decidedly uncomfortable.

"You smell of magic, boy. You've had dealings with Uncle Zeke," she stated.

"Yes."

Her gaze turned to one of stern warning. "You have made an oath to this young woman. The magic the Elder has bestowed on you makes that oath more binding than if you were still just the mere mortal you once were. If you are unfaithful or break the oath, the magic will know, and there will be dire consequences."

Viktor felt a need to lighten the somber mood which suddenly befell them all. "I guess that means no more wenching for you, Hezekiah," he teased. "All the more for me."

Grimm walked over and embraced his bride, refusing to rise to the bait. The look of love and tenderness on Grimm's face cut through Viktor like a knife. Part of him rejoiced at the fact his friend had found such a source of peace and contentedness; but another part burned with hurt and jealousy.

Something must have shown on his face.

Brianna, after a glimpse at the vampire, said softly, "Hezekiah, I know you have been a pirate for a long time, and I know you enjoy women. I couldn't have asked for a better lover." She held up her hand to stop her husband, when it looked as if he would interrupt. "Let me finish. I have experienced first-hand just how long it can be between ports. If you come across a woman who strikes your fancy or feel the need to use a brothel, I will not hold it against you."

Grimm blinked at her. He realized what a concession that had to be for her, given her background. Brianna had been raised as the only daughter of a French businessman. She had been in route to America for what both she and her father believed to be an arranged marriage. They'd never suspected that her fiancé was in reality a pimp who used that ruse often to acquire virgins for his brothels.

She avoided that fate when pirates took the ship she booked passage on. The pirates, in turn, fell prey to the crew of the *Incubus*. At the time,

Hell's Dodo

Viktor needed to re-provision and to take prisoners to feed the blood Hunger possessed by him and his cadre of vampires.

Hezekiah Grimm, the vampire captain's human first mate, claimed Brianna as his share of the spoils; but he took her in and protected her from the rest of the pirates rather than rape her, as she'd expected.

In the end, his gentleness towards her and his honorable treatment seduced her. She'd offered herself to him freely.

He smiled and brushed a strand of hair from her face. "Thank you for the offer, love; but Mother Celie is right. I made a vow of faithfulness to you. I have always been a man of my word. That will not change now. Besides, no other woman could compare to you."

He said the words he never thought would cross his lips and be truly meant.

"I love you, Brianna Grimm."

Her smile brightened her face, even as her tears brightened her eyes. "And, I love you. Hezekiah Grimm."

She pulled him down into a passionate kiss.

When the pair broke from the kiss, Viktor cleared his throat for their attention. He said something it pained him greatly to say.

"Hezekiah, it wouldn't be right to keep you from your family. I release you from your duties as first mate. You have more than earned this chance to live in peace."

Chapter 3

As the newlyweds stood in stunned silence, Celie tapped Viktor's leg with her stick. "I want a word with you, boy. Come inside and let's give them some time alone."

Obediently, he followed her into the tabby shack. Once inside, she motioned for him to sit down.

"What is said here will remain private, unless you choose to share it. No sound passes my walls unless I wish it," she said. "Do you think it was wise to discharge Mr. Grimm?"

"No."

"Then why did you?"

He thought carefully about it before he answered. "I didn't want to, but I have never forced my will on Hezekiah. Whether to go back to sea with me or stay here with his bride must be his choice."

She sat looking at him for some time. Her expression remained unreadable. He managed not to fidget. He knew she would say her peace when she was ready.

She apparently thought he'd waited long enough; she gave him a solemn smile. "You have grown, Viktor. I remember a time, not so long ago, when only what you wanted mattered. Yet, just out there, you demonstrated that not only can you willingly put the needs and wants of another above your own, you can care enough about another to even think of it."

He grimaced. "I'm glad they can't hear us. Hezekiah must think I'm growing weak after that."

"Hardly," Celie laughed. "He knows it took real strength for you to make that gesture. A weak man wouldn't have given him a choice."

"Even if he stays with me, I have to face the fact that he is going to grow old and die."

She held up a hand to stop him before he could go any further. "It is not like you to get maudlin, boy. Don't start now. It serves no purpose. Your focus still needs to be on getting to the last three Sisters. I trust you haven't forgotten about them."

"I have not," he replied, stung.

"Then you let Hezekiah Grimm worry about his own mortality. You have yours to contend with. Remember, Juma's curse will kill you if you just let it be."

"Belle has been leery of trying to have a vision that would lead me to the next one. Venoma Noir almost proved more than she could handle."

She reached over and patted his hand. "You tell her she won't have any trouble from the rest of them. That old spider was the only one who posed a real risk to your siren."

"Not quite the only one, Mother," he corrected. "Belle didn't fare too well with

Hell's Dodo

Gloribeau. She almost became trapped as a mortal in her human form."

"Almost forgot about that; but I promise the last three will be no danger to her magically."

"She'll be glad to hear that."

Celie nodded decisively. "Good; we have that settled. Now I just have one favor to ask of you before you leave. This is the real reason I am keeping our conversation private."

That caused him to sit up.

She continued, "When I said there could be dire consequences for Mr. Grimm, should he break his vow, I meant it. Those twins in that girl's womb carry a portion of the magic Zeke bestowed on your first mate. They are witness to his vow. If he breaks it, they will die and take their mother with them."

"I can see how that would hurt him, but I would hardly describe it as dire."

"One drop of Zeke's power unleashed is enough to destroy the world, boy. He gave your Hezekiah two drops of blood. If those babies die because of a broken vow, all of existence may be wiped out. You need to make sure he keeps that promise of faithfulness to his wife."

The next day, Viktor prepared his sea bag and readied himself for the return to his quest. When he went outside he saw Grimm by the fire smoking his pipe. He had his own sea bag propped beside him, packed and ready to go.

"Where are you going?" Vik asked.

"Back with you to the *Incubus*."

"You ought to stay here with your wife."

Grimm smiled and shook his head. "Zeke charged me to stay with you and watch your back, not to mention keep you on course. Brianna will be safe and well cared for here. Until you've found all the Sisters, my place is with you."

A weight lifted from Viktor's shoulders. "Thank you, Hezekiah."

Brianna came out. Both men noticed she'd cropped her hair short.

"Love! Your hair! What have you done?" Grimm exclaimed in shock.

"Oh hush. It will grow back. Here," she said and handed him a coiled braid of her dark brown hair. She'd tied it with her favorite ribbon. "I wanted to give you something to let you know I am with you in spirit, if not in body."

He took it, savoring the silky texture of it in his calloused hands. He raised it to his face and inhaled deeply, taking in her scent.

She turned to Viktor and stalked up to him. Shaking a finger in his face, she scolded, "I understand and approve of why Hezekiah is leaving with you. However, he best be returned safely to me at the end of your journey. If any ill befalls him, I will hold you personally responsible."

Viktor captured her hand and smiled wickedly before placing a gentle kiss on her knuckles. He continued to hold her hand, lightly caressing the tops of her fingers with his thumb. "I will just have to make sure no harm comes to him then, *Madame* Grimm. I would not wish to cause you distress or incur your wrath."

She was flustered for a bit when he released her hand, but she recovered quickly. "See that you do not, *m'sieur*."

"Say your goodbyes, Mr. Grimm. We need to catch the tide."

Viktor piloted the ship out the Savannah River. These were his native waters, and he knew them better than most of the harbor pilots in port. His second mate approached him with a bundle.

"What have you there, Mr. Jon?"

The hulking pirate grinned. "We have a new flag for our collection. Seems the Colonies have united and decided to form their own navy. Several of us were approached by a recruiter when it became known we sailed aboard the *Incubus*. The man was quite excited about the possibility of our joining the push for 'independency,' as he put it."

"I can imagine," Vik chuckled. "A first order ship like this would definitely afford the rebels an edge. What did you tell the man?"

"Told him I'd bring the subject up with my captain and asked him what all would be involved if we joined. He told me that truthfully the pay wouldn't be much, given that most of their budget was earmarked for acquiring or building ships, but that the Continental Navy's primary purpose would be to harass and disrupt British trade."

"Ah, privateering." Viktor nodded his understanding. "If we were a merchantman, it would be tempting; but I've the Sisters to find. We disrupt British trade anyway, among others. I see no need to put myself in the position of having some fool trying to tell me where to sail and who to attack, simply because he decided to call himself Commodore or Admiral."

"I know," Jon-Jon laughed. "Still, the flag might come in handy when we're in Colonial waters."

"Indeed. Good thinking, Mr. Jon. Let's see the thing, then."

Jon-Jon unfurled the bundle to reveal the Continental Navy Jack: thirteen alternating red and white stripes with a snake and the words "Don't Tread on Me" blazoned across it.

"Interesting design. Stow it in the signal locker, Mr. Jon."

"Aye, Cap'n."

Not long after clearing Tybee Island, Vik turned the helm over to Mr. Bland with the order to head for open sea then set anchor. He needed Belladonna to have a vision in order to get a heading on where to search for the next Sister of Power. This meant waiting for her to finish her hunt and return to the ship. Given her skittishness after the dealings with Venoma Noir, he didn't want to pressure her too hard. That would risk losing her cooperation.

While they waited, he pondered over the decision of which crewman he would sacrifice to her. She couldn't have a vision without a sacrifice, and he didn't have any prisoners to give her.

"Sails approaching!" the lookout called from the crow's nest.

Grimm started to give the order to let the other ship pass, when Viktor stopped him.

"You usually don't hunt this close to Savannah," Grimm observed. Viktor handed him the spyglass. Grimm took the hint and peered through it at the approaching ship. "Son-of-a-bitch. It's Harris."

He lowered the glass to see his captain grinning like a madman. "I have to, Hezekiah."

The first mate thought it over. "He's going to run as soon as he recognizes us, and we're facing the wrong way; not that we can't outrun him once we've turned about."

"We won't have to outrun him. I want to use the lame duck gambit. He won't be able to resist doing a closer inspection to gloat over my carcass," Vik reasoned.

"Oh, this is going to be fun." Grimm's throaty chuckle sounded decidedly sinister.

Chapter 4

"Ship on the horizon!" the lookout aboard the *Georgia Belle* called out.

The news didn't surprise Captain Harris. They were approaching his home port of Savannah. It was a busy port. He still looked through the glass to check it out.

The rebellion hadn't really gotten very active this far south, but Royal Navy patrols had increased. There'd been some fear that the Spanish colony of Florida might take advantage of the unrest. Georgia was still a young colony, only founded in 1733. Many feared reprisal for Oglethorpe's failed invasion of Florida in the early years of the colony.

They approached the ship from the aft, yet no name was visible. Harris could only see that it was a large ship. He couldn't determine if it was a ship of the line or a merchantman. Smoke drifted up from the decks and some of the port holes. The main mast doubled over, broken in the middle with the top edge nearly trailing in the water. Only some rigging held the ruined mast to the ship. There didn't appear to be any movement on board or aloft. Harris could just make out the silhouette of a body hanging in the rigging, both its legs missing from just above the knees.

"She looks derelict," he muttered. Louder, he ordered, "Helmsman, approach her at an angle. Something looks familiar about her. I want to see the name."

"Aye, Cap'n."

Within half an hour, they reached a position to identify the ship. When he saw it was the *Incubus*, his first instinct was to order the ship about and flee. He fought the urge, however. He still saw no sign of activity in the rigging, nor were there any voices to be heard save those of his own crew.

"I can't believe somebody took out Bloody Vik Brandee. He has to be dead, though," Harris reasoned with himself. *"Even with the broken mast and smoke, the ship looks to be in too good of shape for him to just abandon it."*

Aloud, he ordered, "Lookout report! What does she look like on deck?" It frustrated him that the warship-turned-pirate towered over his own vessel. He couldn't see the deck of the *Incubus*, even at its lowest at mid-ship.

"Lookout report!" he repeated the order. Why wasn't the man answering? Had he fallen asleep?

He was about to repeat the order again, coupled with a threat this time, when a shadow fell across him, the only warning he got before a sickening, wet thud announced the arrival of the lookout's body abruptly on the deck. It landed knearly at his feet.

Gazing in stunned silence, he didn't notice his nearby crewmen backing away from him in terror. A few crossed themselves. Still looking at the body, Harris ordered, "Get someone aloft. I want to know if Brandee is dead or not before we board that ship."

A hand rested on his shoulder, and a familiar voice spoke next to his ear, "Oh, I am very much alive, Chadwick."

Harris looked over his shoulder to see Viktor's leering face. The vampire grinned at him, fangs glistening and the lookout's blood dripping from his beard.

Harris felt a sudden, wet warmth travel down his thighs. Viktor glanced down and smiled.

"That's what I like about you, Chadwick. You are consistent." Vik then looked at Harris' men. "Listen up, gentlemen. I am sure you have heard of me, Captain Viktor Brandewyne. You may have even heard the rumors that I was dead. As you can see, they were wrong. I have one simple question for the lot of you. Answer me honestly. I will know if you lie. I can smell a lie. If any of you are still foolish enough to do so, I can assure you your death will be neither swift nor painless. Who here hails from Savannah?"

A small handful of sailors raised their hands. Viktor put an arm around Harris' shoulder and guided him along, making a show of inspecting them. He sniffed at the air around each sailor, something which Harris found very disconcerting.

"You've a fairly honest crew, man. I am impressed. However," he paused, "there is at least one liar among them."

Tamara A. Lowery

Viktor scanned the men before singling one out. "You, Wesley Taylor; you are from Savannah, yet you did not admit it. Why?"

"I was hoping you'd forgotten me, Brandee. I've no desire to play your games. If I'd known you were so familiar with this mincing little bastard, I'd not have thrown in with him," the man replied.

"That's too bad, Taylor. You should have been honest. It would have saved your life, and you would have kept your freedom." Vik shook his head. "Those of you from Savannah will be allowed to continue to port with your captain. I have need of the rest of you aboard my ship."

Taylor drew his pistol and fired off a shot at Viktor. The ball struck him in the neck just below the jaw and ear, spraying arterial blood all over Harris. The impact proved enough to make the vampire stumble back a few steps.

"Are you mad?" Harris shrieked. "You just doomed us all, you fool!"

"No, he has only doomed himself," a female voice replied.

All eyes turned to see the siren, naked and in her human form, swinging her legs over the railing as she boarded. Harris and Viktor were the only ones who knew what she really was. The rest of the *Georgia Belle's* crew stared with open lust.

She extended the talons on her left hand as she passed by Taylor on the way to Viktor, lightly raking them along his right arm. The man dropped his weapon and clutched his shredded limb. The toxins released by the siren's fingertips raised blisters on what flesh hadn't been sliced by her razor-sharp talons.

She paused by Harris, smiled and licked a little of the blood off his cheek, even though she knew it was Viktor's and what effect it would have on her.

"Hello, Mr. Harris."

Chadwick Harris dropped to the deck in a faint.

"Viktor, how badly are you hurt?" she asked through the mental link they shared and just strengthened by his blood.

"Luckily, I just fed a few minutes ago," came his mental reply. *"The neck wound is almost closed, but it may be a while before I can talk. Bastard came close to my spine."*

"I can help with the healing." She knelt beside him and kissed him passionately. He soon returned the kiss with fervor. He wrapped his arms around her and pulled her into his lap. She quickly became aware of just exactly how much he was enjoying this.

It didn't bother her to put on a show, but they had an enemy to deal with. Viktor seemed to be of the same mind.

They both stood. Though still soaked in both the lookout's blood and his own, Viktor's wounds had been completely erased. He made one more mental query before addressing his terrified captives. *"Can you make quick work of the man I killed but make a show of it?"*

She nodded, grinning with her true teeth showing. Her month stretched nearly ear to ear to show off the multiple rows of razor-sharp needles she called teeth. *"My pleasure; I'm hungry. My hunt only yielded a couple of small sharks."*

Viktor walked over to Harris and stooped down. He tapped the unconscious man lightly on the cheek. "Get up, Chadwick."

Groggily, the man opened his eyes. "Huh, what happened?"

"You must have had too much sun, man." The vampire offered him an honorable excuse for having fainted.

"Yes, heat stroke," he quickly agreed. "I was feeling rather flushed before losing consciousness."

"Well, you're fine now," Viktor clapped him on the back and threw a companionable arm around his shoulder. "You're just in time for the dinner show."

Belladonna picked up the corpse of the lookout. She knew Viktor was giving it to her to eat because he didn't want another vampire on his hands. He'd already sired eight that she knew of, and one of them had made the mistake of trying to feed on her. He'd learned the hard way that siren's blood is toxic to vampires. Six currently served as members of Viktor's crew, turned on her advice to help him get his Hunger under control. The last one was a peace offering to the head vampire of Louisiana to replace a vampire Viktor killed in self-defense.

Hell's Dodo

"Well, since you've already killed this man, Captain, I can start with dessert," she reasoned.

"Enjoy yourself, pet. You'll have plenty of play time with Mr. Taylor later."

Needing no further prompting, she opened her jaw wide and bit the top of the corpse's head off. The crunching sounds as she masticated bone were very loud. When she started scooping gobbets of brain out and eating it like pudding, several thuds and some retching could be heard among Harris' crew. At least five men dropped to the deck.

Viktor's pirates, acting on a silent command from him, quietly boarded the *Georgia Belle* and surrounded their prisoners. Jon-Jon made sure to hobble Taylor.

As Belle continued with her meal, Harris blanched. Viktor whispered in his ear, "Buck up, man. If you pass out again in front of what men I'm leaving you, they'll never respect you again."

Harris swallowed hard, nodded, and managed to keep his composure, even though he still looked a little green around the gills.

"That's enough for now, pet." Viktor finally relented. "Over the side with it. Mr. Grimm, Mr. Jon, see our guests get aboard safely and dole out a ration of rum. No rum for Mr. Taylor, and I want him secured to the mainmast to await Belle's pleasure."

"Have him stripped, please," the siren requested. "His clothes would just be in the way." With that, she took the remains of her meal and dove into the sea.

Chapter 5

Later aboard the Incubus as it headed back out to sea, Viktor had Wesley Taylor stripped and tied spread-eagle, suspended in the air between the mainmast and the mizzen. Pulleys attached to the two masts allowed adjustments on the tension of the lines binding his wrists and ankles.

As per the captain's orders, the crewmen responsible for the rig drew the lines as taut as they would go without actually dislocating the prisoner's hips or shoulders.

Belladonna, still nude, inspected the rig before she nodded her approval. Normally, Viktor would chide her about the nudity, but he understood that what she planned to do to Taylor would ruin any clothing she wore.

"Make it as excruciating as possible, pet, but make him last at least one day before you end his misery," Viktor instructed.

"Brandee, no, please!" Taylor pled. "I'll pay anything you ask."

"You were sailing under Chad Harris, man. You don't have any money." Viktor laughed then sobered. "No; you tried to take my life. The price is your own."

"May I have him now?" Belle asked.

Viktor nodded.

The siren smiled and walked around behind her victim. Taylor turned his head, nervous that he couldn't see her.

"What are you going to do?" The question died as he screamed. The siren used the stinger cells in her fingertips to draw patterns slowly on his back. Welts and blisters boiled up behind where she touched. Once she finished with the back, she poured a bucket of seawater over it. This had the double effect of reviving him before he could pass out and of setting the chemical burns. She then set out to decorate his arms and legs in a similar fashion.

This went on for hours, until she'd burned patterns onto his entire body. The crew went about their usual business as if nothing was going on and they hadn't heard the screams. In truth, they remained truly oblivious to the ongoing torture session. Viktor used his blood link to the crew to block the torment of Taylor from their minds. It took giving them an extra dose of the rum tainted with the vampire's blood as well as him draining of a fresh victim for Viktor to maintain the block.

Only he, Hezekiah, the siren, and Taylor himself were aware of the torture. Mr. Grimm decided to tend to something down in the ballast holds. The screams were muffled there. Viktor didn't hold it against him. He knew the man wasn't queasy, but what the siren was doing and about to do to Taylor could make any man cringe.

Viktor stayed to watch; he ordered the torture, after all. He hadn't expected this particular level of savagery; but he felt obliged to see it out. It was the stuff of nightmares.

"You surprise me, pet," he said during one of the breaks Belle took to allow the victim to revive. "I half expected you to skin him."

"I was in a creative mood. He was ugly; I decided to make him pretty." She shrugged; the gesture reminded him that she was a creature nothing close to human despite her appearance. "This takes longer than skinning and hurts worse."

"What do you plan now that he's covered with burns? Are you going to fill in the blank spaces?"

"No; I left them blank for a reason. They mark the most sensitive areas. Now that he is tattooed, he needs to be pierced." To emphasize her point, she slowly extended a single talon.

"Oh God, please no," Taylor croaked hoarsely. "Just kill me now and be done with it."

Belladonna returned to her victim with a sweet smile. "God has nothing to do with this, human. The Captain said I am to make your torment last until this sunset. That is what I intend to do. You've made it through the night and half the day. Just think of it as something to look forward to."

She traced the very tip of her talon around one of his nipples, which were unmarked. The node tightened from the stimulation. Taylor whimpered.

"I am in the mood for an appetizer, however," she said. Ever so slowly, she pushed the talon into the aureole until it came out the other side. When she withdrew, blood welled up and began seeping down from the wounds.

The pain obviously wasn't as bad as Taylor must have expected. He gasped at the sensation of her mouth over his abused nipple as she licked the blood from the wound. He even moaned in unexpected pleasure.

Belle rolled her amber eyes up to his face and bit down hard, neatly severing the node.

"Gah! You bitch!"

After she gave his other nipple the same treatment, she loosened a rope to give her better access to one of his hands. She slowly inserted her talon into the webbing between each finger up through the meat of his hand until she hit the wrist; then she ate his fingers and the thumb one knuckle at a time.

She tightened the rope and repeated the process with his other hand and then his feet. After that, she drove her talon into each joint. Moving it with the precision her sonar afforded, she neatly severed tendons and ligaments while sparing blood vessels. The incisions proved only a dull footnote to the pain Taylor experienced as his muscles constricted into tight knots after being cut free of their moorings. His screams almost made it past the barrier Viktor kept around the minds of his crew.

Finally, sunset drew near.

"I saved the best for last," Belle told Viktor. "After this, I will take him over the side and finish him."

Hell's Dodo

"Very well, pet. I have to admit I am amazed he survived this far."

Taylor wept and shook his head as she approached him again. He was unable to struggle. She reached down and grasped his manhood gently. She used no sting and had retracted her talon. As she stroked him, his body responded involuntarily but only partially. Viktor felt the pull of her magic as she unleashed her sexual aura to affect the result she wanted from her victim. Once she had Taylor full hard, she traced the head with a delicate touch. As she reached the small slit, she grasped his shaft firmly with her other hand and slowly extended one talon into his urethra up the full length of him.

His eyes bugged and his chest seemed almost paralyzed. He couldn't draw breath to scream.

She flicked her finger and split him wide open, spraying blood all over her.

He passed out.

Viktor called his mates to the cabin originally intended to be the officers' mess by the ship's designer. It held a larger table than the table in his cabin and could accommodate more charts. For now, however, they merely discussed ship's business.

"Stubby reports we have fresh rations enough to last about three weeks," Jon-Jon informed his captain. "He did say he wouldn't mind adding some fresh vegetables to the stores. He said the cook promised a hearty stew if he could get any."

"Very well, we'll see what we can do, Mr. Jon. If we get any, inform the cook to pickle what he doesn't use for the stew. Vegetables don't keep," Vik replied.

He suddenly grew very still; the only warning they got of anything amiss. Grimm noticed and asked, "Captain, what is it?"

"Belladonna."

An uncharacteristic wariness about the captain did not escape the first mate. He eased one of his pistols into his lap. It was only a single shot, and he was pretty sure it wouldn't kill her; but it might give Viktor an edge if the siren decided to attack.

"Enter," Viktor summoned before she could knock on the door.

Belle came in fully dressed and with a hesitant air about her. She seemed bothered by something.

"Miss Belladonna, is something the matter?" Zachary Brumble asked solicitously. She'd bedded the captive-turned-navigator a couple of times, and he was besotted with her. She held no similar attachment for him; she had merely used him to fulfill a need.

She ignored his question and met Viktor's expectant gaze. "I had a vision; but it doesn't seem very helpful."

"Describe it, pet."

"I could not see the Sister. All I got were images of a hot, stone-walled room with a low ceiling. There was a furnace or oven built into one wall. There were shelves and a table holding bowls, pots, pans, bags of flour and sugar, and baskets of eggs. There seemed to be the murmur of many voices coming from another room. I saw no one. I also got no sense of location or direction."

"Well, that is frustrating," Vik sighed.

She nodded. "Yes, it is. There was a residual sense of her power, but it wasn't very strong. Wherever this place is, I seriously doubt she is still there."

"If we can figure out where it is, it will still be a place to start," Viktor reasoned.

Zach spoke up again. "Did this place have shallow round pans with a type of pastry dough lining them?"

"I am not sure what you mean," she admitted. "I don't keep up with what you humans call what you eat. I don't know what pastry dough is."

Viktor gently nudged her mind, mentally asking her to share her vision with him. Since it involved magic, he remained cautious about just "looking."

She opened her mind to him and let him see what she had seen.

"She did. It is definitely some kind of bakery kitchen. Since no fruit is in evidence, I would say someone was making egg pie," he announced.

Zach brightened. "I may know the place, but I could be wrong."

"Where, Mr. Brumble?"

"There's a little tavern in Salem I used to love to visit. They have the best egg pie I've ever eaten. As addictive as it was, I wouldn't be surprised to learn there was witchcraft behind it."

"What was the name of this tavern?" Grimm asked.

"The Dragon and the Dodo."

Belle's mood seemed to lighten a bit. Through their link, Viktor knew she'd been worried that she'd failed him.

Zach saw her relax and smiled. He rose and took her hand in his to kiss it. "I am glad to be of service, my dear. I could not bear to see you so sad."

Before she could respond, Viktor frowned and released the block on Zach's perception of what had been done to Taylor. The young navigator's face paled in horror. He quickly stumbled away from her, cupping himself.

"That was cruel, Captain," she said.

"I would rather have him fear you than continue to moon over you in that insipid fashion, pet. Do not forget. You are mine."

"As if you would let me," she retorted with mild bitterness.

Chapter 6

To Commodore Critchfield something felt vaguely familiar about the man he'd found in Amherst. The purported vampire hunter, only in his early thirties, seemed much younger than Critchfield expected.

Britt Westin was the man everyone in that port directed him to, however. All reports credited him with the most extensive knowledge of the various legends and accounts of vampirism. Most of academic society generally considered Westin to be quite mad, as well. He actually believed the stories.

In fact, only the Commodore's intercession kept him out of prison and allowed him to escape the noose or a lifetime in an asylum. He had been arrested and about to be brought up on charges of murder for the staking and beheading of two prostitutes and one of their clients. He'd claimed they were the undead. The whole incident probably would have escaped notice if not for the fact the "client" Westin executed turned out to be a minor police official.

Critchfield still wasn't sure why he believed any of the bilge about blood-sucking creatures of the night. Lady Carpathia just had a convincing way about her.

Tamara A. Lowery

Since returning to New Providence, no word of Brandee's activities came to his attention. He remained unsure whether to believe the pirate had dropped from the face of the earth or merely left no survivors or witnesses to his piracies. Given the rogue's reputation, Critchfield felt inclined to believe the latter explanation.

To while away the time, and because it was the main reason he had Westin aboard, he decided to have his vampire expert teach him everything he knew about the creatures.

"Well, sir, I will warn you that I may tend to run on a bit. I am very passionate about the subject," Westin told him.

"Currently, I have plenty of time, sir," Critchfield assured him.

The man nodded his understanding and launched into a treatise, clearly delighted to have an interested audience.

"The legends about vampires vary from land to land. There are a few details, though, that seem to be held in common: they are reanimated corpses which require human blood to function; they are highly flammable; sunlight can cause them to spontaneously combust; and holy or blessed objects or holy water will burn them like a firebrand."

"Interesting; are there other weaknesses to the creatures?" Critchfield prompted.

"A few, but they vary according to the source," Westin conceded. "A few have proven false, such as garlic, running water, and mirrors. I believe the creatures have deliberately spread misinformation about themselves to lure hunters into a false sense of security."

His voice grew distant, some old nightmare lurking in his eyes as he added, "That is how the bitch lured my father to his death."

"So, you have a personal reason for hunting vampires."

"Yes," Britt's eyes shone bright with hate. "They took my family from me and tried to use their powers to cover it up."

"A moment, please," Critchfield stopped him and rang for the cabin boy. When the boy arrived, he ordered, "Fetch some cheese and bread from the fresh stores we just laid in; oh, and a couple of limes, as well."

"Aye, sir." The lad nodded and left on his errand.

The request briefly distracted Westin. "Limes? Forgive me, Commodore, but that seems an odd garnish for cheese and bread."

"It's more complimentary than you would think, Mr. Westin. Any kind of citrus helps stave off scurvy, therefore it is valuable aboard any ship." Critchfield told him. "I prefer to cut up one and crush the pulp into a glass of gin or white wine. It's good with rum, too."

"I will keep that in mind."

The cabin boy soon returned with the requested food. After placing it on the table and setting out the flatware, he went to one of the cabinets and got out two glasses. Once they were placed before the Commodore and his guest, the boy went to the liquor cabinet and returned with a flask of white wine.

"Thank you, Paul. That will be all."

"Aye, sir."

As soon as the boy left, Critchfield continued the conversation. "These holy objects, do they have to be from a particular religion?"

"Actually, no; it depends on the user's faith. I will add the caveat that unless the object has actually been blessed and sanctified, it cannot repel the creatures without true faith to back it up. Doubt will get you killed," he answered.

"I see. What about these false weaknesses?"

"There is a grain of truth in them, but they are not proof against vampires," Westin told him. "The inability to cross running water except at high or low tide is the only one that is a total fallacy. Garlic is only a little more offensive to them than it is to a living man. Vampires seem to have heightened senses, much like those of an animal. They also do have an aversion to mirrors, but not for the reasons stated in legends."

"Oh? I am unfamiliar with vampire lore, Mr. Westin. Please, enlighten me to what the legends say and what the real reason is."

"Well, according to legend, a vampire casts no reflection because it has no soul. Whether or not a vampire has a soul, I cannot say, but it does cast a reflection, just as a chair or rock does. The true reason they avoid mirrors is because of their reflection. Vampires have a natural glamour they cast to make themselves appear attractive. Their reflection shows the truth of their unholy, undead nature. If you can look at a vampire's reflection, it will give you a partial immunity to the mind games they play. I will warn that if you are close enough to capture their reflection, they are close enough to attack you. A vampire's speed, agility, and strength are vastly greater than those of a mortal man."

"Will they attack if they are unaware you have seen their reflection?"

"I am impressed by your question, Commodore. Most people never think to ask," he said. "They might; it depends on their motives at the moment. It would be difficult to hide the knowledge from them. They seem able to sense emotions and lies. It is a given that if they do know you are free of their glamour, they will attack."

"What about these mind games?"

Westin pushed his food away and downed the remains of his wine in one gulp. "I will need something stronger to drink. This involves the destruction of my family."

Chapter 7

"Of course," Critchfield said with a nod. Rather than ring for the cabin boy again, he got up and took the wine flask back to the liquor cabinet. He retrieved a bottle of scotch and returned to the table. "This batch is fifteen years old; strong and smooth."

"Thank you, Commodore."

Once Westin downed about half the glass, his eyes focused on some distant point in the past, and he began his tale.

"For several years, I believed my father had killed my mother. The memory of it still seems so real. His business took him abroad for months at a time. During those absences, one of our neighbors paid court to my mother. Mr. Tucker was a man of disrepute, but my mother was an honorable woman. She rebuffed his advances."

"That much is fact and the basis for the lies and false memories the vampire wove. The best and most believable lies are based on truths, merely twisting them to the liar's purposes."

"The false memory is of my father returning home to accuse my mother of being unfaithful, of being a whore. They argued. He struck her and pushed her. She hit her head on a shelf and crumpled to the floor in a pool of blood. He then took me out of the house but forced my little brother to stay behind, claiming he wasn't his son."

"It wasn't until years later that we learned what really happened. A powerful vampire murdered my mother and brother. She was about to feast on me, but my father arrived home in time to save me from her. He said she let us go because it was so close to sunrise."

Critchfield found himself both interested and puzzled. "How is it you came to learn the truth?"

"My father discovered it shortly after he started hunting the creatures. He had captured a newly made vampire and kept it for a while to study it before dispatching the wretch and freeing its soul from Hell. One of the things he'd learned was how they can implant false memories to hide their activities."

"He went to a priest for absolution and cleansing. It was then that he was able to recover his true memory. He took me to the same priest. I was absolved and cleansed, but I still cannot remember the truth. The priest said it was because I was in the vampire's thrall for too long before being rescued. He feared she may have permanently erased the memory of the true events of that night."

"And you accepted this, the word of a priest you didn't know and that of the man you believed had killed your mother?" Critchfield sounded dubious.

"I did, and I do, sir," Westin affirmed. "Not at first, of course, but as my father began training me to hunt, the truth became evident. He allowed me to observe and study specimens he would capture, always careful to make sure they were new enough to have not come into their full power, and always using the proper precautions."

"When I was in my late teens, *she* resurfaced. Neither of us had ever encountered a vampire so powerful. Although she barely looked to be older than me, she had to be ancient. No other vampire we had ever encountered had been able to capture my will in such a way I couldn't fight free. I knew she had to be the one that had murdered my mother and brother."

"My father used a mirror to detect her true nature. I was close enough to see the reflection, but my father was closer to her. Faster than my eyes could follow, she travelled from across the square to his side. She did not attack him right away. Instead, she smiled up at him, even knowing we could see through her glamour. She reached into a burlap bag she was carrying and said, 'Nolan Westin, you and Father Brian have been causing quite a nuisance among my people.' She then pulled out the priest's head from the bag."

"Father and I stood transfixed, unable to move. I cursed myself for not wearing my cross outside my clothes where she could see it. At least Father had his out, but it would not glow."

"She whispered something to him almost too low for me to hear. Once I could make out what she was saying, I realized she was using her demonic magic to alter his memory again."

"What did she say to him?" Critchfield asked, caught up in the tale for the moment.

"She said, 'Your faith is corrupt, Nolan. You have lied and murdered without repentance. You killed your wife and abandoned your youngest son, not I. I was not there. In fact, I did not know of your existence until a couple of months ago. Your little trinket is of no use to you. You might as well drop it in the dust.'"

"And he did?"

"Yes; he gave up the only protection he had. She hadn't actually touched him before that. The minute he dropped his cross, she embraced him as if he were a lover. He submitted to her will and allowed her to bite him and drain him dry. It took quite a while for him to die. I still remember the horrible slurping sounds and her growls."

"When she finished with him, she looked at me and said, 'I have not been given orders for your death, and I am sated for now. In truth, you serve a purpose. Some of my kind make fledglings indiscriminately, drawing undue attention and creating too much competition for prey. Hunters, like you, thin the ranks, culling out the weak and foolish, allowing the strong and cunning to thrive in discreet obscurity. Do not think I have rewarded this man with the immortality my kind enjoys. He has caused me trouble and is now mine to punish for eternity.'"

"She came at me, and I don't remember anything after that. I came to myself after sunrise in my own room. I have been tracking her ever since. I almost caught up to her in Vienna a few years ago. The shock of seeing the creature that had once been my father with her gave them enough time to escape."

Hell's Dodo

"The last I had heard, she had taken ship in the Black Sea and was bound for the Caribbean."

Critchfield gave a wry smile. "So, you had an ulterior motive besides escaping the noose for agreeing to come with us."

"Yes, sir, I did. It is my hope that I can pick up her trail again," Britt said with a nod. "She calls herself after the mountains of her native land, Lady Carpathia. She is petite and deceptively fragile-looking, with a striking beauty if you can't see past her glamour. Her hair and eyes are dark, and her skin is milk white. Even without the glamour, she is stunning. I can only guess that she was magnificent when she was still alive."

"Interesting, Mr. Westin." He pulled out his timepiece and checked it. "I hate to cut this short, but I have a staff meeting with my fellow officers and the captains under my command. With the punctuality I demand from them, it wouldn't look good for me to be tardy."

"Of course not, sir. I fully understand."

Critchfield poured himself a whiskey and brooded. Quite a lot of information stirred in his mind, clamoring for attention.

He learned from his captains that the Colonials had escalated their little rebellion. The fools were actually trying to form a navy of their own. He wasn't too concerned about that. The rebels did not have the ships, discipline, or resources to pose any real threat to the Royal Navy. The way he viewed it, they would be named brigands and pirates and dealt with accordingly.

The thing he kept puzzling over more and more was why Carpathia would direct him to someone with a grudge against her. He realized he was going to have to accept that creatures such as vampires existed, fantastical as it seemed, if any of this was going to make sense.

She wanted him to learn about vampires, so he wouldn't be caught unaware by anything Brandee threw at him.

It looked more and more as if hunting the pirate would prove a daunting task. If half the man's reputation was to be believed, he was already a formidable opponent. Now, Critchfield had to add that Brandee had possession of the sister ship to his own pirate hunter, the *Quicksilver*, and the superhuman powers of a vampire.

The Commodore had never been one to back down from a challenge, and he wasn't about to start now.

Chapter 8

Viktor decided to try out his new flag and sailed the *Incubus* right into Salem Harbor. It was common knowledge that Massachusetts served as a hotbed for the rebellion -- or revolution, depending on who one talked to about it.

The ploy worked, although it did make the ship the talk of the town. Prudently, he followed Mr. Grimm's advice and masked over half of the gun ports. No sense revealing her true might to those who did not need to know.

Zach led them to The Dragon and the Dodo tavern. At Viktor's request, Belladonna remained on the ship. Zach remained skittish around her, and the captain didn't need him distracted. He seriously considered manipulating the man's memory so that he had a healthy fear of the siren but not so much that he couldn't function around her.

The tavern wasn't quite what the pirates expected of a port town. Several families made use of the common room; only a few lone sailors were scattered here and there among the crowd. It was evident from how they carried themselves that none of the serving wenches were sporting women, either.

Zach smirked at the look of disappointment on Jon-Jon's face. "The Puritans have always had a strong influence in Salem, Mr. Jon. Not to worry, though; there are places here that are more to your liking."

"If we have time for it," Viktor reminded. "We're looking for a Sister, not a whore, right now."

"Aye, Cap'n," Jon-Jon nodded, shaking off the urge to pout over the possibility of no sporting in this port.

The pirates followed their captain's lead and found an unoccupied table rather than their usual habit of just taking a table whether it was occupied or not. Viktor didn't want to deal with angry locals. His Hunger wanted badly to rise, and it took a bit of concentration to keep it under control.

It wasn't long before a server approached them. "Good morrow, sirs. What may I get for you?" she asked politely. She blushed a bit when she noticed Jon-Jon's leer.

Viktor kicked him under the table and said, "My navigator tells me you serve a good egg pie here."

She beamed at him. "It is the best, sir. We also serve an excellent local ale, if I may suggest it."

"That will be fine, lass."

Once she was away from the table, Jon-Jon rubbed his shin and said, "Ow."

"I already said we may not have time for sport, Mr. Jon."

"Aye, Cap'n, but she's nice and plump. A man can at least look, can't he?"

Hell's Dodo

"Just look for now, then."

Before long, the girl returned with a tray full of mugs of beer. "There you go, sirs. We have a batch of pies cooling now. They're about this big," she said, making a circle with thumb tips and finger tips touching. "Will two each be enough, or would you like more?"

"We'll start with that and see where it goes from there."

"I'll have the baker put another batch in the oven. I've a feeling you will want more," she said with a smile.

Jon-Jon drained the tankard and clapped it down on the table during the exchange. "Bring me back another ale if you would, lass." He winked at her.

Once again, she blushed and smiled. Nodding, she left the table again.

"Mr. Jon." Viktor's voice held a note of warning, but an amused quirk played at the corner of his mouth.

"All I did was ask for more drink, Cap'n." The second mate tried to look innocent. "Can't help it if I'm thirsty."

"Mm-hmm."

They were all chuckling over the exchange when the young woman returned to the table with a large platter of pies and another tankard of ale. She set the platter down before she set Jon-Jon's beer down. When she did, she leaned over enough to brush against his arm and give him an eyeful of her ample bosom.

Before she could move away, he grasped her wrist firmly but gently. He placed a gold piece in her hand and let his fingertips just brush her palm. "Thank ye, lass. What's your name?"

"M-martha," she replied, flushing bright red.

"I'll know who to ask for the next time I'm in port, then, Martha." He smiled and released her.

She returned to the kitchen to fetch another table's order, fanning herself as she went.

Vik pinched the bridge of his nose, sighed, and shook his head. "It's like telling a fish not to swim."

"Aye," Grimm agreed. "Willoby would try to wench even in his deathbed."

Jon-Jon grinned. "That I will, but I'll have the lass atop me. Wouldn't want to crush the poor thing when I die of pleasure."

A few heads turned at their roars of laughter, but quickly went back to their own meals. A group of sailors ashore was a common enough sight to not draw lingering attention.

The pirates set to eating. Just as Viktor was about to take the first bite, he felt a growing warmth under his shirt. He frowned and set down his spoon to reach into his shirt. He drew out the milky crystal he wore suspended from a silver chain. It seemed to pulse in his hand.

He held the Elder's stone closer to the pie, and it grew warmer in his hand and began to glow ever so softly. It did not, however, glow bright enough to draw attention.

Hell's Dodo

"We're on the right course, but the Sister is not here," he observed.

"I agree, Captain," Grimm concurred. "That thing gets as bright as the full moon in the presence of their magic."

"Indeed; still there is some kind of spell connected to her at work here." He slipped the chain off and waved the crystal over their pies. "These should be safe to eat now."

Viktor put the stone back on and tucked it back into his shirt. He then commenced to eating his own pie.

They all agreed the pies were the best they'd ever had, even without the enchantment on them. Martha was a bit surprised, when they didn't order another round of pies.

They had the chowder, instead.

Tamara A. Lowery

Chapter 9

"That was good!" Vik declared of the food. Now he wanted to meet the cook as well as the baker. The Elder's stone had not reacted to the chowder, so he knew the enjoyment was from the cook's skills and not some enchantment.

When Martha returned to the table, he handed her enough coin to cover the cost of their meal three times over. Catching her eye, he smiled. "That was an excellent meal. If it is not too much trouble, I'd like to meet the kitchen staff to give them my compliments."

A faint emerald glow emanated from the living vampire's eyes. Viktor wasn't taking a chance on getting an argument.

"Of course, sir," Martha said. "Just follow me."

She led them back to the kitchen. Viktor opened his link with Belladonna and mentally asked, *"Is this what you saw in your vision?"*

The siren replied back from the ship, *"Yes! That is exactly it! But, I don't sense the Sister anywhere in this port. She wouldn't be able to shield her presence at this range."*

"I know, pet. There was a spell in the pies that the Elder's Stone reacted to, but it was weak."

He cut the connection and looked around for anyone working in the kitchen. At first, it seemed as if no one was there, although some movement could be heard from a storeroom that let off the room opposite the door to the common room.

The sound was quickly followed by a burly man toting a sack of flour back into the kitchen.

"Hullo, Martha. If you're not busy, fetch me another basket of eggs and a jug of molasses from the storeroom," he said; then he noticed the four men standing in his kitchen. "Can I help you gentlemen?"

"Perhaps," Viktor replied. "We are looking for the cook and the baker for this fine establishment."

"That would be me on both counts," the man said with a nod. "Nathan Trundle; what can I do for you?"

The vampire smiled without revealing his true nature. Through the blood bond he maintained to keep his crew in line, he sent Zach to watch the back door and Jon-Jon with Martha with orders to keep her occupied for a while. The second mate chuckled as he left the room, and Viktor guessed just how the large pirate would fulfill his order.

"I'll help you carry those, lass," Jon-Jon said with a leering smile and gave her a wink. She rewarded him with a bright blush.

Grimm had no such connection with the Captain, but he knew Viktor's mind just the same. He surreptitiously moved to block the door from the dining area.

Hell's Dodo

"My compliments to you, sir." Viktor smiled and bowed. "That was the best meal I've had in a very long time."

"Thank you, sir." Nathan returned the smile, but he wore a look of caution on his face. The disbursement of the others had not been lost on him. "Might I ask your name?"

"Viktor Brandewyne, at your service." Vik felt some gratification to see a small flicker of fear in the man's eyes. "I noticed something special about your pies. Where did you get the recipe?"

Nathan blinked at him. Clearly, that was not the subject he had expected after hearing the notorious pirate give his name. "What?"

"The recipe for your egg pie: where did you come by it?"

"Old family recipe; the Trundles have been bakers for generations. The secret was passed down to me by my father," he replied with a nervous laugh. "Is that what you came for? I was afraid you were here to rob me."

Viktor's mouth quirked up at one corner. "It is still early. Why did you just lie to me, Mr. Trundle?"

"I didn't...," he started to protest.

"Yes, you did." Viktor used his inhuman speed to move to stand nearly nose-to-nose with the baker. To his credit, the man held his ground. "There was an enchantment on those pies. You did not get that part of the recipe from your father."

Nathan Trundle stared up at Viktor Brandewyne, ready to be indignant over being called a liar. He never even realized when his will fell prey to the vampire's emerald eyes. "No, sir, I did not get the recipe from my father. He was not a baker and rarely ever went into a kitchen."

"I thought as much. Who taught it to you, and what makes it different from any other recipe for egg pie?"

"I don't like to tell people how I came by the recipe. Given this town's history, it wouldn't be good for business to be known to have associated with a witch. Auntie Clarissa was always kind to me. She used to run the Dragon and the Dodo. I hired on with her as a lad to help my mother and sisters out while my father was out with the whalers. Auntie taught me how to cook and then made me the cook when my father died. She knew the extra income would help my family."

"It was during the cooking lessons that I learned her secret. She was a witch. I would see her adding odd ingredients or muttering strange words, when she thought I wasn't looking," he continued. "I'd been the cook here for three years before she caught me watching her. She'd gone into the storeroom, and I had taken the opportunity to go to her work table to see what ingredients she had just put in some bread dough. She came back out of the storeroom before I'd expected her to."

"'So, you know what I am,' she'd said. 'How long have you known?' 'A few years,' I'd answered."

"And what did she do to you?" Vik asked.

Hell's Dodo

"She asked me if I'd ever told anyone, even my family, about her magic. I assured her I hadn't; then she warned me not to try any of her spells on my own. After a year, she decided she could trust me. She called me to the kitchen and locked all the doors. She then gave me a small loaf of bread and told me to eat it. I did so, and she watched to make sure I ate the entire thing."

"Once I finished it, she smiled and told me I would not be able to remember any of the secret ingredients I had seen her add to food to cast her spells.... She said they were too dangerous for a mortal to wield."

"However, there was one spell she said she would teach me as a reward for my faithful service. She told me, also, that she was giving me the tavern as my own business. The spell would guarantee that I always had customers, provided I never divulged the secret."

"Is this the spell on your pies?" Viktor asked.

"Yes, but only on the egg pies. Auntie was clear about that. The pie recipe is common enough. The secret is adding a drop of blood to the custard. It will make people crave the pies. She did tell me that the type and size of eggs used would affect the potency, however."

"I see. What became of the witch? I know she is not in this port."

Nathan's expression grew puzzled, as if he wasn't sure if he really believed what he was about to say. "It seems like a dream now, but two years ago, she said, 'He is coming;' then she turned into a bird and flew south with a flock. I

have neither heard nor seen anything of her since
that day."

Chapter 10

It surprised Viktor he hadn't detected the blood in the egg custard. Perhaps it dissipated when the Elder's Stone neutralized the spell connected to it.

"Mr. Grimm."

"Aye, Captain?" the first mate responded.

"How would you compare the meal we just had with our shipboard fare?"

"There is no comparison. I thought we ate well, but this man's cooking far surpasses anything I've ever eaten aboard any ship."

Viktor smiled and clapped Nathan on the shoulder. "Your Auntie Clarissa was right. Now that you've told the secret of the pies, you won't have any more customers here."

He frowned. "Damn; I tried to keep it secret, really I did. Don't understand why I just blurted it out to you."

"Not to worry, Mr. Trundle," Vik assured him. "We've a place for you aboard the *Incubus* as the new ship's cook. Good food will do wonders for the crew's morale. If there are any special utensils or crockery you wish to take, I suggest you gather them now."

"I'm being conscripted?" he asked.

"In a manner of speaking."

"Captain, someone's coming," Grimm warned. "I think it's the other wench."

"Let her in, Mr. Grimm," he instructed. Moving lightning fast, he went over to where the latest pies were cooling. He pulled out the crystal and used it to negate the spell already in place; then he poked a tiny hole in each, using his dagger to prick his finger, and placed a drop of his own blood in the pies.

"That won't work," Nathan started to protest.

"Trust me, Mr. Trundle, it will," Vik grinned at him, not bothering to hide his fangs. He renewed his mental grip on the man's will to prevent him from warning the young woman entering the kitchen. He then played the man like a puppet.

"Where is that slattern, Martha?" the woman growled as she stormed into the kitchen. Grimm closed the door behind her. Only then did she notice the other men in the kitchen with her employer. "Oh!"

"Agnes, I have a treat for you and Martha," Nathan said. "She can have hers when she returns from the storeroom."

Minding her manners in front of strangers, Agnes said, "Thank you, sir; but there are customers waiting for their food, and Martha has been gone for a while."

Hell's Dodo

"They can wait a little longer. You both have worked hard. You deserve a little break. Please, have a pie." He handed her one of the altered pies.

"Really?" Agnes' demeanor changed drastically. Apparently, Trundle rarely allowed them to have a pie. It was usually a special reward. She wasn't about to let him change his mind. "Thank you, sir!"

She took the pie and looked uncertainly at the strangers. Used to maintaining a servant's mentality, she felt it would be rude for her to eat it in front of them.

"Don't mind us, lass," Grimm assured her. "Go ahead and enjoy it while it's still warm. We've already eaten."

She needed no further prompting. Going to a stool in one corner of the kitchen, she attacked the pie with the greed and gusto of a starved child.

Viktor sent a silent hint to Jon-Jon to finish up his sport and bring the wench back to the kitchen. He sensed some reluctance from his second mate, but the man remained obedient.

Shortly after, Jon-Jon emerged from the storeroom with a flushed and disheveled Martha. It didn't take her long to spot Agnes with a pie.

"She got a pie?" There was an upset tone to her voice.

"I saved one for you, as well, Martha," Nathan assured her.

Agnes piped up around a mouthful of pie, "She's been whoring again. She doesn't deserve it. Let me have her pie."

"That is enough, Agnes," her employer chided.

Martha snatched the pie set aside for her and moved to another corner of the kitchen as far away from Agnes as possible. Viktor and Grimm watched with wry amusement.

Speaking low enough that only his first mate could hear, Vik said, "Makes you think they're both related to Belle. I'm surprised they aren't growling at each other."

"I know," Grimm replied, his voice equally low. "Makes me wonder what the spell would have done. It reminds me of how opium smokers or hashish users behave if they've gone without for a long time."

"Aye; or a vampire that has gone too long without feeding." Viktor's comment let Grimm know he now had a better understanding of the first mate's former compulsions and addiction that led to their parting company years before. Viktor would like to sit and talk with his friend about it, but not here or now. Other business needed attending to.

Both women wore a brief look of confusion when they finished eating. Agnes broached the subject first.

"Did you make these?"

"I did," Nathan replied.

Hell's Dodo

"Have you changed your recipe, sir?" Martha asked. "They are good, but they don't taste quite the same."

"No, they don't," Agnes agreed. "Still, they do taste better than the ones Miles Hawkins makes when you are sick. He swears he follows your recipe to the letter, but they're never as good."

Nathan smiled. It was an old complaint. "He just doesn't know my secret ingredient, and he never will. You are right, though. These are different. I tried a new secret ingredient," he told them.

"But why?" they asked almost in unison.

Viktor drew their attention. As expected, a temporary blood bond had been forged by the eating of pies tainted with the vampire's blood. "It was my idea. Mr. Trundle shall be accompanying us back to our ship. I suggest you find a new cook."

"I'll send a boy over to fetch Miles," Agnes said with a nod.

"Shall I go back to waiting tables?" Martha asked.

"Yes," Viktor confirmed. "Say nothing about where or with whom Mr. Trundle has gone until three days from now. Then, if anyone asks, you may tell them that he is part of Viktor Brandewyne's crew now."

"Very good, sir; I hope you have a good voyage."

Nathan just gawped as his employees went about their business as if noting was amiss. The vampire had released him from his thrall for the moment.

Noticing his new cook's stunned expression, Viktor grinned and said, "I told you it would work."

The crew carefully avoided mentioning the names of any of the mates on the lists while the harbor pilot was aboard. They knew the captain didn't want to draw undue attention. The *Incubus* drew enough attention as it was. Given some of the conversations heard around the docks, messengers had probably already been dispatched to inform both the rebels and the Royal Navy that the Continental Navy now boasted a ship-o'-the-line.

The rebels would use the story to boost morale.
The British would hunt for the ship, not that they weren't already. Either way, Viktor didn't have time to deal with the delays and distractions either navy could cause him.

Once the pilot disembarked, Grimm approached his captain. "What course do we set now?"

"South, Mr. Grimm. Trundle said she turned into a bird and flew off with a flock. That is the direction we need to go if we hope to catch her trail."

Chapter 11

The *Shining Star* put in at New Orleans. Samantha Brumble hoped she could find fresh news of Brandee's whereabouts. She preferred to find him and ransom back her brothers while she still had money to ransom them with.

At Captain Bainbridge's suggestion, they started asking around for news of Brandee in the taverns close to the docks. They got varying results. Some said Bloody Vik Brandee was dead. Some said they could tell exactly where he was, for a price.

These, Sam and Bainbridge ignored. Chances were the blackguards just wanted coin and would tell whatever lie they thought would do to get it.

They heard rumors of multiple sightings, though. Brandee had been seen in New Orleans, but no one proved willing to say when. He had also been reported all over the Caribbean, as well as around Africa and several islands in both the Indian and Pacific Oceans.

None of this helped pinpoint where he was most recently.

Bainbridge saw how Sam grew ever more frustrated with the lack of progress. However, one tavern in the Quarter gave her some hope. Their inquiries were met with fearful hostility. Both she and Bainbridge agreed that these people had seen the pirate recently.

They approached the barkeep. Bainbridge placed coins on the bar and said, "We're looking for information on the whereabouts of Viktor Brandewyne."

The man glared at them. "Who wants to know?"

"George Bainbridge and Sam Brumble."

"You don't say? Brumble? That name sounds familiar." He rubbed his chin as if trying to remember. It kept them distracted enough not to notice a slight figure leave the bar and slip out. "Can't, for the life of me, place it; but I know I've heard it before. Oh well, it'll come back to me, I'm sure. Tell you what, if this pup here can drink two cups of rum without passing out, I'll tell you what I know."

"Bring out the bottle," Sam said with determination.

Bainbridge gave her a worried look. "Sam, you don't have to do this."

"Yes, Captain, I do."

Setting a less than clean cup and a bottle of rum on the bar, the barkeep barked with laughter, "Let the lad have a go, Cap'n. Maybe it'll put some whiskers on that girly face."

Samantha smirked a bit at the remark. Before he could pour for her, she grabbed the bottle. Pulling the cork with her teeth, she poured the cup to the brim. It sloshed a bit when she picked it up.

Hell's Dodo

She took a deep breath through her nose and drank the cup straight down.

The barkeep watched her with a raised eyebrow as she set the cup down. She quickly filled the cup again and drained it.

She set the cup back down, let her breath out, and recorked the bottle. She swayed for a moment, dizzy from holding her breath, but quickly recovered. She then shot the barkeep a triumphant sneer.

"Be damned if ye didn't do it, lad," he grinned, impressed.

"The trick is not to breathe," she said. "That way, you can drink it fast without choking."

Bainbridge scowled. "You've been spending time with the riggers."

"I have. Robbins taught me how to drink and play dice," she confirmed. Her tone turned mildly flippant as she began to feel the effects of the rum.

"I'll have to see to it that he gets more work. Obviously, he has too much idle time."

The barkeep interrupted them. "So, ye're lookin' for Bloody Vik Brandee? Why? Are ye pirate hunters? There be easier prey than that one."

"No, we're not pirate hunters!" Sam rounded on him. "Although we are hunting a pirate. Does that make us pirate hunters, Captain? Never mind; that'sh irreverent."

"Irrelevant," Bainbridge corrected her. His tone held a note of worry over how quickly the rum acted on her.

"What he said," she jerked a thumb at him, never taking her eyes off the barkeep. "Brandee has my brothers. I want them back."

The barkeep had been watching her with a bemused smile. "Has he sent you a ransom note, lad?"

"Well, no."

"You might as well forget about getting them back, then. If Brandee hasn't asked for ransom, they're either dead or part of his crew. He's not in the habit of letting men leave his crew — alive, that is. Are you sure Brandee has them?"

Bainbridge spoke up. "Aye; I was there when he took the oldest brother hostage."

"Yet here you stand." Clearly the man didn't believe him.

"Brandee has some sort of grudge against their father. He wanted my employer to know who was taking his sons," he explained.

The barkeep looked at them in silence for some time. Finally, he spoke. "I don't know where Brandee is now, but he makes this port every year or so. Go to Madame Thibideaux's and ask for Celine or Angelique. They may be able to help you. That's usually where he stays when he's in port."

"A brothel?"

"The upstairs, aye; the street front is a juju shop."

"Thank you." Bainbridge put more coin on the counter. It quickly vanished into the barkeep's apron.

Hell's Dodo

They left the tavern. They'd passed the shop in question on their way there. Bainbridge stopped Sam when she started to barrel towards the place.

"I think you should go back to the ship, Sam. I can ask around at Madame Thibideaux's," he said.

"Captain, I am not afraid of a brothel or some witch," she protested, her face flushed. "Besides, I've never met a whore before. I'd like to know why a woman would do that."

"No," he kept his voice stern. "You are drunk, Sam. Your judgment is not what it should be. Your brothers would never forgive me for exposing you to such wantonness. I'll take you back to the ship; then I'll return to see what I can learn."

"Neither of you are going anywhere, mates," a snide voice said from behind them. "That's Brumble."

"You are under arrest. Come with us," a burly *gendarme*, one of four, ordered.

"Arrest?" Sam replied incredulously. "For what? We've done nothing wrong!"

In answer, the closest *gendarme* hit her in the stomach with a cudgel. She doubled over, the air knocked out of her. She collapsed to her knees and vomited up the rum she'd just had.

"Sam!" Bainbridge knocked the man back before he could hit her again. The other three promptly ganged up on him. One of them managed to knock him unconscious.

☠

He came to in a holding cell. Samantha lay sprawled on the floor next to him. He checked her but could find no bruises or broken bones. He could only surmise she passed out after the blow to her stomach.

"Sam; Sam, can you hear me?" He patted her face in an attempt to wake her.

"Hmmm? Wha'?" she began to stir. "Oh!" She rolled to her stomach and dry heaved for a few minutes. Finally, she sat up and huddled in on herself, sniffling and wiping her eyes. "Don't ever let me do that again."

"I tried to stop you this time, remember?"

"Oh. You did; didn't you?" She gave him a weak and apologetic smile. She looked around at their surroundings and asked, "Why are we imprisoned?"

"I don't know," he replied. "I remember them saying something about you being a Brumble."

"Do you suppose Thom or Zach got into trouble here?"

He shook his head. "Not while they were still free. Your father is extremely intolerant of any employee, be they hired or blood kin, casting an ill light on the business. They wouldn't have risked a flogging over something stupid enough to get them jailed."

"Yes, he would be vicious enough to do that to them, wouldn't he?" She scowled.

Hell's Dodo

The sound of a key scraping in the lock of the door to the cell block interrupted their conversation. Both looked warily toward it. Some *gendarmes*, a rat-faced character, and an older, well-dressed man entered and approached them.

The fancy held a kerchief over his nose, apparently not caring for the general funk of the cells or their inhabitants. Sam and Bainbridge barely noticed it, having grown accustomed to the smells aboard a ship. Fresh water was too valuable to be wasted on regular hygiene at sea.

"Etienne, neither of these men is the one who took my daughter," the fancy said through the kerchief.

The *gendarme* in question clouted the rat-faced man on the back of the head. "Garner, you cur, I ought to lock you up for trying to get good reward money for the wrong men," he growled.

Garner rubbed his head and whined, "But, I heard the older one call the lad Brumble."

Sam approached the bars but didn't get too close. She recognized Etienne as the one who'd struck her in the stomach. "Sir?" she addressed the fancy. "Am I to understand that you believe a Brumble kidnapped your daughter?"

"Yes, lad; he came into my home under the false pretense of brokering a business arrangement with his family's trading company. He then seduced my daughter and spirited her away. Now, his father will not honor the agreement and claims his sons have turned pirate and betrayed him."

Her face flushed bright red with anger. "He misinformed you, sir. My brothers were taken hostage by a notorious pirate; but neither of them would ever do what you claim. Could you describe the man?"

He looked at her closely. "Your brothers? What is your name, lad? The senior Brumble only claimed to have two sons."

"In that, he spoke truth. I am Samantha Brumble. I am trying to find the pirate who took my brothers so that I may ransom them. My companion is George Bainbridge, captain of the *Shining Star*. Now, please, describe the man who deceived you. I can tell you if it truly was one of my brothers."

"Not so fast, *Mademoiselle* Brumble." Clearly, he didn't trust her yet. "If I describe the man, you may easily lie and say it was not your brother. Rather, you describe your brothers to me."

She didn't even hesitate. "Zachary is the oldest and favors our mother, as do I. he stands about as tall as Captain Bainbridge and has dark blond hair and grey eyes. Thomas favors my father and has been said to be the very image of him when he was a young man. He is close to the same height as Zachary, but has ginger hair and blue-green eyes. Oh, and he freckles in the sun."

The man looked shaken. He actually stumbled a bit.

"Lord Mayor, are you well?" Etienne asked as he steadied the man.

Hell's Dodo

"*Oui.*" He shook it off and regained his composure. "Open the cell and release them. They are innocent of any wrong doing."

He returned his attention to Sam and Bainbridge. "My apologies, *mademoiselle*, Captain. The men you described do not match the description of the man who presented himself to me as Thomas Brumble. He was a tall man with black hair and beard and the most striking green eyes."

"Our quest is the same, sir," Bainbridge said, his face pale. "You described the pirate who took Miss Brumble's brothers. Viktor Brandewyne's grudge against their father must go deeper than we realized."

"Brandewyne, did you say?" The mayor blanched. "If that is who took my daughter, I fear I will never see her again. I thought he had been reported dead and stricken from the lists."

"Sadly, the reports of his death were in error. The man has the devil's own luck at cheating death. He is devious, as well. When Zachary and I encountered him, he had a man-o-war and a crew decked out as British Royal Navy. He drugged us and used that influence to get us to surrender half our cargo, provisions, and stores, and to get poor Captain Brumble to sail off with him. He sent me back with a message for my employer that he had taken his sons in partial payment for the ill-treatment of someone he called Jim Rigger," Bainbridge told him.

The mayor absorbed this information and said, "I see; perhaps it was for the best that *Monsieur* Brumble refused to honor the false trade agreement. If Brandewyne bears such a grudge against him, it would not be safe or prudent to do business with him. I am puzzled as to why he would take my daughter and demand no ransom, however. I have not done him or any of his crew any harm that I know of."

"If and when we find him, I will ask after your daughter, sir," Sam said.

He smiled at her, but it was a sad smile. "I appreciate the thought, *mademoiselle*. Perhaps it would be better if you never find him, however. I fear you would only suffer the same fate as my Melanie. *Non*; it would be best for you to return home. I am sure your father misses you very much."

"Thank you for your concern, sir; but that is something I will not do. If we are free to go, we have a few more inquiries to make."

"As you wish. Etienne, escort them out."

Chapter 12

Jeorge looked up irritably at the vampire standing by patiently. "This had better be important, Claire. You know how I hate to have my breakfast interrupted."

"Forgive me, my lord." She bowed, studiously ignoring the human who lay limp in her master's arms. "There has been word from our hounds that someone has been asking after Captain Brandewyne."

Jeorge dropped his victim and stood; his full attention on his underling. "What details do you have?"

"There are two humans: one male; one female masquerading as male. The name Brumble was heard, and they were picked up by the *gendarmes* and taken to the Lord Mayor. Our hound in his personal guard reports that they were released just moments ago, and his lordship now knows it was Brandewyne who took his daughter, not Brumble. No mention was made of vampires, so we do not believe the humans know his true nature and think him merely a pirate."

"I see; you and Guillaume track them and see where they go. If prudent, bring at least one if not both of them to me," he ordered.

"As you wish, my lord." Claire bowed and went in search of Guillaume.

"Well, that could have gone much worse." Sam shuddered once they were back on the streets of New Orleans. Etienne pointed them toward the docks after escorting them outside. The hint was not lost on them.

"Aye, it very well could have. Makes me wonder if any other Brumble & Sons crews have run into trouble because of that bastard's stunt," Bainbridge grumbled.

"It would be a good idea to send Father a message to warn the fleet," Sam reasoned.

He looked at her for a moment. Finally, he said, "I know better than to try to talk you into going home without Zach or Thom; but that is the first time in months I've heard you mention your father without rancor in your tone."

Samantha sighed and looked down. "Perhaps it is because of how the Lord Mayor took the news of who had really taken his daughter. I have hurt Father. Part of me feels bad about that, while another part of me is unrepentant, saying he deserved it for the way he sacrificed my brothers. I do understand why he did it, but I still find it hard to forgive him."

She remained silent for a while before she continued, "I do not wish him continued suffering. I will not go back until I've found my brothers; but I believe it will do Father good to know I am alive and well. I will send him a post before we leave port."

Bainbridge placed a hand on her shoulder and offered her a warm, if sad, smile. "You are a good daughter, Samantha Brumble. Never doubt that. If old Tobias ever thought otherwise, he was a fool. Now, I think it best if you go on back to the ship. I'll stop by this Madame Thibideaux's and see what I can learn."

She nodded. "I think you're right, Captain. I will see you when you return to the ship."

She headed toward the docks, and he angled off in the direction of the French Quarter.

Sam had barely gotten out of sight of Bainbridge, when someone tapped her on the shoulder. She turned to see a young woman a little shorter than her, smiling at her. Thinking the woman had mistaken her for a sailor, she said, "I'm sorry, miss, but I have no coin."

The woman smiled wider, revealing long, sharp canines. "That is a moot point, Samantha Brumble. There is someone who wants to meet you."

She moved faster than Sam could see. Sam only had long enough to wonder how this woman knew who she was before her vision darkened.

She came to in an opulent bedroom. A quick self-inspection revealed that, although lying on the bed, she remained fully clothed. That brought a sigh of relief.

"Where am I?" she wondered aloud.

Tamara A. Lowery

"For the moment, you are a guest in my home." The unexpected voice startled a yip from her.

She edged away from the lad sitting in the chair next to the bed. She wondered how she had not noticed him before he spoke. "Who are you? How did I get here? Why am I here?"

He smiled, tight-lipped, at her and said, "I am Jeorge. Claire brought you here, and I wish to know why you seek Viktor Brandewyne."

"Do you have a surname, Jeorge?" She eased her hand behind her back. She kept her marlin spike and knife tucked back there.

"I did once, but it has been so long since I've used it, I am afraid I've forgotten it. Oh, are you looking for these?" He waved a hand at the two tools on the night stand. "We feared they would be too uncomfortable for you to lie on, so I had Claire set them aside."

Sam fought not to panic. She was unarmed, true, but she was not defenseless. Growing up with two brothers and no mother had seen to that. This young man had offered her no harm, so far; and she was pretty sure he hadn't taken advantage of her while she'd been unconscious. She decided she would ride this out and see where it went.

"You say someone named Claire brought me here? I remember a woman stopping me on the way back to my ship. Somehow, she knew my name. The next thing I remember is waking up here."

"Ah, yes," Jeorge gave an unconvincing look of apology. "Regrettably, it was necessary to render you unconscious before bringing you here. This is a secure location, and I wish to keep it so. I have few enemies, but the ones I do have are dangerous."

She scowled at him. "You could have just blindfolded me."

He shook his head. "It would have taken too much time to convince you of the necessity or even agree to come here. Now, please, it is important to me to know why you seek Brandewyne. Do you know what he is?"

Sam couldn't hide her anger. "He is a vile, black-hearted pirate! He has targeted my family over some slight my father supposedly did to someone by the name of Rigger, whom Father doesn't even remember! The bastard has my brothers, and I want them back!"

"A pirate; is that all he is?"

Something in the way he asked the question gave her pause. She realized she dealt with no mere boy. He was something more, but she wasn't sure what. He held an almost a predatory air about himself.

"Isn't that enough? I obviously haven't found him yet, so I don't know. What else would he be?"

Jeorge peered at her. She noticed he seemed to be scenting the air. His behavior, as far as she was concerned, was decidedly odd.

She started to back away from him again. Just as she reached the other side of the bed and set her feet on the floor, he was out of his chair and standing close enough to almost touch her. She let out an involuntary yelp and almost fell back onto the bed. Her anger melted into fear.

"What are you?" Once again, she tried to back away from him. She soon found herself trapped against the wall.

Jeorge leaned into her, his eyes dilated and lips parted. The tips of long, sharp canines peeked out, just visible to her. Sam noted that his eyes seemed to have an eerie glow. Gazing into them, her fear vanished as if it had never been.

He took a step back, confident that she would no longer offer resistance. "That is better. Are you still frightened, child?"

"No; but I do not understand what is going on."

"You truly don't know what I am or what Brandewyne is beyond a mere pirate and brigand," he stated rather than asked. "Do you know what a vampire is?"

She frowned as if struggling with a faint memory. "I think I have heard the term before, but I am not sure exactly what it is. I have been warned that he was more than human, some dark creature of evil."

Jeorge sighed. Her vague knowledge might slow things down, and he'd hoped to be done with her before dawn. "Very well; I shall attempt to explain. Hopefully, you are a clever enough girl to grasp it quickly. I am a vampire, and, luckily for you, I have already fed tonight. Your fear earlier was quite — appetizing."

Hell's Dodo

She tilted her head. "You eat people? I thought those were called cannibals."

"No," he laughed. "I do not eat flesh. I feed only on blood, preferably human blood. Sometimes, I have found it prudent to drink from animals instead, to avoid discovery by those who hunt my kind."

"Are you saying that the pirate I'm looking for is such a creature? Is that why you wanted to know why I am hunting him?" she asked.

"Partially, yes."

She shook her head. "Even though I have encountered some inexplicable phenomena during my search, I never truly believed the rumors that he was some supernatural creature. It is not uncommon for pirates to spread lies and rumors about themselves to frighten their potential victims. Until just now, I did not believe in vampires. I've certainly never encountered one before."

"Actually, *ma Cherie*," he laughed, "you have encountered at least one vampire before. It is plain that he or she blocked your memory of it, however."

"What are you talking about?"

"You have been closer to Captain Brandewyne, or perhaps one of the vampires he made, than you think. There is a scent about you that bears his touch; yet it has a distinctly feline flavor to it," he told her.

Unbidden, her mind flashed back to the large black cat she had not seen since the night she dreamed she'd been ravished. Jeorge saw the memory, mild telepathy with his prey being one of his gifts. He saw the recognition and realization flicker in her eyes. His smile widened.

"Claire will help you disrobe. I see no bite scar on your throat therefore it must be somewhere else." At his silent bidding, the woman Sam saw earlier on the street entered the room.

"Do not touch me!" Sam's anger forced back the vampire's influence.

"You will not be harmed; I give you my word," Jeorge reassured her, impressed at her strength of will.

"Perhaps not, but you would humiliate me!"

He suddenly stood right in her face again with his fangs bared and his eyes flashing. He grasped her chin and forced her to meet his gaze. His voice came out as a firm growl. "Another time this might have been amusing, but dawn draws near, and you try my patience. I may not be your master, but I am very old and very powerful. You will do as you are told!"

Sam whimpered as she felt the full force of the vampire's will. At last, she realized how easily he could kill her; and she would be powerless to even defend herself.

Silent tears slid down her face as Claire helped her remove her clothing. In truth, she needed the help. She seemed to have lost the ability to perform even the simplest movement on her own.

Hell's Dodo

Once Sam stood nude, the female vampire posed her in a spread-eagle stance. Sam found herself unable to even follow Jeorge with her eyes as he slowly circled her. Her gaze remained locked straight ahead. She became very familiar with the wallpaper pattern.

Jeorge examined her thoroughly, lifting her arms, looking over her back, and even lifting her breasts to see if she had been bitten under them. Finally, he scooped her up as if she weighed no more than a kitten and laid her on the bed. He spread her legs apart to get a better look at her inner thighs.

"Ah, there it is," he said, finally finding the unique scar left by fangs. "Claire, bring in Melanie and a measuring rod."

"Yes, my lord."

Claire left the room and returned shortly with another vampire and the required tool. Jeorge measured the space between the fang marks on Sam's thigh and compared it to a similar scar on Melanie's throat.

Frowning, Jeorge observed, "They are not the same. Melanie, can you confirm that she was bitten by a vampire of your sire's bloodline?"

Obediently, Melanie leaned over Sam and sniffed at the scar. Samantha wanted to writhe and scoot away as the vampire's hair tickled her skin.

Finally, Melanie stood straight and said, "Yes, my lord; his scent is there, diluted by cat. I am reminded of the black cat he retrieved my necklace from before he kidnapped me."

"Odd; I have never heard of anyone being able to turn an animal. Even if it were possible, it would not be wise." He frowned in puzzlement. "Also, the spacing is too wide to have been done by a cat."

He gazed at Samantha. Her tears had stopped, and amazed understanding must have shown in her eyes. Memories which formerly seemed dreamlike and disjointed to her now made sense.

"You have thought of something, child. You may get dressed now."

Free to move again, she quickly gathered up her clothes and put them back on. She then moved cautiously around the bed, keeping a wary eye on the vampires as she did so. When she reached the nightstand, she retrieved her knife and marlin spike and tucked them back into their customary positions at the small of her back.

She remained acutely aware that Jeorge allowed her to regain the weapons. Obviously, he did not view them as a threat to his well-being; having seen his speed and felt his power, she had to agree. She still felt better for being armed again.

"Now then, child; what memory or realization did Melanie just spark in you?" he asked once he saw she was more relaxed.

"Several; but before I tell you, I want your guarantee that I will be returned to my ship unharmed."

His mouth quirked up into a half-smile. "That has been my intention, provided you did not prove difficult. You have my word."

Hell's Dodo

She nodded in acceptance of his pledge; though she did not fully trust him to keep it. "First, I realized that she is the reason I was beaten and jailed by the *gendarmes*. They thought I had something to do with her disappearance. You are the Lord Mayor's daughter, are you not?" The last was addressed to Melanie.

"I was," the vampire in question responded. "Why would they think you had something to do with my kidnapping?"

"I am Samantha Brumble. Viktor Brandewyne used my brother's name to gain entry to your house."

Melanie gave her a look of sympathy. "I fear your brother Thomas is dead or one of us. My sire told me he had killed him."

"If your father killed him, why was I put through all that?" Sam clearly didn't understand.

"I did not say my father," Melanie corrected her. "Viktor Brandewyne is my sire. He made me a vampire. He killed your brother."

"He killed Thomas?" Tears came unbidden to her eyes. "What about Zachary?"

"I do not know. He made no mention of any Zachary. As I said though, Thomas may be vampire, like I am. My sire did mention he had made a handful of his crew vampires. Your brother may be among them."

"But you said he killed my brother."

"Yes, just as he killed me." She held her hand out, palm up. "See for yourself. I have no pulse."

Sam grasped her wrist and almost dropped it instantly. The flesh felt icy to her touch and looked pasty white compared to her own weathered tan. She found no pulse.

Melanie reached up and caressed Sam's cheek. "You are so warm and alive," she whispered. She eased closer until her mouth was but a breath from Sam's ear. "You smell delicious."

"Melanie; enough." Jeorge's voice remained calm and even, but there was power behind it. The female vampire stood several steps away from Sam within the time of a heartbeat. "Go to the cellar and pick out a meal. This one is under my protection."

"*Oui*, milord; forgive my brief lack of control." Melanie curtsied and left the room.

Samantha shook herself, as if waking from a dream. "What just happened? Where did she go?"

"I sent her to feed before she could attack you," he told her. "You said you realized several things. What else besides recognizing who Melanie was?"

"Oh," she said, amazed that she had gotten off course. She wondered how it had happened. "The large black cat; there was one on the *Shining Star* that seemed to have taken a liking to me. He would curl up in my bunk every night and follow me around. I had a strange dream one night that he turned into a handsome young man and ravished me. He told me he could help me find Brandewyne. The dream felt so real I had Captain Bainbridge help me search the crew for my attacker. We found no one aboard who fit the description, and I never saw the cat again. Is it possible it wasn't a dream?"

He stared at her without moving for several minutes. She found it unnerving. Finally, he spoke. "It is possible; though if true, this cat or man is a very rare vampire. The ability and knowledge to change forms has been lost to my kind for over a thousand years. If you do find Brandewyne, it will be because he lets you. I am sure he is aware you are hunting him."

"He is," she confirmed. "Zachary left a letter for me with a tavern girl in Havana warning me to stop my search."

"I would advise you to heed that warning, *mademoiselle*. It seems that Viktor Brandewyne is more powerful and dangerous a specimen of vampirekind than perhaps even he suspects."

He looked down at the floor as if troubled. When he looked back up, she fell for the ruse and met his gaze.

"Sam! Where have you been? We've been looking all over for you," Bainbridge chided worriedly.

She looked up to see him approaching her on the street. "Captain? I was on my way back to the ship. I still have that letter to father to write and I'm starving. I thought you were going to Madame Thibideaux's. What happened?"

He frowned as he reached her and started probing her head, checking for lumps. She tried to wave him off, irritated and confused by his behavior. "What are you doing?"

"That bastard of a *gendarme* must've hit you harder than I thought. You've been missing for a day, lass. I went to the whore's place of business last night. The watch said you'd never returned to the ship. Can you remember anything?"

She stared at him, her face pale with shock. How had she lost an entire day? "The last thing I remember was a strumpet approaching me. I shooed her off, telling her I had no coin, and was headed back to the ship just as you came up to me."

He shook his head at her. "Let's get you back to the ship and have the doctor take a look at you. You can take care of the letter after that. I think you should stay away from rum from now on, Sam. It obviously has an ill effect on you."

"Ugh! Don't even say rum!"

Bainbridge smirked. "That's what I thought. Once you've been checked out, fed, and your letter posted, I'll tell you what I found out at Celine Thibideaux's."

Chapter 13

The *Incubus* reached the Caribbean just in time for the sugar and rum convoys. While Viktor had his quest, he still captained a pirate ship. He had his crew to think of, and old habits died hard.

"Mr. Grimm."

"Aye, Captain?" The first mate's demeanor held a quiet eagerness. He knew his captain well.

"Consult Mr. Brumble about which ports his father's ships do rum trade with. The lads look a bit thirsty, and they've been idle too long. Some exercise will do them good."

Grimm couldn't hide his grin. "Aye, Captain, that it would." He quickly left to find the navigator.

Belladonna sauntered over to lean against the railing. "He's still frightened of me, you know," she stated.

"Grimm? Cautious, maybe; but I don't think he's frightened of you."

She scowled at him. "That's not who I meant, and you know it. Zach is still afraid. Granted, he's not as terrified as he was in Salem, but I still spook him. That is not a good thing."

"And how do you figure that, pet?" His smirk let her know he disagreed and thought she was only pouting over the loss of her playmate.

"It makes him look, smell, and act like food," she told him. He saw in her eyes just how serious she was.

He blinked. It never occurred to him she might start seeing Brumble that way. He found himself forced to admit the thought of having a tempting morsel waved in one's face yet being forbidden to eat it must be torturous. Belle had done nothing to deserve such treatment from him.

He used the blood bond he held over his crew to make a slight alteration in Brumble's perception of the siren. Shortly after, Grimm returned with the former trader.

The man smiled and nodded at her but gave no other reaction. Viktor could smell no fear from the man.

"Better, pet?" Vik asked as Belle headed for her cabin.

"Much; thank you," she replied and disappeared down the ladder.

"Ah, Mr. Brumble, what can you tell me?"

"According to the charts, we're not far from Aruba, Captain. There are a handful of sugar plantations there which have an exclusive contract with Brumble & Sons. They ship some sugar and molasses; but they specialize in rum. There is a distillery on the island they run as partners," he replied.

Hell's Dodo

"Now that does sound promising," Grimm said with a grin.

"Indeed, it does," Viktor agreed. "Mr. Brumble, we need to know when the rum shipments are going out and from what port."

Zach nodded and held up a chart tube. "I anticipated that, Captain. In my spare time, I have been plotting out charts of all the main B & S trade routes, as well as the unofficial ones run through a few dummy companies."

"I am impressed, Mr. Brumble. What possessed you to do this?" Vik asked.

"Piracy agrees with me, it seems. I am sure Father believes I threw in with you willingly. Why disappoint him?" he said with a shrug.

"Could be worse, lad." Grimm clapped him on the shoulder. "You could be barking mad, like old Mudstick."

Zach smirked. "There is that. I grew up hearing horror stories of the man. Father always worried I would turn on him like Grayson Chapelwaite turned on his family."

"Were there warning signs, like you buggering anyone or anything that stood still long enough?" Grimm joked.

Zach laughed. "Hardly! No, Father has just always been paranoid."

"Gentlemen," Vik drew their attention back to the subject at hand, "Let's go to my cabin and coordinate our plan of attack."

Vik had the *Incubus* lay in wait along the trade route. One of the smaller islands hid the ship from view of potential prey. They planned to wait until the convoy sailed past the island, then sail around to intercept. To get the timing right, he sent Lazarus aloft in his raven form to keep an eye on their prey.

The *Dutch Girl* led the rum convoy from Aruba headed toward Boston. Her captain, a thin, fractious man named Lemuel Gordon, always prided himself on bringing in cargo on time or under time. Though not as physically violent a captain as his employer, Tobias Brumble, he nonetheless presented as a puritanically strict man. He did not mind shipping spirits, since they were a profitable cargo; but he did not partake of them nor permit his officers to do so while aboard, either. He made the concession of allowing the crew a daily ration of watered-down rum or gin, though, to avert the risk of mutiny aboard his command.

For that same reason, he did not ask his officers to abstain in port. Captain Gordon was nothing if not practical. He knew the value of good officers outweighed his distaste over what was rarely viewed as even being a vice.

His current first mate and quartermaster, Lockland Stoud, proved a prime example of that policy. The man loved his spirits, but abided by the captain's rules. Gordon could not remember having a more able mate. The grizzled, gruff sailor had seen more than his fair share of trials at sea. Gordon trusted his judgment.

Hell's Dodo

"Mr. Stoud, what make you of that?" he said and pointed out the ship-o-the-line clearing the island to starboard. "She appears to be changing course to join us."

Dutifully, Stoud looked over at the approaching ship. He then got out his spyglass for a closer look. While he did this, Gordon observed, "I thought we'd received word a few months back that we would no longer receive any military escorts in pirate waters, what with the unrest being stirred up by those rebels."

Stoud grunted and lowered the glass. "Aye, Cap'n; we did. That's no Navy ship, either, or I miss my mark. Never knew a Navy commander yet who would allow his men to have uniforms that ill-fitting; and a ship that size usually sails with a few escorts. Looks like we've run afoul of pirates."

"Are you sure, Mr. Stoud? What pirates have ever laid their hands on a ship-o-the-line like that?" Gordon said incredulously.

"There's one. Heard about it on me last ship; but I don't think the word's gotten to all the B & S ships, yet." Stoud frowned and looked through the glass again. "Aye; and that's the very ship I heard tell about: *Incubus*. God in Heaven help us."

Gordon saw his first mate grow ashen, a sheen of terror in his eyes. "Who is her captain, Mr. Stoud?"

The answer came in a shaky whisper, "Bloody Vik Brandee. Oh God, I need a drink."

☠

Tamara A. Lowery

The *Incubus* never even fired a shot. Before they had a good shot on the merchant ships lined up, the lead ship hove to and ran up a flag of surrender. The three ships following her did likewise. Although their captains didn't have the information the captain of the *Dutch Girl* had, they realized they would never be able to outrun the warship, let alone stand in a battle against her.

Viktor's pirates, under the guidance of Grimm and Jon-Jon, soon began the process of transferring the cargo over to the *Incubus*. Meanwhile, the vampire ordered all the captains and mates brought to him.

The men arrived in the officers' mess only expecting to hear demands or possibly to be executed. What they didn't expect was the sumptuous meal laid out before them. Mr. Trundle had been very busy in the galley.

"Gentlemen, please be seated," Viktor said with a wave toward the table. "Mr. Trundle has worked very hard. It would be a shame to let such a feast go to waste."

This caused some uneasy murmuring, as the merchant captains and mates seated themselves around the large table. The food smelled and looked good, and a good cook at sea was hard to come by.

Viktor waited for them to be seated; then, with a genial smile, no hint of fang showing, said, "I am Viktor Brandewyne, captain of this fine vessel. You will excuse the absence of my first and second mates, Hezekiah Grimm and Willoby Jon. They are busy shopping, as it were. However, my navigator, whom I am sure you are all acquainted with, Zachary Brumble, will be joining us, as will the lovely Belladonna."

He enjoyed the various reactions this announcement garnered. Captain Pembroke, of the *Island Runner*, spoke up in indignation. "Young Captain Brumble was taken by pirates a few years back. There was never any ransom demand; he is assumed dead."

Zach took that as his cue to enter the cabin. "No, Harold, I'm not dead, although my brother, Thomas, is."

This news was greeted with a mixture of sympathy and suspicion — and murmured speculation about why one brother was spared and the other was not. For the most part, Zach ignored it, having expected it of them.

Viktor moved over to one of the side doors off the cabin and rapped at it. "Belle, pet," he said, "I know you are out there. Don't keep our guests waiting." Though his words remained polite, they held an undercurrent of impatient irritation.

As one, the men rose when she entered. She wore a teal silk gown which set off her creamy complexion and dark, blood-red hair. The low-cut, tight-fitting bodice, lifted and displayed her ample bosom.

Lockland Stoud found his voice first among them. Even Viktor had been momentarily stunned. "Belle, love, you haven't changed a bit. Doubt you remember me, though," the grizzled old sailor grinned.

She peered at him for a moment before recognition set in. She broke into a beaming, mischievous smile.

"Lockland! How could I ever forget you? You'll want to keep that one, Captain. He's one of the most able seamen I've ever met." Her laugh held a wicked, throaty tone.

"Is there something I should know, pet?" Vik raised an eyebrow at her.

"Later, in private," she replied impishly.

Only she saw the heat in his eyes, as he held the chair for her. Along the mental link they shared, he told her, *"I look forward to getting the information from you, pet."*

"I'm not your pet." She gave her token rebuttal.

He noticed during the course of the meal that the siren showed an amazing grasp of table manners. *"You've been practicing, pet,"* he thought at her.

She replied in kind, *"Brianna made me a project of hers. She convinced me that she could help me blend in among humans other than sailors. After realizing we might have to deal with more polite society, thanks to Jeorge, I agreed to let her teach me."*

"Remind me to thank Hezekiah for taking a fancy to her." Aloud, he said, "I don't believe I've seen that dress before, Belle. The color suits you."

"Thank you, Captain. Brianna gave it to me shortly before the wedding. She said she doubted it would fit her anymore, but that it should be a perfect fit for me."

"Oh, it is. I shall have to find you some suitable jewels to go with it."

She smiled at him before pushing back from the table. He took the cue and rose to help her with the chair, so her skirts would not tangle with it. The rest of the men stood, as courtesy dictated.

Smiling, she told them, "It has been a pleasure to meet you, gentlemen. Now, if you will excuse me, I am sure you have business to discuss."

They murmured their pleasantries to her, as she left. Once she was gone, the cabin boy brought in a decanter of brandy and a case of cigars.

"Now, gentlemen, let us discuss my terms." Viktor poured a glass of brandy for each man and had the cabin boy distribute them and the cigars around the table. He noticed that Captain Gordon pointedly would not touch either.

"Is there a problem, sir, that you do not accept my hospitality?" Vik asked.

Lemuel Gordon looked at him with an icy stare. "I do not imbibe, sir, nor do I have any fondness for tobacco. I merely carry it as cargo."

"I see." Viktor's eyes began to glow slightly. "You prefer to keep your blood pure."

"I do, sir." He continued to meet Viktor's gaze.

"Very well, I will not conscript you to my crew. A piratical life would not suit you, I deem."

"No, sir; it would not."

"Bring Mr. Gordon a flagon of water," Viktor instructed the cabin boy. The lad immediately left to get it. "Will that be satisfactory, sir?"

"Yes, thank you."

"Now then, gentlemen, I will start by telling you that some of you will be invited to join my crew and some of you will not. Of those not invited, one will be permitted to leave this ship alive." He waited for the announcement to sink in.

Gordon spoke up, "Are we to be ransomed, then?"

Viktor laughed, no longer bothering to hide his long, sharp canines. "Who would pay it? Not Tobias Brumble, I'd wager. Why, I've heard reports that he told the Royal Navy his sons conspired with me and willingly became pirates, which is simply not true. Yes, his sons serve me, but they were conscripted and did not willingly betray their father."

He shook his head, still chuckling. "No, there will be no ransom demands. Do not worry, however; I still have a use those of you who will not be invited to join my crew."

This clearly puzzled Gordon. He also found the complacency of his fellow captains quite disturbing, more so that the pirate's unnatural teeth. It was well know that most of the legendary pirates were given to theatrics.

Hell's Dodo

"If not for crewmen or for ransom, what possible purpose would imprisoning or murdering us serve?"

"You especially, Mr. Gordon, carry something I value far more than gold." Viktor smiled at him. "I need your blood thanks to a nasty little curse I picked up in Hispañola. In fact, I think I may have a little sample now."

The merchant captain looked about for something to use as a weapon. "Pembroke, Barton, Stoud, your assistance!"

"Hold him." Viktor's voice carried power. It traveled through the new blood bonds formed when the merchants drank the brandy tainted with the vampire's blood.

They had no choice but to obey.

"Harold, what is wrong with you?" Shock and betrayal filled Gordon's voice as his compatriots grabbed him and immobilized him. "I never imagined you would throw in with pirates."

Pembroke held his arm but gave him an apologetic look. "I'm sorry, Lemuel. I don't want to do this; but Captain Brandewyne wills it."

Gordon glared at Stoud, who held his other arm. "I won't forget this, Mr. Stoud. You will never serve aboard another merchant ship!"

"Already found another ship, Cap'n Gordon." Stoud didn't look phased by the threat. "Pirate, merchant, makes no difference to me, 'cept pirates are more fun and don't begrudge a man a drink or two."

Barton, who stood behind him, grabbed his forehead and forced him to bare his throat. The remaining men sat stoically in their seats awaiting Brandee's pleasure.

Viktor moved to stand in front of the shorter man. His Hunger shone in his eyes, but he did not try to force his will on Gordon, yet.

"I don't believe I've had unpolluted blood before. The majority of my victims have been the sort of people who wouldn't be missed."

"What have you done to them to make them turn on me?"

"Oh, there was something in the brandy," Vik replied. Before Gordon could say anything else, the vampire attacked.

Chapter 14

Viktor decided to put in at Cartageña to offload the sundries they had no use for. He kept the rum, but most of the sugar and molasses just took up valuable cargo space. It was far too much for the cook to use.

It also proved to be a good port to release Harold Pembroke in.

Viktor knew that worry for his sister had been eating away at Zach. The man was a good navigator, and Viktor didn't want him distracted. Zach's will was strong enough that Vik didn't want to rely solely on the regular dosing of the special rum to keep him in line. He let Zach pick which man to spare. He then implanted a compulsion in Mr. Pembroke to find Samantha Brumble and try to convince her to go back home. There would be no ransom. Viktor said to tell her she would suffer her brother's fate if she continued to pursue the pirate.

He omitted the fact that she would suffer it regardless. Her fate had been sealed the moment Jim Rigger fed on her.

Pembroke encountered Thomas Brumble during the voyage from the islands to Cartageña. The experience disturbed him deeply, since he hadn't been under Viktor's influence at the time.

He would stress the warning.

Satisfied with the price Grimm got for the illicit cargo, Viktor divvied up the gold and gave his crew some time in port.

Grimm, of course, had not been happy with the price. He knew of at least five other ports where he could have gotten double or triple the amount; but they were all north of their current location, the opposite direction from where Viktor needed to search for Auntie Clarissa.

"Hezekiah, don't look so sour about it," Vik reasoned with him. "The cargo cost us nothing, we got plenty of provisions, since the ships were fresh out of port, and we got some extra hands. The gold was adequate to let the lads enjoy themselves ashore without over-indulging, and don't forget the rum."

Grimm shook his head, smiling. "You're right, Vik. When looked at that way, it was a good prize. Come to think of it, that is only the second time either of us has taken an entire convoy. Didn't even have to fire a shot."

"Exactly."

"I guess I'm just missing Brianna," Grimm sighed. "I don't even have the urge to go wenching. Has she really civilized me that much?"

"All the more wenches for me," Vik joked. "I don't know if she's civilized you that much, Hezekiah. You still like to drink, smoke, and commit mayhem. She does seem to have had a civilizing effect on Belle, however."

Hell's Dodo

"Oh?" Grimm raised his eyebrows questioningly. "Is that a good thing or a bad thing?"

"Good, so far; and interesting. She has nearly mastered table manners. She even wore a dress without being asked to. Usually, it is a fight to get her to wear anything as tight-fitting as the bodice on that gown was."

"I didn't know she even owned any dresses."

Viktor smirked. "Your wife gave her one of hers: the teal silk. First time I've seen it, though."

Grimm's eyes darkened at the memory. He chuckled. "She wore it for me a couple of times. I couldn't wait to get her out of it, either. Belle has more bosom than Brianna. I can imagine the visual effect."

"Aye." Vik's chuckle matching his first mate's in lustiness. "I think she could have shown her true smile while wearing that dress, and not a man in the room would have noticed or cared."

They both laughed.

Grimm found a game of dice not long after going ashore. Confident that his first mate would gamble all night, Viktor went in search of a bottle and a wench.

As an afterthought, he summoned Lazarus. "Lazarus, come forth."

Mrrrow? The large black cat materialized in front of him.

He squatted down to rub the cat's ears and said, "Jim, I need you to fly back to Mother Celie's. Hezekiah is troubled about his wife more than he will admit. He turns into an old hen when he worries. Just look in on Brianna and see how she's coming along."

Lazarus rubbed his cheek against Viktor's hand, purred, and dissolved into a smoky mass. A moment later, he rematerialized as a raven, cawed once, and took flight.

Satisfied, Viktor headed toward the more affluent parts of town. He had a mind to seek out and seduce some land owner's daughter or wife. The challenge added more sport than merely paying at a brothel.

Barely an hour after sunset, he spotted a woman he thought worth the effort. He found her absolutely stunning. Petite, she stood just a little shorter than Belladonna and had dark hair possibly as black as his own. The pure whiteness of her skin made it seem to nearly glow in the starlight. Fine, delicate features gave her face an aristocratic air.

Viktor's first thought upon seeing her was, *"I want."*

As he watched her, he wondered why she ventured out after dark unaccompanied. Her mannerisms clearly marked her as an aristocrat rather than a whore. Something quietly dangerous about her movements intrigued him. He soon recognized her as some sort of predator.

A breeze wafted from the direction of the bay and carried her scent to him: vampire.

Hell's Dodo

That explained the pallor. Granted, Viktor still sported his weathered sailor's tan; but he remembered how pale Jeorge and his people had been. Even the six crewmen he'd turned paled to a ghostly shade of white. He guessed it had to do with them being dead, where he was not.

The wind shifted a bit, and she scented him. She turned her head and looked directly at him, then smiled. He found it both inviting and predatory at the same time.

He gave her a matching smile. Having bedded both Gloribeau and Belladonna, he knew the sport would be more intense with a magical being than with a mere human woman.

They advanced towards each other.

At Captain Wormsloe's insistence, the *Lorelei* put in at Cartageña a few days prior to the arrival of the *Incubus*. The smaller ship tied up at the docks. The draft of the *Incubus* forced Viktor to anchor in the harbor, close to the mouth of the seaway.

Unaware that her prey was so close, Carpathia took the opportunity to hunt in the city. At first, she stayed near the docks. Bodies of sailors and harbor workers were easily disposed of. She grew tired of such fare after a couple of nights and decided to seek out victims in some of the better areas of town.

While wandering an affluent neighborhood, she felt eyes upon her. A change in the breeze brought her the scent of a healthy male in his prime. She detected a hint of the sea about him, but not like a common sailor. He smelled cleaner than that.

She smiled at him and was rewarded with an answering smile just as predatory as her own. She could see his body temperature rise in key locations as blood rushed to them.

As they approached each other, Carpathia thought he looked absolutely delicious.

Viktor couldn't resist testing his power of compulsion on her. He could sense her trying to use hers on him. Her eyes shone with an un-light, they were so dark. It was the kind of darkness that promised to wrap itself around you like a warm, protecting blanket.

Viktor recognized it for the trap it was. *"She thinks I am human,"* he thought. *"This is going to be fun."*

Carpathia stopped a few feet from her prey and tilted her head in confusion. Not only was the strikingly handsome stranger not falling to her will; he blasted her with a power of his own. She could feel it like a warm sea breeze caressing her skin as his eyes blazed with emerald fire.

She grew cautious. His power fired both her lust and her Hunger. To take him and then take his power would be magnificent; but until she knew what manner of being he was, she would not allow herself that indulgence. Some creatures were dangerous to drink from.

Hell's Dodo

"You are not human. What are you?" She kept her distance, her senses alert for a possible attack.

Viktor found her accent fascinating. "I could ask you the same thing, vampire," he replied playfully. He carefully kept his fangs hidden.

"How do you know what I am?" she asked with narrowed eyes.

In response, he darted around behind her, or tried to. She spun with him, keeping him in front of her. He smirked and gave her a mocking half-bow. "It seems we are evenly matched, pet."

The pure arrogance of his statement both infuriated her and aroused her. That she couldn't figure him out drove her curiosity wild.

"What are you?" she asked again.

"Someone looking to enjoy what the night has to offer." He daringly reached out a hand and brushed her cheek with his fingertips, lust shining in his eyes.

Thia went dead still. It was the only way she could keep from reacting to his touch. Even knowing what she was, he still wanted her and showed no fear at all. She couldn't remember the last time a man had been that way toward her after learning how dangerous she truly was. That went further toward seducing her than any words ever could.

Viktor's smile was almost smug. He could tell she wanted him. Her emotionless mask was just that; a mask. She couldn't hide her scent. Even the walking dead could exude that muskiness of arousal.

He chuckled and started to step in closer. He was so concentrated on the vampire before him that he barely noticed the siren's approach.

"There you are. I've been looking all over for you," Belladonna said. Spotting the vampire as Viktor turned to face her, she added, "Who is she?"

Carpathia took advantage of the momentary distraction to take flight.

When he turned back to ask for her name, he found no one there. "Gone, it would seem. You frightened her off, pet."

"Good and I'm not your pet. You don't need to be dallying with vampires. It will only lead to trouble," she grumped.

"You worry too much, Belle."

In her consternation over the mystery, Carpathia went after easier prey. She got herself invited into a family's home and proceeded to murder the entire group, glutting on their blood.

As she finished off the children, whom she saved for last, she finally could think rationally about the encounter.

The male had looked and almost smelled human, yet he clearly wasn't. A siren, of all creatures, had come looking for him and acted very territorial about him.

Thia had found one reference to a male siren during her studies of vampire lore and law centuries ago. It seemed the only logical explanation for his immunity to her powers and his lack of fear. Siren blood was instant true death to any vampire. He knew he was safe.

She now knew she was safe from him, as well. Sirens didn't eat vampires. They preferred living flesh or that fresh from their own kill.

This could prove interesting.

Later, aboard the *Incubus*, Belladonna lit into Viktor in his cabin. "What were you thinking?"

"That I was looking for sport. That vampire showed potential for some fine sport, indeed," he replied unapologetically.

"You know better than to get mixed up with other vampires, Viktor."

He rolled his eyes at her. "I very rarely use this port, pet. It is not important to me. I'm not worried about having to deal with the local version of Jeorge."

"Viktor, there's a good chance that the vampire you encountered tonight is not local. I was looking for you to tell you I spotted the *Lorelei* in port. That's the ship I stole Robert from. The vampire who is hunting you is in this port." Her voice held genuine worry.

He misread it as jealousy, which he found amusing but irritating, as well. "All the better; if that was her, I can find out why she is hunting me. She doesn't even know I am vampire, yet. She kept asking me what I was."

"You are determined to seek her out again, aren't you?" Belle frowned.

"I am."

She glared at him for a few minutes before speaking. "Then you are a fool." She turned and stormed off only to find him blocking the door. She didn't even have time to back away from him before he had her jaw in his grip. The look he gave her was not friendly.

"I am many things, Belle, but foolish is not one of them. Never. Forget. That."

He released her and stepped aside, a tacit dismissal. She rubbed her jaw where the imprints of his fingers were fading. Deliberately, she walked past him and out of the cabin, quietly shutting the door behind her.

Chapter 15

Viktor didn't see Belladonna for the remainder of the time the *Incubus* remained in port. He found her pouting annoying but not particularly surprising. It wasn't the first time she'd avoided him. He figured she would show back up once they headed out to sea.

He went back out the next night, searching for the vampire. Checking the direction of the wind, he went to the side of port that was downwind and tried to catch her scent. After about half an hour, he finally picked up a faint trace of it.

The scent remained elusive, almost disappearing at times. If he hadn't seen the *Lorelei* in the harbor on his way into town, he would have thought it was leftover scent from the previous night.

Finally, it grew strong, accompanied by the aroma of fresh blood. She was stationary and feeding. Viktor proceeded cautiously.

He located her in an alleyway. From his rooftop perspective, he could see her using a long, serrated dagger to remove her victim's head. Silently, he dropped down to street level.

Some faint rustling of cloth or a brush of power alerted the vampire. In a split second, she stood facing him with her blade to his throat.

"Who are you?"

He gave her his most wicked smile, still concealing his fangs. "Don't you mean *what* am I?"

"Your name," she growled in response to his arrogance.

He took a step closer to her, allowing the blade to bite into his skin. A thin trickle of blood began to flow from the small wound. He leaned down and captured her mouth with his.

Her lips were soft and moist with the fresh blood of her victim. The taste of it threatened to wake his Hunger. He growled and deepened the kiss, clasping her to him and trying to steal every stray drop without cutting his tongue on her fangs.

Despite herself, Carpathia's eyes fluttered closed at the intensity of the kiss. *"No wonder sirens are so dangerous,"* she thought. The stranger's lips were soft and warm and tasted slightly of salt spray and… was that the taste of blood mingled with liquor? Her shock at feeling his fangs with her tongue caused her to drop her knife.

"How can he be vampire?" Her thoughts raced. *"He is warm and living. His skin is tanned dark from the sunlight. His heart beats. His magic feels strong, but he does not smell like a vampire; and I cannot sense him!"*

Hell's Dodo

Viktor finally broke the kiss. He threw his head back and loosed a shuddering sigh. Her power danced along his skin.

"That was worth it!" he laughed.

"Your name, please." He saw she gazed up at him with curiosity, as if she had never encountered anything like him before. He'd had similar reactions from human women after he'd seduced them. To get this reaction from a being as magically powerful as the creature he now held boosted his ego and arrogance even more.

He released his embrace and stepped back to give her a half-bow. He watched her face carefully as he replied, "Viktor Brandewyne, at your service."

For a split second, she went very still. Other than that, she showed no reaction to the name. It was enough, though. It confirmed she was the vampire looking for him.

She smiled up at him. "I am Lady Carpathia." She thought, *"So this is the creature I have been sent to destroy. He is strong; perhaps even a match for me. I will have to resort to deception and seduction, if I am to find his weaknesses and exploit them.*

"Carpathia; what an intriguing name." He smiled. "It suits you, pet."

"You do not know me well enough to speak with such familiarity." Her words said she was incensed, but her tone sounded coy rather than insulted. A wicked little smile played at the corners of her mouth. "Perhaps we should remedy that."

"Not so fast, milady!" he teased. "I must be wooed."

She stood there with her mouth open, flabbergasted. After some sputtering, she finally blurted, "You kissed me, sir! I am the one who should complain of an over aggressive suitor!" As an afterthought, she added, "And you owe me something for stealing the last tastes of my meal."

Viktor grinned. "I am a pirate, pet. I take what I want." With that, he launched into flight.

In order not to lose him, Thia quickly scooped up her knife and sheathed it without cleaning it. She launched into the sky after him.

Viktor led her on a merry chase through the sky over the city. Had he really been trying to elude her, he would have led her into the rigging of the ships in the harbor. He would have bet she wouldn't have been able to navigate among the sheets and shrouds as adeptly as someone who'd worked them all his life.

He finally came back to earth in an alleyway behind one of the local brothels. Carpathia alit a few yards away from him, eyeing him for any signs he might take off again.

He grinned like a rambunctious young boy and said, "That made me Hungry. How about you?"

Hell's Dodo

She blinked, caught off guard by the question. "Um, yes actually, now that I think about it."

"Do you want a man or a woman?"

"I have no preference."

"Very well, I'll surprise you."

While she wondered what he was up to, he turned and went in the back door of the brothel. Carpathia stood there in stunned silence. About ten minutes later, he emerged with a naked woman on one arm and a man, naked from the waist down, following behind.

"Hold these two for a moment, pet. I'll be right back." With that, he disappeared back into the brothel.

Still puzzled over what he was doing, she took the minds of the two humans to keep them from running. Shortly after that, she heard his voice coming from the street front.

"Thank you, Madame. There'll be a man at the dock waiting to row them over," she heard him say.

A female's voice answered, "Normally I do not send my *chicas* out, *señor*, but you have been more than generous."

"It is only fair that my crewmen who have to stay with the ship have some sport. Their crewmates have been spending their pay freely enough in port."

"You are a good *Capitan, señor. Gracias* for your business."

When he returned to the alleyway, Carpathia had to ask, "What was that all about?"

"I purchased a fresh meal for my cadre. I don't usually let them off the ship. Besides, it will give the crewmen who stayed behind some sport.

Something else bothered her about his recent actions. "Who invited you in there?"

"No one."

"So you have been here before, perhaps when you were alive?"

He grinned at her consternation. "No; it has been probably a decade since I've been in this port. This particular establishment did not exist then, as far as I know." He gave her no further information. "Now, shall we take our meal to the roof so as not to be observed?"

Viktor took the bodies and beheaded them before he dumped them beyond the harbor's mouth. Something would eat them.

By that time, sunrise loomed close by. Carpathia returned to her hidden daytime resting place in her cabin aboard the *Lorelei*. Although she found it painful to do so, she could remain "alive" past the appearance of the daystar in the sky. She spent over an hour going back over the evening's encounter with her reason for being in that part of the world.

She found Viktor Brandewyne to be both arrogant and charming. He was also quite an enigma to her. Although clearly a vampire, he felt and smelled like he was alive. His power level far exceeded what a vampire his age should have been able to attain; for instance, his abilities to fly or to hold more than one victim at a time in thrall. He had also done something she had never seen another vampire, not even her master, do. He had entered a dwelling uninvited.

No wonder her master wanted him dead. Viktor was powerful enough that she knew even she should fear him.

Yet, she did not fear him; rather, she found that she wanted him. She wondered if she could bend him to her will.

She hadn't forgotten the idea that had blossomed in her mind when she'd encountered the mermaid he'd turned and sired a child on. Perhaps his magic was powerful and different enough to revitalize her womb. A child from such a union would give her the power and leverage to break free from her master, perhaps even overthrow him entirely.

Viktor returned to the ship and found Hezekiah already aboard and waiting on him. He felt glad of it, since it saved him the trouble of looking for his first mate. Hezekiah Grimm was the only member of his crew not bound to his will.

"Hoy, captain," Grimm greeted him. "Murph arrived with a boatload of wenches about an hour ago."

"Aye, Hezekiah; they're for sport for the watch before they go to the cadre. Have the lads that aren't occupied with the wenches to ready the ship to sail. I've called the crew back. High tide is in about two hours."

"Aye, Captain."

Viktor wasn't sure if it was his bond with the siren or his own sense of self-preservation that prompted him to recall the crew and depart Cartageña. He knew there would be attention, if not repercussion for emptying that brothel. Not knowing the rank or position of its regular clientele, he was unsure of how severe or how far such repercussions would reach. Some men were very particular about their whores.

He felt it a good idea to put some space between himself and the beautiful vampire, as well. He found her extremely attractive, more so than was natural for him. Until he could figure out if the effect came from just their magic interacting or if she actively tried to bewitch him, he didn't want to get too close.

Already, he'd behaved around her like some besotted schoolboy. He'd acted almost foolishly, a thought which brought him a sharp reminder of Belladonna's rebuke. It puzzled him. He never had a woman, regardless of species, affect him like Carpathia had. He almost resented her for it.

She, however, left him with a veritable boatload of lust that he needed to vent. A quick mental check of the crew revealed a few who hadn't finished with the wenches.

A few minutes later, one of the men brought him a woman.

Chapter 16

Britt found life aboard a Navy ship to be tedious. It wouldn't be so bad if he had something to do other than regale the Commodore with accounts of his years hunting vampires. At first, he'd thought Critchfield would aid him in his crusade. Now, it felt more like he was just an oddity for the entertainment of the naval officer.

Thankfully, he didn't have to sleep below decks with the crew. The stench of unwashed sailors permeated the gun decks. Combined with the Caribbean heat, it made them almost unbearable to be on.

During a particularly hot week, even the Commodore couldn't take it anymore. He called his officers to a meeting and bade them order the men to rig a bathing sail.

Britt had never heard of such a thing and asked his bunkmate about it. "Commander Turlington, could you explain to me what a bathing sail is?"

Turlington grinned at the slightly younger man. "A godsend, if you ask me. We take one of our largest spare sails and tie floats around the edge of it; then we drop it in the water behind the ship and tie it off."

"Why?" Britt asked, still confused.

Tamara A. Lowery

The Navy man realized someone who'd never been a sailor might not understand right away. "Fresh water is too precious to waste on bathing. The bathing sail gives the men a place to swim, wash, or cool off in relative safety from shark attacks. If a man can't swim, we lower him down close to one of the floats. He can hang onto it to keep from drowning."

"Oh!" Britt brightened. "I'd like to take advantage of that, too. I'm starting to get as ripe as some of those poor blighters below."

Within a couple of hours, several of the crew of the *HMS Quicksilver* turned the sea black with months of accumulated grime. Officers and seamen alike enjoyed the refreshing coolness of the water. A few remained clothed, but most stripped down completely.

Britt and Turlington, along with a few others, shared one of the longboats back to the save-all nets which had been lowered over the side to allow the men to climb back aboard. Normally, the nets just served to catch any cargo that dropped during loading.

Although used to seeing scars on the sailors, the Commander's scars still shocked the vampire hunter. They wrapped the man's groin and inner thighs. He wondered how the man hadn't been ruined by them.

Back in the privacy of the cabin they shared, Britt broached the subject. "Pardon my asking, but how did you get those scars on your legs? I'm surprised you can walk."

Hell's Dodo

Turlington blushed. "There's quite a tale to go with these." He finished pulling up his trousers and tucked in his shirt. As he pulled on his boots, he told his bunkmate the story.

"I was lucky the wounds weren't deep. The scars look worse than they are. I'd been sent by the Commodore to return Bloody Vik Brandee to the lists of wanted pirates. He'd been reported dead, lost at sea by the captain of the *HMS Bonnie Mae* a year or so earlier. That report had been in error, of course."

"On our return trip, we were under orders to relay the warning to any ships we encountered. One supposed merchantman turned out to be pirates in disguise. During the battle, they got in a lucky shot and exploded our powder magazine. I clung to wreckage for nearly a day. A passing ship, the *Lorelei*, rescued me. They told me there were no other survivors."

"The Lady Carpathia, a passenger, tended my wounds. She stitched the cuts in my skin shut while I was unconscious or delirious. Thankfully, none of my muscles were damaged."

Turlington's eyes dilated and his voice grew husky. "She was an amazing woman."

Britt arched an eyebrow in an attempt to hide his recognition of the name. "You seduced a noble?"

"Hardly." He laughed. "She seduced me. Lady Carpathia showed just how decadent Eastern European women can be, Mr. Westin."

"What did she look like?" Britt wanted to be sure it was the same creature he'd been hunting for years. The possibility the vampire used the name of an innocent human as an alias always existed. He'd heard of such before.

"Oh, she was beautiful beyond belief. I've never met a woman like her. She had hair like black silk and skin as smooth and soft as eider down and white as milk. Oh, her eyes, her eyes… like staring into the heart of night itself…." His face grew slack and his gaze unfocused.

Britt frowned worriedly at him. "Commander, are you well?"

It took a few moments for Turlington to respond. 'Hmm? Oh? Sorry, my mind must have drifted."

"You look a bit peaked. Perhaps you should lie down for a while."

Turlington shook his head. "No; I'm fine. I do think I'll head back up on deck. The sea breeze will clear my head."

"Very well."

Britt waited a few moments after Turlington left the cabin. Quickly and quietly, he gathered his belongings together and packed them into his sea bag. He stowed the bag under his bunk and went in search of Commodore Critchfield.

Mr. Westin, what may I do for you?" Critchfield asked when the cabin boy ushered the vampire hunter in. He could tell something agitated the man greatly.

Hell's Dodo

"Commodore, some disturbing information has come to light. I believe Commander Turlington has encountered the vampire that murdered my family."

"How did you come to this conclusion, sir?"

"His description of the woman he says rescued and returned him to this ship matches what I know of her. When he described her, he went into a trance, which is consistent with the mind control vampires are capable of. And then there are his scars. What are the chances of wounds from a powder magazine explosion being that extensive but only skin deep? Why are they only limited to his groin and thigh? Wouldn't they be on other parts of his body, as well? Why are there no burn scars?"

"No sir; I believe that his Lady Carpathia is the same one I've been hunting, and that she has contaminated and altered the Commander's memory. I have encountered false scars made to disguise fang marks before," he concluded.

Critchfield stared at the man for a while. He'd wondered how long it would take Westin to figure things out.

Smiling a most unpleasant smile, he said, "So, now you know. It does explain much about the lady. However, Thia directed me to seek you out because of your knowledge of vampires. Whether you like it or not, you owe her your life. You were headed for the gallows, remember."

Horror filed Britt's face. "She got to you, also?"

"If you mean she bit me, no. For reasons of her own, she hunts the pirate, Viktor Brandewyne. We both want him dead. It is my duty, after all. She told me what he has become and directed me to find you, so I could learn how to defeat him."

"I see."

Critchfield took a step toward him. "Now that you know, can you be trusted to aid me?"

"I will help you hunt this pirate. If he is truly vampire, I will help you destroy him. That she wants him dead tells me he is dangerous." His face remained stony. "I do have one requirement."

"Oh? What, pray tell, is that?"

"The next port we put in at should have a priest. Both you and the Commander need to confess and be cleansed of the Lady's influence. Commander Turlington, especially, is in danger. If he dies before he can be cleansed, he will rise as a vampire and murder your crew without remorse to satisfy his blood lust."

"Very well. I will take your warning into consideration. If you see Mr. Turlington on your way back to your cabin, please inform him I wish to speak with him."

"Thank you. I will."

Britt woke from a nap to find Joseph Turlington standing over him.

"Commander?"

Hell's Dodo

In answer, the man struck him on the temple with a belay pin.

The sound of water lapping against wood worked its way into his subconscious. He dreamed the bunk was afloat under the stars. After a while, he realized it was a boat rather than his bunk, and he wasn't dreaming.

He sat up, and pain lanced through his skull. He discovered a tender lump crusted with blood above his ear. He couldn't, for the life of him, think of how he got there. It just made his head hurt worse. He looked around. The Milky Way let him know where the sky and sea met. He saw no lights other than the stars. The *Quicksilver* and her crew had abandoned him at sea.

136

Chapter 17

Viktor enjoyed pirating along the northern coast of South America. The Spanish colonies and ships always yielded good prizes. It did not ease his frustration over a lack of heading for continuing his search for Auntie Clarissa, though. No knowledge of her could be found in any of the ports he put in at.

He reached along the bond he shared with the siren. *"I hope you are hungry, pet."*

He felt her responding enthusiasm. *"Always!"*

Viktor stood, hands on the railing, studiously not looking at her. He wanted to, though, badly. Belladonna leaned back against the railing beside him, completely nude in anticipation of the swim ahead of her.

Crewmen had already headed below or aloft at the sight of her. They knew her nudity signaled bad things for them.

"Are two enough for a good vision?" Vik asked, still looking out to sea.

She knew he hated giving up any of his crew to her. "Yes; this is true sacrifice and not expendable prisoners. The vision will be clear."

She turned and climbed up on the rail. "I will be merciful and kill them quickly."

He did look at her then. She saw gratitude in his eyes. She smiled and dove into the sea.

He reached through the blood bond he used to control his men. Two pirates moved reluctantly to the railing. They stripped and jumped overboard. Once clear of the side, Viktor released his power over them completely.

They entered the water screaming.

He saw a hump in the water arrow toward the men. Desperately, they tried to swim away from it. The siren struck quickly. She struck them in the neck just below the skull, first one and then the other. Death came instantaneously.

Just as quickly, she pulled the bodies beneath the waves.

"You look troubled, Vik." Grimm poured drinks for his captain and himself. While he had rum, Viktor opted for the blood-brandy blend with the least liquor; a sure sign the vampire's Hunger was piqued.

Viktor took the glass with a nod of acknowledgement. The first mate could tell he forced himself to sip it slowly rather than quaff it.

"Aye, Hezekiah; I don't like sending any of the lads to Belle, but it would be me killing them in another week." Vik took another sip. "I probably wouldn't stop at two, either."

Hell's Dodo

"Your Hunger is getting that strong?"

"Hezekiah, this is the worst it's been since I went after Jorgen."

Grimm nodded and frowned. "Belle told me how Zeke influenced it to test you. I'm glad you were able to overcome it and get that bastard before he could deliver me to the gallows."

"So am I." The vampire finished the glass, got up, and refilled it. He downed it quickly and refilled it again.

"Intercept Belle when she returns and have her give you the coordinates. Don't let her come in here. She'll want to."

"Vik? Are you all right?" He took a step toward his captain.

Before he could react, the vampire tackled him. He stared up at his friend and barely recognized the ravenous creature that pinned him.

Viktor grasped his hair and yanked his head to the side. Grimm grunted in pain. The angle his neck was forced to was agonizing. He knew it wouldn't take much more pressure to snap his spine.

It was all he could do to hold the creature off; but for how long? If Viktor thought to break his arms, he would be defenseless.

"Viktor, no!" Belladonna yelled from the doorway. She sent a psychic punch that knocked the vampire off his victim and halfway across the cabin.

With a snarl, Viktor returned the blast with one of his own. The siren hit the bulkhead hard enough to leave an impression. She crumpled to the deck, stunned.

Grimm used the distraction to get to his feet. He never considered running away. Belladonna just saved his life. He owed her.

Viktor made a lunge for the siren. Grimm tackled him from the side. They crashed into the table. A free-form mix of boxing and wrestling ensued.

Belladonna shook her head to clear it. She heard the men fighting before she saw them. The first mate seemed to be holding his own. She moved to the cabinet where Viktor kept his most prized possessions. She extended her talons and picked the lock. It didn't take her long to find what she was looking for.

"Hezekiah, get him in a headlock, if you can!"

"Of course, lass," he grunted. "Anything else you want while I'm at it? The King's left nut, perhaps?"

"Just do it so I can get this on him." She frowned and held up an emerald-encrusted cross.

"Put that back!" the vampire growled. Rage contorted his face into something almost unrecognizable.

While Viktor focused on the now-glowing cross, Grimm managed to get behind him. He reached his arms under his captain's and laced his fingers behind his head. The siren darted in with inhuman speed and draped the chain around his neck. She barely avoided getting bitten for the trouble.

The change in Viktor was immediate.

He relaxed and stopped fighting against Grimm. His face grew calm. "You can let me go now, Hezekiah. The danger is past."

Grimm couldn't see his face. He glanced up at Belle, who nodded at him. Trusting her, he released his captain.

"Damn, that was close. I almost had no warning," Vik said. "You both need to get out of here. Pet, if you know any binding spells, put them on the cabin to keep me in. The cross is draining fast. It won't protect you for much longer. Give Hezekiah the heading. Hopefully, getting to the Sister will make the Hunger abate."

She looked at the first mate. "Make course for the southern coast of La Grande Isle del Tierra del Fuego." She turned back toward Viktor. "I am staying. The only spell I have which will contain you requires it."

He frowned. "I don't like that. I don't want to hurt or kill you, pet."

"You won't." Her words sounded confident, but a flash of uncertainty flickered in her eyes. "Mr. Grimm, it's best that you aren't in here for this. You might get caught in the spell."

"I don't like leaving you alone with him, lass, after what just happened; but I understand. I'll go find Brumble and get a course charted." He turned and left the cabin.

Once they were alone, Vik looked pointedly at her. "He had a point, pet. There is a hint of fear about you."

"I only hope I can complete the spell before the cross' power wanes too much. Lie down on the bed."

He sat on the edge of the bed and felt her open the link between them as wide as it would go.

She began to sing.

Grimm and Zach Brumble spent hours going over the charts. They couldn't find their destination on any of them. The best they could determine, Tierra del Fuego lay south of the Straits of Magellan.

They would have to sail into uncharted waters.

"We have a couple of dedicated trade routes that pass through the Straits," Zach said. "The natives are naked savages. Other than a couple of outposts at either end of the straits, we never got any reports of any kind of settlements or villages."

Grimm nodded. "Aye; I passed that way a few times. Never saw the first hut, just scattered fires dotting the land at night. At least the sea ice won't be bad by the time we get down there."

"Sea ice? I thought it got warmer the further south you sailed."

The first mate smiled indulgently at the younger man. "You would think so, but after you pass the Tropic of Capricorn, it starts to get cooler, like sailing far north. The bottom of the world is just as frozen as the top. The seasons are backward, too. It snows in the middle of summer and gets hot and green in winter."

Zach squinted at him. "Are you sure you're not just japing me?"

Grimm chuckled. "You'll see, mate."

Days later, Vik slowly woke. He blinked up at the ceiling of his cabin. He realized he'd been asleep, but it was now an odd sensation to him. He'd only slept once since Mamaan Juma had cursed him. That had been after he first bedded Belladonna.

What he didn't know was why he'd been asleep now, nor for how long. He remembered Belle singing to him....

Everything came back in a rush. He remembered nearly killing Hezekiah, then Belladonna joining the fight. She'd put the cross on him to calm his Hunger. It worked for a bit, but weakened fast. The last thing he remembered was jerking her into the bed and attacking her just as she sang the last few notes of her spell.

He sat bolt upright. The siren's limp form lay next to him. Her skin felt cool to the touch, but she still breathed. He saw no blood or fang marks on her anywhere.

He released a breath he didn't realize he'd been holding.

"Of course you didn't bleed her, you idiot," he muttered to himself. "You're still alive."

Gently, he stroked her face. "Time to wake up, pet." She didn't respond. "Belle?" He lightly slapped her; nothing. Shaking didn't work either.

He tried to reach her through their bond. She still didn't respond, but he saw why and what had happened. When she'd opened the link wide to make the spell more effective, it had trapped her in it with him.

He remembered an old story he'd read as a boy. He thought he now knew how to wake her from the magic-induced sleep. It would either work, or it wouldn't.

He cradled her in his arms and kissed her tenderly. At the same time, he called out to her mentally. *"Belle, wake up; please."*

Her eyelids fluttered, and she kissed him back. Finally, she opened her eyes and smiled up at him. "Hello."

"Hello to you, too. You had me worried, pet."

"It was the only way I could be sure the spell would work. I see your Hunger has abated."

"Or the cross recharged while we slept," he said.

She lifted it on its chain to get a better look. "No, it is depleted. It won't recharge as long as you wear it. The sleep did you good." She gave him a half smile.

"How long have we been asleep?"

"I have no idea."

He smiled and shrugged. "It doesn't really matter. I sense that all is going well with the ship and crew." Without warning, he pinned her to the bed and loomed over her.

"Viktor?" Her voice held a hint of fear. "You know my blood is deadly."

"Blood isn't what I'm hungry for, pet." He slid a hand into her breeches.

"Oh." She smiled and relaxed.

The sounds from the captain's cabin grew quite loud.

"Sounds like the Cap'n is up," Jon-Jon said with a chuckle.

"Aye," Grimm replied. "In more ways than one."

They both grinned knowingly.

Tamara A. Lowery

Chapter 18

"Cap'n, boat in the water to starboard!" the top lookout cried down to the deck. Every man aboard the *Shining Star* not on a specific task moved to that side of the ship.

"Helmsman, bring us alongside," Bainbridge ordered.

"Aye, Captain." The man made a slight adjustment to the course.

The riggers trimmed the sails, letting the wind out of them. The ship slowed as it approached the drifting smaller craft. Once alongside, they could see a prone figure in the bottom of the boat.

"Ahoy! Do ye need assistance?" a sailor called down. They got no reply or sign of movement.

Sam came up on deck to see what was happening. "I felt the ship slow; is something the matter, Captain Bainbridge?"

"We've come across a drifter." He waved a hand toward the starboard side.

As she moved to look over the rail, one of the sailors hollered to the helm. "There's a body aboard, but he looks to be dead."

"Is he swollen up?" Bainbridge called back.

"No, Cap'n."

"Send a crew down to bring him and the boat up."

"Aye, Cap'n."

Within minutes, a crew of four lowered one of the *Shining Star*'s boats. When they reached the water, they untied and rowed over to the drifter. Once they secured it, two sailors transferred over and inspected its contents and passenger.

"He's alive!"

"Beck, go fetch the doctor," Bainbridge ordered.

Sam watched as the men tied the boat to the block and tackles and hauled it up to the davits. The deckhands swung the davits in and unhooked the boat so the tackles could be lowered to bring their own boat up.

The ship doctor arrived shortly and set about his examination of the unconscious man. He directed a couple of sailors to carry the man below; then he climbed the stair to the helm.

"How is he?" Bainbridge asked.

"I'm surprised he is alive. Going by his sunburns, he's been in that boat for nearly a week. I'd say without food or water for most of it. He's fevered, but I imagine it is from thirst and starvation rather than disease. If he makes it through the night, I would say his chances are good."

Bainbridge turned to Sam and was about to speak. Her reaction to the rescued man stopped him short. She had finally gotten a good look at him as the sailors carried him below, and she had flushed bright red. Immediately after, she blanched dead white and looked about to faint.

"Sam?" he gripped her arm to steady her. He shook her a little, when she didn't respond. "Samantha?"

"I need a closer look at him, Captain."

"That's actually a good idea," the doctor said. He hadn't seen her reaction. "He'll need someone to nurse him to health if he lives. I would think you would be the best choice for that, Miss Brumble, rather than one of these gobs."

"Ah, yes," Bainbridge said. "Why don't you get him settled into the passenger cabin, Grogan? I need to speak with Miss Brumble privately."

"Of course, Captain."

Sam followed the captain to his office. With the door safely shut, he turned to her and asked, "What is it about this man that has you so shaken?"

Rather than meet his gaze, she focused on a point on his desk. "Remember when I was so sick? I thought a man had come to my bunk and ravished me."

"I remember. We looked over the entire crew but found no culprit. I'd never heard anything that night, so we determined that it had only been the delirium of your illness."

"I know. I am not sure and will need a closer look at him, but I swear the man just rescued looks like the man I remember." She finally looked at him with frightened eyes. "Either that, or I am going mad."

In a rare show of affection, he reached out and cupped her cheek. "You are not going mad, child. I don't see how this could be the same man, but I have encountered stranger things in my travels. Now, let's go have a look at him. If he is the man, I'll find someone else to nurse him to health; then we can decide his punishment."

Sam nodded her consent.

She looked at the unconscious man for some time. She touched his hair to check the texture. She lifted an eyelid to see the color of his eye. He showed no response to this treatment. Finally, she lay down next to him briefly.

The last made the doctor raise a questioning eyebrow at the captain. Bainbridge quietly shook his head and put a finger to his lips.

Sam stood back up and looked at the two men rather than the one on the bunk behind her. She shook her head.

"This is not the man. The hair is almost the same, as is the face, but his eyes are lighter, and he is taller. I will nurse him."

"What man? What are you talking about, Miss Brumble?" Grogan clearly found her behavior and words confusing.

"This man resembles the one Miss Brumble thought took advantage of her that time she was severely ill, Roger," Bainbridge explained.

"That is odd, indeed."

Hell's Dodo

"I know," Sam said. "Do you have any special instructions, doctor?"

"Oh, yes." He handed her a small hourglass and pointed to a keg secured in the corner of the cramped cabin. "This is a half-hour glass. Give him half a cup of water every turn of the glass. You may bathe his face and neck as often as you see fit. I've ordered the cook to make some broth. Only give him a few spoons full at a time along with the water.

"Why so little at a time and only broth and water? If he has been without for several days, he will be thirsty and starving when he wakes," she said.

The doctor nodded. "Aye, I know. However, his stomach will not be able to handle solids for a couple of days. As for the amount, it has been my observation that the gut shrinks inside a man who has been fasting. He could drink more at a time, but he would not be able to retain it for long and would evacuate it."

"Oh; that would be unpleasant and a waste of water."

"Exactly,"

Shortly before dawn, she finally managed to get the man lucid enough to take liquids. She hadn't wanted to pour water or broth into his mouth while he'd been unconscious. She'd feared he would choke on it. Instead, she bathed his face and neck with a damp rag frequently through the night.

Tamara A. Lowery

Finally, his eyes fluttered open. They were dull with sleep. He was extremely weak, and she had to lift his head to the cup. She gave him a few sips of water, a few sips of cooled broth, then more water.

When she took the cup from his lips, he passed out. The same thing happened a half hour later. The third time he woke, he found his voice.

"Where am I?" he rasped and collapsed into a coughing fit.

Sam waited for the cough to subside before she gave him more water. "You are aboard the *Shining Star*."

He tried to reach for the cup when she pulled it away. She held it out of his feeble reach. "I know you are thirsty, but the doctor said not to let you have too much at once. He warned that your stomach would reject it. You may have some more at the next turn of the glass."

He looked at her pleadingly. She gave him a gentle smile and shook her head. "It's not as long as it seems. Why don't you get some more rest?"

He let out a frustrated sigh, gave her a hurt look, and closed his eyes.

She laughed at him. "I have two brothers. Pouting will get you nowhere with me."

He grunted, but gave her no more argument.

Sam woke from a doze with a start. She hadn't meant to fall asleep, but she was so tired. Staying up to tend her charge took its toll.

Hell's Dodo

Her charge! Had she missed one of his water intervals? She looked over at the bunk to check on him. It was empty.

"Where did he get off to?" she wondered aloud.

A tap drew her attention. She realized it was the sound that woke her. In the corner, a figure lay crumpled on the deck. Nearby was the chamber pot. Her patient tapped the lid of the pot against the deck.

"What are you doing over here?" she asked as she tried to help him sit up.

"Had to use the privy. I didn't want to wake you, lad."

She didn't bother to correct his mistake. She'd been keeping her hair shorter and wearing shirt and trousers ever since she'd gone to sea in search of her brothers. At first, she'd done it to hide her gender. That was no longer an issue. She kept the practice up because she found it practical.

None of that caused her current silence, however. The realization that the man was bare from waist to knee stunned her. It looked like his breeches got tangled about his legs when he'd lowered them to use the pot. She reasoned that he must be too weak to pull them back into place, now.

"Do you think you can stand, if I help you up?" she asked, a blush starting to color her cheeks. He nodded.

She put the lid back on the pot and put his arm over her shoulders. Braced between her and the wall, he managed to get his feet back under him. He remained unsteady. She let him brace on her shoulders while she untwisted his breeches and pulled them back up. She tried not to look at his dangling sex, but it drew her eye almost instinctively. It hung almost directly in front of her eyes.

Her face flushed bright crimson. As she stood to help him back to the bunk, she turned her face and hoped he wouldn't notice the blush. If he did, he didn't mention it.

Just before she got him to the bunk, his legs gave out. It caught her off guard, and they both tumbled to the deck. He landed on top of her. Her head made contact with the deck hard, and she blacked out for a moment.

He came to the realization she was female. He tried to scramble off of her but lacked the strength. "Help!" His voice came out as a weak croak, impossible to hear beyond the confines of the cabin.

Sam came to. She saw his vaguely familiar face and felt the weight of his body on hers. She panicked.

"No! Not again! Get off, get off, get off, get off! No! No! No! No!" she screamed as she beat at him.

Her cries, unlike his, were heard by others. The doctor and the cabin boy ran into the cabin. Grogan stopped the boy just as he was about to kick the patient. He could see the man was too weak to lift his body off of Samantha's

Hell's Dodo

"Cease that caterwauling before you wake the entire crew, woman," he barked at her. "Freddy, help me get him off of her and back into his bunk."

"But Doc, he was attacking Miss Brumble," the lad protested.

"He was doing nothing of the sort. I was on my way to relieve her, so she could get some sleep. I heard the unmistakable thump of a body hitting the deck."

The man breathed a sigh of relief that the doctor grasped what had happened. "I am sorry. I did not mean to harm or frighten you, miss," he managed to say. "I would also like to apologize if I embarrassed you earlier."

Sam picked herself up but winced at the sore spot on the back of her head. Before Grogan could ask her to clarify the patient's remark, she looked at the cabin boy. "Freddy, please take the chamber pot and empty it over the side."

"Aye, miss." The boy picked up the lidded receptacle and headed out of the cabin with it.

Once he'd closed the door, she sat down and returned her attention to the two men. "I owe you an apology, sir. When I came to, I thought you were someone else."

"What exactly happened?" Grogan demanded.

She flushed but met his gaze. "I dozed off. When I woke, he was on the deck next to the chamber pot with his trousers tangled around his ankles. I helped him to get up and restore his dignity. I almost had him back to the bunk when

155

his legs must've given out. I think I hit my head when I fell under his weight."

"I see. I will have to check that out to assess the damage. You have an uncanny ability for banging your head on things, Miss Brumble, I must say."

The patient stared at the deck. "I truly am sorry, miss. If I had known you were not a lad, I would have asked you to call for the cabin boy."

"I've taken care of my brothers before, when they were sick. It was awkward, but no harm was intended."

"Who did you think I was that frightened you so?"

"I don't know the man's name. In truth, until I saw you, I thought he had been the product of a fever dream. A couple of years ago or so, a man who resembled you very closely entered my cabin and ravished me. No one ever heard anything, and he couldn't be found anywhere aboard the next day."

He frowned and looked concerned. "You say he resembled me. Did he look older than me with slightly graying hair?"

"No; he looked to be a young man."

"Oh, then it must have been a chance resemblance. I thought for a moment you might have encountered the creature that had once been my father." He seemed relieved.

His remark puzzled Sam, however. "Who are you, and what do you mean 'the creature' that had once been your father?"

Hell's Dodo

"Oh, I'm sorry. I guess there hasn't been a chance for introductions. My name is Britt Westin. Explaining about my father would take quite a while, however," he said.

The doctor interrupted them. "The tale will have to wait, then, Mr. Westin. You need to recover your strength, and Miss Brumble needs to return to her berth and get some sleep. I imagine Captain Bainbridge will wish to speak with you later, sir."

"Of course; my apologies Miss Brumble, doctor." Britt looked relieved that he'd been reprieved for the moment. The conversation had taken its toll on his weakened body.

Before the doctor returned from shooing Sam out, Britt was asleep.

Tamara A. Lowery

Chapter 19

As Samantha slept, she dreamed of a large black cat then of a lad who was really an old man. She remembered none of it when she woke.

She got dressed and went in search of Captain Bainbridge. She found him near the helm.

"Ah, there you are, Sam," he greeted her. "Dr. Grogan told me about the scare you had."

She looked chagrined. "Yes, I overreacted I am ashamed to admit."

"It can happen to anyone," he whispered. She gave him a dubious look then her stomach rumbled. He smiled at her. "We'll stop by the galley on the way to speak with Mr. Westin."

"Good afternoon, Mr. Westin. Welcome aboard." Bainbridge shook the man's hand and pulled up a couple of chairs, one for Sam and one for himself. Britt sat on the bunk. Dr. Grogan stood nearby. "I am Captain Bainbridge. You've already met Miss Brumble and Dr. Grogan."

"Yes, thank you, captain. May I ask what vessel this is?"

"You are aboard the *Shining Star*, a merchantman. Miss Brumble's family owns it."

Britt looked at her, his expression one of curiosity. "Does all of your family set sail, then?" he asked.

"That is a very tactful way of asking why a woman is found to be part of the crew of a merchant ship, Mr. Westin." Sam smiled sardonically. "Ordinarily, I would never have put to sea. I seek my brothers, Zachary and Thomas Brumble, to ransom them from the pirate Viktor Brandewyne."

He paled enough to worry the doctor. "I believe this conversation might have to wait until you have fully regained your strength, Mr. Westin," he said.

"No; I have some dire information about this pirate," Britt countered and shook his head. "It may sound outlandish; please do not think this is some nightmare borne of exposure."

Bainbridge's chuckle held no humor. "I doubt it would be any more outlandish than some of the things we have encountered since starting this hunt."

That seemed to reassure Britt. "I have reason to believe that this Brandewyne is a vampire, a creature that feeds on human blood."

"Are you sure of this?" the captain asked, suddenly intense.

"Without meeting him, I cannot say; but I was betrayed by one who believes he is. The man who sought my counsel hunts Brandewyne. He learned from me all he could about vampires; then he set me adrift when I learned he was in league with another vampire I have hunted for years."

"A vampire hunting a vampire; hunting Brandewyne, you say. Perhaps that sailor wasn't as mad as I thought."

"Sir? You have heard of the creature?"

"Aye," Bainbridge confirmed, "but at the time I thought her to be allied with Bloody Vik Brandee rather than hunting him. Not long after running afoul of the pirate and him taking Zachary prisoner, we encountered a ship we were to have rendezvoused with. The crew had been slaughtered in a most gruesome manner; but hardly any blood polluted the decks. The only survivors were a cabin boy who had hidden in a cabinet and two men who had tied on lifelines and gone over the side. One man died without awakening. The other and the boy both told of a woman they said came aboard with two men and asked the captain about Brandee. She'd said she knew he was dead, when they told her he'd been stricken from the lists as lost at sea, presumed dead. She still wanted to know where he was. They said she and one of her companions were responsible for the slaughter of the crew."

"You say this creature is in league with the man that marooned you? Who is he?" Sam asked.

"Commodore Nathan Critchfield."

Her face darkened. "I should have slit his throat instead of his cheek." She spat. "He has no honor."

"Now, Sam, think for a moment. He has cut his own throat if he is in a partnership with her. If she is the same one, it was Critchfield's own fault the venture failed. She killed the ones who were to buy the goods," Bainbridge reminded her.

"Goods that the pirate had already taken, along with my brothers; oh, this just makes my head hurt. I wish Father had never entered into that partnership with him."

"I am sorry to have brought you such distressing news, Miss Brumble. If I may be of service in any way, please let me know," Britt said.

She blushed at his words. "No need to apologize, Mr. Westin. It is good that you told me. I give you my word you will not receive ill-treatment from any on this crew."

Dr. Grogan cleared his throat. "That should include refraining from taxing the patient's strength any further today," he chided. "The cook has fresh broth for him with fine diced meat in it. Why don't you fetch it, Miss Brumble?"

"Of course." She nodded and left for the galley.

Bainbridge said, "I stand behind Miss Brumble's word. You are welcome aboard for as long as you like. If you feel you must leave to continue your own hunt, we will take you to a safe port. Now, if you will excuse me; I have duties to attend to."

Britt appreciated the fact the doctor allowed him to have something with more substance to it than mere broth. Not only did the new batch have meat in it, the cook added flour to thicken it.

"This is good, but I don't believe I can eat what's left in the jug," he told Sam. "It would be a shame to waste it."

"Dr. Grogan said it might be a few days before you could handle full rations," she said. "Do you know how long you were on that boat?"

"No; I was unconscious when they set me adrift with no sign of ship or land when I came to. I ran out of food and water within a couple of days. I grew senseless a few days later and lost track of time."

She frowned. "The bastard would have been kinder to kill you outright rather than condemn you to such a slow, tortuous death. Forgive my language. It has grown a bit colorful during my recent years at sea."

"No need to apologize. Please, have the rest of the broth. I'm not able to eat any more, and it is too good to throw out. Besides, I feel quite sleepy now."

She smiled. "Thank you, Mr. Westin. I believe I will. You go ahead and rest. Perhaps tomorrow, if the weather holds, the doctor will allow you up on deck. Some sun and salt air will restore your appetite, I'll wager."

"Perhaps it will." He returned her smile.

Britt woke feeling rested and markedly stronger. To his surprise, he found Sam sound asleep, curled up on the deck between the chair and the bunk. She mumbled incoherently when he tried to rouse her; but she did not wake.

Suspicious, he sniffed the jug the broth had been in. He recognized a scent he'd missed earlier; laudanum. He doubted Sam had known it was in the broth or that the doctor thought she would eat any of it.

He got up, stepped over her and went to the cabin door. He saw no one in the corridor, so he closed the door. He felt sure the doctor would be by to check on him eventually.

He thought about picking Sam up and putting her in the bunk, but doubted he had strength enough for something like that yet. He settled for putting his pillow under her head and covering her with his blanket.

She smiled in her sleep and nuzzled into the pillow. It brought a smile to his lips. Sleep gave her features a softness that was hidden when she was awake. He liked it. He wondered if she realized how pretty she was. If so, she definitely wasn't vain about it. He liked that, as well.

He got a drink from the water barrel then lay back on his bunk. The gentle rocking of the ship helped him drift back to sleep.

Over the following weeks, Britt returned to full health. He taught Sam and Bainbridge about vampires. Sam taught him what she'd learned about seamanship and navigation. They also shared with each other the stories about their quests.

Hell's Dodo

Sam got a clearer idea of the true danger to her brothers and what kind of monster she was pitting herself against.

Britt learned his hostess was an exceptional, brave, and intelligent woman who would never be content to sit back and let the men handle her problems for her. Every day, he grew to admire and respect her strength and determination to continue on her chosen course, despite obstacles and opposition.

Bainbridge noticed the interaction between the two. He doubted old Tobias would approve of Samantha's growing interest in the young man; but he felt they were going to be good for each other.

Chapter 20

Viktor felt grateful for Belladonna's weather magic. The winds, seas, and storms grew violent only a few days after the *Incubus* passed the point where the coast turned southwest. The siren sang up favoring winds and calm seas.

Finally, they reached the Straits of Magellan. Belle could sense the Sister to the south. After sailing several days along the coast of a large uncharted island, fires were spotted along the coastal mountain sides.

"You will find her about a day's hike inland," she told him. "I would go that far with you, but I need to hunt."

"I understand, pet." Vik caressed her cheek. "You spent a lot of energy to get us here so swiftly and safely. I wish you a good hunt."

She gave him a tired smile, stripped where she stood, then went over the rail. Part of him wished he could go with her. He felt his own Hunger growing.

He knew better than to hunt this close to a Sister of Power, however. He didn't know if any of the locals belonged to her or not. Taking the wrong prey could have dire effects on his quest.

"Mr. Grimm."

"Aye, Captain?"

"Have Mr. Jon and Mr. Bland put together a landing party to hunt for fresh meat. You and Mr. Brumble gather two days' worth of provisions for the three of us. Belle said the Sister is about a day's march inland."

"I'll let them know." Grimm left to carry out the orders.

"We're being watched, Captain," Zach said about four hours into the hike.

"I know, Mr. Brumble. Eyes have been on us since we came ashore. The natives are very good at blending in with their surroundings."

"They stand out, if you know what to look for," Grimm commented. "Poor buggers don't have a stitch on. Don't see how they're not freezing to death."

"We saw the fires last night, Hezekiah. The cold doesn't seem to bother them during the day time." Viktor sniffed the air. "It smells like they may rub some sort of fat or oil on themselves, too."

Zach seemed nervous. "Do you think they might attack?"

Vik grinned. "No, or they already would have. They've probably never seen white men before and don't know what to make of us."

They continued on for quite a while in silence. The natives seemed content to merely watch the pirates.

Hell's Dodo

The sheer bounty of the frigid waters amazed Belladonna. She saw creatures she'd never encountered in more temperate or tropical waters. She'd thought the cold would be inhospitable to her; but it proved not to be a problem. Apparently, as long as the water was briny, her powers remained undiminished.

Still, she needed prey; preferably something large. Immense schools of fish swam past her; she deemed them too small and too much trouble. She would use nearly as much energy catching enough to restore what she'd lost already.

A large creature, nearly half the size of a human, darted past her in pursuit of the fish. Several more followed. It took her a moment to realize they were birds. About four of five of them would do; but she didn't pursue them. They reeked of the Sister's power.

She moved on, a little closer to shore, to hunt. She sensed large forms moving in the water there.

She found native women diving for fish and shellfish. Again, she did not pursue. The Sister's protection wasn't on them, but Belle knew it would not help Viktor to anger the natives.

Meanwhile, her hunger grew. If she didn't find suitable prey soon, she would be driven to kill indiscriminately.

The scent of fear traveled through the water. Belle's hunger flared. The vibrations indicated a swimmer as large as if not larger than her siren form. The fear came from the human females; but the siren was not the cause of it.

She saw them scattering and swimming desperately for the surface. She saw what chased them.

One of the largest species of seal she'd ever seen closed in rapidly on a young girl.

Belladonna extended her talons and arrowed for the larger predator. She hit it from beneath with enough force to knock it up and away from its prey. Her dorsal fin knocked the girl away. Talons sank into the skull and thorax of the seal. For good measure, Belle opened her mouth to its widest and tore out the mammal's throat. A cloud of crimson quickly spread through the icy water.

"Captain, we're going to have to set camp and build a fire," Grimm said.

"Are you afraid the natives will attack in the dark, Hezekiah?" Vik laughed.

"No; like you said, if they were hostile, they already would have done so. "It's the cold that worries me. My fingers and toes are already numb. I doubt I could use a weapon right now. We need to thaw out."

"Are you of like mind, Mr. Brumble?"

"Aye, Captain. It seems the bottom of the world can get just as cold as the top, as Mr. Grimm warned me. I've heard of men's extremities freezing so badly as to turn black and break off."

"Very well, that hollow looks like it will be a good shelter from the wind. We'll make camp there."

Hell's Dodo

They put their sea bags down where he'd indicated. Zach took a small hand spade and carved a bare patch into the turf for a fire. Viktor and Grimm gathered up wood. Once in place, Grimm used his tinder box to get the fire going.

He was about to put his flint and striker away, when a feminine hand snatched the tool from him.

"I haven't seen one of these in years!" a petite, nude, dark-haired woman said.

The three stared at her, dumbfounded. Not even Viktor saw or heard her approach. The vampire recovered first.

"You are Auntie Clarissa?"

"You are the One!" Her eyes grew large and frightened. She dropped the striker and took a step back. In a blink, she vanished, or so it seemed.

A small, dull green hummingbird hovered where the witch had been. He sensed it was about to dart away. Viktor spoke a single word.

"Lazarus."

A raven coalesced out of the growing darkness and knocked the smaller bird to the ground. Before it could recover, the raven morphed into a large black cat and pinned the hummingbird.

Just as quickly, the small bird returned to a human form. Lazarus sat on her chest and seemed to smirk down at her.

"Get it off me, please!" She sounded almost hysterical. She could not hide her fear of the cat.

"If you give your word you will not try to run or fly away, I will call him off," Viktor stated his terms.

"Yes, yes, just please get it away from me!"

"Lazarus, return."

Obediently, the cat stretched, showing his claws, stepped to the ground, and leapt to his master's shoulder.

Grimm offered her a hand up. Silently, he removed his coat and wrapped it around her. She smiled up at him almost shyly and stepped closer to the fire. He returned the smile.

Clarissa eyed the cat warily and made sure to keep the flames between them. "So, you are the One who will change everything."

"So I've been told." Viktor nodded. "Not that I know or really care what that means. You know I need a token of your magic to go toward freeing me of my curse."

"You have no interest in changing everything? I thought that was why you needed my magic. I did not know you were cursed." She looked confused for a moment but shrugged and said, "Very well; give me this man as my lover, and I will give you what you need." She indicated Grimm with a nod of her head.

"No."

She blinked at him. "No?"

"Captain, I don't mind..," Grimm started to say. Viktor held up his hand to stop him.

Hell's Dodo

"No, Hezekiah. I have never known you to be an oath breaker. I will not ask you to become one on my behalf. It would not bode well for your wife and children." He turned his attention back to the Sister. "Besides, Mr. Grimm is not mine to give. He serves the Elder."

Even by the dim light of the fire, he could see her pale at the revelation. He found it surprising that she hadn't been able to sense that. Was she truly the Sister of Power, or was she a servant only, albeit a powerful one?

He caught the tell-tale scent of low-level magic. She was hiding her true power and knowledge — and lying to him. He silently thanked Belladonna for teaching him how to detect such deceit.

He decided it was time to make her fear real.

In a blink, he set Lazarus on the ground and moved around the fire to her side. Before anyone could react, he scooped her up, laid her on the ground, and pinned her beneath the weight of his body.

She gave a startled gasp, but smiled up at him. "If I cannot have him, I will accept you as a lover. Stay with me, and I will give you what you need."

His pupils dilated. Her scent told him she was not lying to him this time. He grinned lustily and let his fangs show. He felt her body go from pliant to tense.

She hadn't realized he was a vampire.

"A tempting offer, pet, but one I cannot accept. If I stay with you, my curse will destroy me." His

173

smile turned evil and he allowed enough of his own power to leak out that his eyes began to glow. The emerald light tinted her face.

He dipped his head down until his lips brushed her ear. She gave a shuddering sigh despite her fear.

He whispered, "My Hunger is growing stronger, Clarissa, and my control is growing weak. I suggest you name a new price for your help before I decide to see if drinking you will gain me what I seek."

Finally, she released her own magic.

"Get off of me!"

Her power lifted and threw him toward the fire. Only his reflexes saved him from landing in the flames. Instead, he hovered there for a second, then lit back on solid ground.

He kept his expression neutral and watched for her reaction.

Clarissa glared at him. "I was a fool to underestimate you, Viktor Brandewyne. Yes, I know your name. I knew it before your conception; and you were a fool for underestimating me."

"I am many things, witch, but a fool is not one of them," he countered. "I knew that you were hiding your power, and I knew you were not really frightened by me or Lazarus — at first. That is why I forced your hand."

"Why should I help you? You have refused to meet either of the prices I have named."

Hell's Dodo

"You have named false prices. They look simple enough on the surface, but once met, they would prove to be traps that would have consequences more dire than I am willing to accept."

"Very well; I will name my true price. Since this is the third price named, I ask for three things to be brought to me in exchange for my help; refuse and you forfeit your right to ask anything of me."

"Agreed."

"You must bring me an egg of the dodo, an egg of the dragon, and at least one drop of blood from the Dragon's Daughter."

A sea bird swooped low with something in its beak that glinted in the firelight. Clarissa held out her hand. The bird screamed and dropped its prize. She caught it and handed it to him.

Viktor examined the small cut crystal bottle. Much like his silver vial, it had a latching cap made of silver. He looped the attached cord over his head. "This is for the blood, I take it?"

"Yes."

With that, she once more transformed into a hummingbird and darted away into the night.

Grimm picked up his coat where it had fallen and put it back on. He looked at Zach, who seemed a bit shaken by the recent events. He looked back at his captain. He had a feeling he knew what was about to happen.

He snapped his fingers in Zach's face. "Look alive, Mr. Brumble! The Captain has need of ye."

"Oh? Aye, sir." Zach stood and looked expectantly at Viktor.

Vik frowned. "What are you driving at, Hezekiah?"

"I've seen the signs before, Captain. Your eyes give it away. You need to feed. Why else did you have Brumble come with us? All I ask is that you try not to kill him. He's a damn good navigator and mate."

"Actually, that idea had not occurred to me. I just didn't want to run the risk of Belle returning to the ship before we did and finding him. You know how she can be after a good feeding."

"One of the reasons I've always avoided her in situations like that," Grimm confirmed.

"Still, you are right; I do need blood. I think a small amount should suffice."

Chapter 21

"That didn't take long," Belladonna said when she returned from her hunt to find Viktor already back aboard the *Incubus*.

"She showed herself at our campfire."

The siren detected some tension in his voice. She sniffed the air. "You need to feed."

He scowled at her. "I did feed — on Brumble, as a matter of fact. He's sleeping it off in his cabin."

"You. Need. To. Feed. The locals are not under Clarissa's protection; only the birds are."

"No, I need to hunt further away." He shook his head. "These people may not belong to her, but I do not want to face a hostile reception when we return."

"You have a point. It would cost unnecessary time. We're not that far from the straits. I'll see if I can scout out a ship making the passage."

"Good. As soon as Mr. Jon's hunting party gets back aboard, I'll set sail toward the northern side of the island."

The next day, Grimm knocked at the door of the captain's cabin.

"Enter."

Viktor sat at his navigation table with three bottles on it; two of blood brandy and one of gin. "Ah, Hezekiah, I was just about to send a lad for you. Have a seat and pour yourself a drink. We need to talk."

Grimm paused for a moment. "Should I be worried?"

The vampire grinned unnervingly. "Not as long as my blood stores last."

"Oh, well then." He breathed a sigh of relief. The captain was in a good mood. He sat down opposite and grabbed the bottle of gin. "What do you want to talk about, Vik?"

"Eggs." He took a swig of the blood brandy and made a face, as if the taste didn't agree with him. "What the hell is a dodo? I know the name of that tavern in Salem was the Dragon and the Dodo, but the paint on the sign was so faded, I could barely make out the dragon's shape. I can only assume the bluish splotch opposite it was once an image of the dodo."

Grimm shrugged. "Haven't a clue. Never heard of the beast before. Why didn't you just agree to her first price?"

Viktor took a longer pull on the bottle. He looked down at the table. "It was a trap. So was the second one. They sounded too easy. The Sisters don't work that way. Even Glory's task was difficult, and she liked me."

"Aye, she liked you enough to upset Belle." His masculine chuckle said he wouldn't have minded going a round or two with Gloribeau, himself.

"It was worth it; but giving you to Clarissa would not be." He sighed. "Mother told me not to tell you this; but I think you have a right to know. I have no control over what you choose to do."

"What are you getting at, Vik? If old Celie told you not to tell me, maybe you shouldn't."

"No. You need to hear this, Hezekiah. Do you remember how La Forte's daughter held some of the magic he stole from Venoma?"

"Yes, and it made that crossing miserable."

"Your children that Brianna carries hold some of the magic Zeke forced on you. They heard your vow to forsake all other women for their mother. If you break that vow, they will die in the womb and take her with them."

Grimm paled and took several swigs from the gin bottle. To his credit, he didn't lose his breath from it. His eyes did tear up and turn red, though.

"Damn. Thank ye for telling me, Vik. And to think, my sweet Brie offered to release me from that vow, but I wouldn't let her."

"Aye. Funny how our words and actions can trap us."

"Aye. That it is." He changed the subject. "I heard Belle had returned, but I haven't seen her. Also, before I forget again, the helmsman wants to know if we have a heading."

Viktor concentrated on the bond he had with all of his crew save for his first mate. He'd ordered a round of rum tainted with a few drops of his blood for the crew right after Jon-Jon and his hunters had returned. Forming the bond that way wasn't as strong as feeding on them would have been, and it was temporary; but he didn't run the risk of ending up with too many vampires on the crew.

He found the helmsman and directed him to head for the straits. "Taken care of. Belladonna went to the straits of Magellan to see if there are any ships making the passage. We need to take a prize."

"That'll make the lads happy. A good bit of pirating keeps 'em fresh and battle-ready. Good thing you dosed them when you did. Mr. Jon reported seeing a bunch of the local wenches swimming about. He knew Belle was on the hunt, so he kept his gang out of the water; but the lads are a bit randy. A prize will take their minds off their cocks for a while."

"I follow your tack, Hezekiah. When we get back to civilized ports, I'll give them a day or two to get in some wenching."

"Thank you, Vik. They'll be glad of the news."

They drank in comfortable silence for a while. Finally, Grimm looked at his captain. Viktor's expression made him smirk.

"You've thought of something."

"Aye. I just remembered Jeorge has an extensive library. Some of the texts are quite ancient."

"You think you might find something there to help you?"

Hell's Dodo

"I hope so. I need to find out what a dodo is and where I can find one. Dragons are a problem, also. I have to accept that they are as real as all the other mythic beasties we've encountered. Next thing you know, one of these bitches will have me chasing sea serpents."

Grimm grimaced. "Don't fancy that idea. Heard tales of serpents big enough to swallow a ship whole. I'd hate to think they were real."

Viktor chuckled at his friend.

Lazarus sat on the table in Zach's cabin. He sensed that the man was closer to death than the Captain thought. He knew Viktor hadn't taken that much blood, but the cold had taken its toll on Zach's body. His lips were blue.

The cat hopped off the table and padded to the cupboard. Standing on his hind paws, he pawed at the latch until he got it open. Once open, he grabbed a woolen blanket in his jaws. Because of what he truly was, he had more strength than a real cat. Getting the heavy blanket was not an issue. Leverage or the lack thereof made the task of pulling the thing over the sleeping man difficult.

Lazarus managed to get it in place. He resumed his position on the table and kept watch.

Belladonna found no ships making the passage. The onset of winter and the steady drift northward of sea ice made the straits too treacherous to risk.

She returned to the *Incubus* to find out what heading Viktor meant to take. She knew her weather magic would be needed.

Zach woke two days after the encounter with Clarissa. He remembered the strange bird-woman flying away, but nothing after that. He wondered if it had only been a dream.

He nearly fell when he tried to get up. His whole body ached, and he trembled with weakness.

"What is wrong with me?" he said aloud. His voice sounded raspy and hoarse.

"Meh?" Lazarus sat up and blinked at him. He then stretched, jumped to the deck, and slipped out the partially open door.

Zach's stomach rumbled.

"Ah, pet, I was hoping you would return quickly," Viktor greeted the siren.

She frowned. "I couldn't find a ship for you. The seas are already slushy. Most captains don't want to risk getting iced in and starving their crews — or freezing to death."

"I guessed as much," he said. "Have you recovered your strength enough to speed us north? I'd just as soon we didn't find ourselves in that predicament, either."

She nodded. "Yes, but if we don't find a ship soon, we'll have to get to a port to hunt."

Hell's Dodo

"I know. I plan on wearing my emerald cross for a few hours every day to help keep my Hunger under control."

"Be sure to give it ample time to recharge in between wearing it," she cautioned.

"Yes, mother." He rolled his eyes, and she giggled at him.

Lazarus picked that moment to materialize. "Mrowrrr!" he growled.

"What?" Belle asked.

Viktor got the visual the cat sent him. "I understand, old friend." He rang a small hand bell, and a cabin boy appeared at the door.

"Cap'n?"

"Run to the galley and tell Mr. Trundle to whip up something hearty and hot for Mr. Brumble. He's been ill and needs to regain his strength."

"Aye, Cap'n." the boy darted off to fulfill his orders.

"I should go ahead and sing up a wind." The siren headed for the door. Viktor caught her hand and tugged her back to him. He smiled down at her, heat showing in his eyes.

"Not so fast, pet. There's something you can do for me, first."

He leaned down and kissed her.

Tamara A. Lowery

Chapter 22

They raced the ice north.

The winds called up from the south by the siren's song were polar winds. They brought the deadly chill of the southern winter season. From a bird's-eye view, it looked like the floes and sea slush pushed the *Incubus* ahead of them.

After a week of this, they finally reached warmer waters. They still found no trader vessels to prey on. It took another week to reach a civilized port; Montevideo.

While the port held some Old World elements, for the most part it was an outpost against the wilds. A certain lawlessness that appealed to the pirates permeated the place. The established traders and merchants stayed in at night and posted guards. The taverns and brothels welcomed a much rougher clientele. More genteel folk chose to dwell in Buenos Aires, across the bay from the fortified, city.

To the vampire and the siren, Montevideo proved a rich hunting ground.

The crew of the *Incubus* took advantage of the port's amenities, as well. Mr. Grimm saw to it that any coin taken from Viktor's victims was redistributed among the crew. They, in turn, spent it on women, food, and drink.

A week of hunting put the vampire's Hunger at bay. He even replenished his blood stock on board for himself and his cadre of vampires.

Restored and resupplied, they once again sailed north.

Somewhere off the coast of Brazil, a few of the men enjoyed an evening on deck playing dice and swapping lies. Among them, Jon-Jon and Lockland Stoud vied over which had seen and done more.

"Aye, I bedded that wild wench once," Stoud said after Jon-Jon recounted how Belladonna had left welts on some of the crew when they'd refused her advances.

"Bilge! I don't believe it! Cap'n would'a killed ye for it, I'd wager," Sniff piped up from his perch low in the rigging.

"He's right, Stoud. The Cap'n doesn't share," Jon-Jon agreed. "Besides, why would she pick an old barnacle like you to play with?"

"Heh, a lot you know, Mr. Jon," he cackled. "Doubt he'd gut me over something that happened when he was still a pup. Oh, I was a pretty thing in my youth. Belle saw me out fishin' one day and took a fancy to me. We spent a glorious month or more on some uncharted island. Oh, I tell ye, mates, she is insatiable, that one! T'was lucky to get out wi' me manhood intact, I was."

Hell's Dodo

Jon-Jon snorted. "You were lucky to get out alive, mate. Don't you know she likes to play with her food?"

"Aye, I know; but y'see, I knew what she was from the moment I saw her. Knew she weren't a mortal lass nor even a mermaid. I c'n read, and I've read the right books. No mate, I knew she was a siren and a man-eater right off. Made her vow not to harm or eat me afore I agreed t'go off with her." He tapped his temple and winked. "I know a bit of magic meself and knew the right words to make her say to make it stick."

"Still don't believe it," Sniff protested. "She wouldn't have been more'n a child or babe when you were young."

The siren in question walked by at that moment and overheard much of what was being said. "Hah!" she laughed. "I'm much, much older than I look, troll."

Stoud leered and winked at her. "They don't believe I've had you, Belle."

She gave the sailors a wicked smile. "You were just too good to eat, Lockland. I still have fond memories of those three months."

Jon-Jon pounced on the discrepancy. "Ha! I knew it was a lie! He said he bound you with magic from eating him and that it was only a month or more."

"Mr. Jon, three months is a 'month or more.' My lovers tend to lose track of time," she corrected. "He did make me promise not to eat him as long as the tides flowed in and out." She paused and grinned wide with her true teeth showing needle sharp. "Of course, there is that brief moment between the tides, when they flow neither way."

While the other men laughed nervously, Stoud smiled calmly and coolly replied, "Why do you think I made sure we were too busy for you to attack, luv?"

"Your stamina was quite impressive; almost as impressive as the Captain's." With that, she sauntered off about her business.

Every eye in the group followed her until she disappeared below deck.

"Saucy wench if ever there was one," Stoud commented to no one in particular.

"I still think you're a liar, Stoud; but damn, you're good at it," Jon-Jon said.

"No more a liar than you are, Mr. Jon," he shot back, unruffled.

The second mate grinned and handed him his flask. "That proves it. Everyone from here to Boston knows I'm the biggest liar to sail the seas."

"That's only because Anvil is an honest man. He's the only one bigger than you I've ever seen," Stoud referred to the giant who served as the ship's blacksmith.

He took a long pull on the flask and handed it back. Jon-Jon frowned and peered into it. He upended it over his extended tongue and only got three drops to come out.

"Dammit, I'm going to have to see if Mr. Grimm will front me some more gin. I already owe him for two barrels," he grumbled then shrugged. "Oh well; so you already knew sirens were real before coming aboard. What about vampires?"

"You have me there. I'd heard stories, mind ye, but I'd never seen proof of 'em until I met the Cap'n. There are other beasties I've seen in m'travels, though: mermaids, devil fish big enough to sink a sloop, snakes big enough to swallow a man whole, even dragons and a kraken."

"You did not see a kraken… did you?" Sniff said.

"Aye." Stoud nodded. "Bitch damn near sank us. I was aboard a trader about three days out of Nippon headed south to the Indies."

"You mean you were smuggling," Jon-Jon said. "Everyone knows they aren't fond of white men."

"Their emperor and his warlords might frown on trade with whites; but our captain had a woman in a fishing village who would procure cargoes. He wouldn't let us go ashore except to load up. Warlord near her village got wind of it and tried to shut us down. She met us at the pick-up point and begged us to take her with us. Said she'd be killed for bringing dishonor on her family if she stayed."

"Did ye take her?"

"Aye; Cap'n said it was bad luck to have a woman on board, but he didn't think she deserved execution. There was some grumbling, but we went along with it; then the accidents started happening. Knots came undone for no reason, ropes broke on calm seas, and two experienced riggers fell. One broke both his legs when he hit the deck. The other fell into the sea and was lost. When the giant beast attacked the ship, we knew we'd been cursed."

A touch of sadness shadowed his face briefly. "We lost six good men that day. The beast pulled two from the rigging and bit them in half with its terrible beak. Four more were crushed when it toppled the mainmast."

"Me and some of the mates went to the captain and demanded he turn over the woman. He refused. Said it wouldn't be Christian. Th' first mate pointed out that she was a heathen, and the beastie was obviously sent by some heathen god to punish her. The captain was threatening to charge us with mutiny, when the wench came out of his cabin."

"She placed a hand on his arm and shook her head. Her English weren't so good, but we could understand her. She said the monster had come for her and would kill us all, if she didn't give herself up. She walked over to the rail, shucked off her fancy robe, and dove over the side. The beast let go of the ship right away and disappeared back into the deep."

There was silence from his crewmates for a few moments.

Finally, Jon-Jon broke it. "That made me thirsty. Think I'll go find Mr. Grimm and see if I can wheedle some gin from him."

Hell's Dodo

"You wanted to see me, Cap'n?" Stoud said from the doorway.

"Aye, Mr. Stoud. Come in." Viktor poured himself a glass of blood-brandy. He motioned to another bottle and glass. The liquid was clear. "Have a drink."

"Thank ye." He unstoppered the bottle and filled his glass. His face lit up when he sniffed the contents. "Cognac; I'm honored."

"I hear you've seen dragons," Viktor got right to the point. "Is this true?"

Stoud took a sip and considered his captain for a moment. He'd had captains take him to task for the tales he told in the past. Somehow, he didn't think that was the case this time.

"Aye; I've seen creatures that were known as dragons," he confirmed. "They're not really like the ones in the old legends, nor even like the great wyrms the Chinee worship. They're more like giant lizards."

"Like 'gators and crocs?"

Stoud tilted his head to the side and waggled his hand. "A little. They can get as long or longer, and they can swim, but they're more likely to stay on land. They're as fast as snakes, and they can climb trees."

"Interesting." Viktor took a sip and watched the older man over the rim of his glass.

"Is that really blood? How do you keep it from clotting?"

Vik smirked. "I like you, Mr. Stoud. You don't dance around a question."

Stoud shrugged. "Dancin' never got me anywhere 'cept maybe a whore's bed every once in a while. Are you going to answer the question, Cap'n?"

The vampire laughed. "Very well; yes it is blood, Mr. Stoud; human blood mixed with brandy to preserve it. It is not as potent as fresh, but it keeps me and my cadre from draining the rest of the crew."

"What do you mix with the blood for them?"

"What makes you think they don't get the same?"

Stoud just looked at him. Finally, he said, "Never met the captain yet, be he merchant, Navy, or pirate, that didn't eat better than his crew."

"Very astute; rum."

"Makes sense. Rum is much cheaper than brandy, and they were already used to it when they were alive."

"Indeed, Mr. Stoud. What else can you tell me about dragons? I need to find one and acquire a dragon's egg."

"We've a long sail ahead of us, then. They only exist on a few islands in the East Indies."

Viktor downed the remains of his drink, slammed the glass down on the table, and refilled it. "Damn. Why am I not surprised? These bitches never make anything easy."

"They're female, Cap'n. What did you expect?"

Hell's Dodo

"Precisely."

Stoud took a pull on his cognac and savored it. When he set his glass down, he said, "One more thing about these dragons: their teeth aren't as sharp as a 'gator's or croc's, but their bite is deadly poisonous. It's not a quick death, either. One of me mates got a bare nick of a bite on his hand. It swelled up, which didn't surprise us, but then it turned red and later black. The surgeon took the hand at the elbow, but it was too late. The rot had already got in the poor blighter's blood. He was dead in a fortnight."

"Duly noted, Mr. Stoud. Is that all you know about the creatures?"

"Aye, Cap'n."

Viktor drank a little more, obviously lost in thought. Stoud drank in companionable silence.

"What about a dodo; have you ever encountered one?"

Stoud blinked. "Can't say as I have. Not sure I've ever heard of the beastie before. What is it?"

"Either a bird or a lizard; I'm not sure. I just know that I need a dodo egg, as well."

"Sorry I couldn't be of more help."

Viktor finished his glass. He did not refill it. Head cocked to one side, he regarded his crewman. His eyes glowed softly.

"I remember that look, Cap'n," Stoud said warily. "You had that look right before you killed Lemuel Gordon."

"No fear, Lockland Stoud; I'm not going to kill you. I'm going to ensure you will be a permanent member of my crew. When you do die, you will rise again and join my cadre."

Before Stoud could react, Viktor moved behind him for the better angle and bit deep into his throat. Just as quickly, he released the man and choked down a single swallow of blood.

"That was it?" Stoud's voice held both surprise and a touch of humor.

Viktor made a face as he returned to his seat. "Gah! You taste of gin."

He grinned at the vampire. "Old Billy said you didn't have much of a taste for gin or cheap whiskey."

"You sailed with Billy Black?"

"Aye; I spent a few years aboard the *Nightshade*. Made a few smuggling runs with him too, back when you were still working at the Black Flag."

Viktor peered at him. "I thought you looked familiar. I remember he'd disappear for a few days every few months, always right after you and a few others would show up."

"Always felt good to get one over on those Navy boobs."

"Aye, it does, doesn't it?" Viktor grinned. "Now I'm even gladder to have you on my crew, Mr. Stoud. Get with Mr. Brumble and see what charts we have of the East Indies. If you can pinpoint the correct islands, he can work out a course to them for when we leave New Orleans."

Hell's Dodo

"Aye, Cap'n."

Tamara A. Lowery

Chapter 23

The *Incubus* didn't encounter a single ship between Montevideo and Trinidad. The lack of prizes to take forced Viktor to put in at Port-of-Spain, the island's main port. They needed supplies.

As before when they'd made port, the vampire found his Hunger to be near ravenous. He decided to take a few days to hunt. The crew took advantage of the extended stay to do what sailors do when in port. Grimm made sure they had instructions to keep a sharp eye for any plunder that might bring a good price in New Orleans.

"The *Lorelei* is in this port," Belle informed Vik before he left to hunt. "Be careful. I'd ask you to avoid that vampire, but it would do no good."

"Jealousy does not become you, pet."

"It's not entirely jealousy, although that is part of it. She is far more dangerous to you than you realize, Viktor. I suspect she is older than Jeorge. If that is the case, her power may surpass yours. Vampires don't survive that long by accident."

He could see she really was worried for him. He cupped her cheek and kissed her gently. "I will be careful, pet," he whispered. He turned and launched into the air.

The siren stood looking up after him. She could still feel the softness of his lips on hers. Something soft brushed against her foot. She looked down to see Lazarus.

"Keep him safe from himself, if you can," she told the cat. She ran to the rail and dove into the bay, not bothering to shuck her clothes first. Shredded fabric floated to the surface of the water then sank from sight.

Thia found it maddening that no word could be found of Brandewyne or the *Incubus* for months. Her frustration was uncharacteristic. She had been an elite hunter for millenia. She knew how to wait her prey out and lull them into a false complacency until they revealed themselves. Something about the pirate made him different.

There had finally been a sketchy rumor that the *Incubus* had been spotted headed south down the eastern coast of South America a few months previous.

The *Lorelei* ported in Trinidad for supplies and to allow Thia to hunt. Captain Wormsloe warned her hunting would not be good further south.

Their second week in port, the captain waited for the vampire to emerge from her daytime compartment. The very second the sun vanished below the horizon she burst from the hidden recess in her cabin.

"I know that scent! He is here or has been recently."

Hell's Dodo

Wormsloe nodded. "Aye, m'lady; the *Incubus* made port today. I urge caution. Brandee may be a young vampire and untutored, but by your accounts, he is powerful. He has always been dangerous, even as a human."

Thia smirked. "I doubt I have anything to fear from a fledgling, especially one that is besotted with me."

He frowned at her. "Do not underestimate him, m'lady. Vik Brandee has always been one to do whatever it takes to get what he wants. He may not be as besotted as you think. Keep in mind he was only a lad of eleven when he committed his first act of piracy."

"Why Captain Wormsloe, one would almost think that you were besotted — and jealous."

"Do not flatter yourself, Lady Carpathia."

Viktor watched the *Lorelei* from the crow's nest of a nearby ship. He made sure to stay downwind. He suspected Thia would detect his scent, but he didn't want her to pinpoint him just yet.

For that reason, he bespelled the sailor on top watch aboard the ship he'd chosen rather than kill him. Blood and death carried scents which called out to a vampire. Besides, he'd made sure to feed well during the daylight, before Thia rose for the evening.

He watched her leave her ship. Rather than heading toward the obvious hunting grounds, she stayed near the docks. It took him a moment to realize she was making for the *Incubus*.

This puzzled him. He hadn't told her the name of his ship, and he'd returned to the ship while she was dead for the day, when he'd encountered her before. There was no mistake that was where she was headed, though.

Port-of-Spain boasted a harbor deep enough to accommodate even the largest merchant vessels. It allowed the *Incubus* to berth at the docks rather than anchor in the harbor.

Viktor did not return to his ship. Instead, he took up an observation post from the roof of the warehouse at the head of the pier. His eyesight and hearing were acute enough to clearly follow Thia's actions and words.

A breeze came across the harbor. As it passed over the warship-turned-pirate and to the docks, it carried an unmistakable scent to Carpathia. She could tell there were multiple vampires aboard. It gave her pause for a moment.

Until that moment, she hadn't sensed these vampires. Cautiously, she reached out with her power, but still she could not feel their power that way. How was Brandewyne able to shield them from her? He hadn't been vampire himself for even a decade, yet. He should not have that level of power. Given *her* age and lineage, no vampire should.

More and more, she saw why her master wanted this vampire put down.

Hell's Dodo

It also made her more resolved to try her wild plan, before she fulfilled her commission. If Brandewyne could breed with her, their offspring would be powerful enough to usurp her master.

She walked up the gangplank to be met at the top by a pirate. "I am looking for Captain Brandewyne."

"Cap'n's gone ashore, but I'd be glad to service ye, lass," the man said with a leer.

Thia cocked her head at him. It dawned on her that she didn't have to hide what she was from him. She grinned wide enough to show her fangs and felt gratified to see his surprise and fear.

"I don't think so." She laughed, turned, and went back down the gangplank.

With the wind still in his favor, Viktor dropped silently from the warehouse roof to the alley between it and the next building. There, he waited.

"I heard you were looking for me, pet."

Only centuries of practice allowed the vampire to conceal her startlement. Her prey appeared every bit the predator she was. He'd made sure she didn't hear or smell him. She already knew she couldn't sense him as a vampire.

She turned to the voice in the alleyway and smiled. "Yes, I have. I had hoped to have more time with you back in Cartageña."

Tamara A. Lowery

He stepped out of the shadows and kissed her boldly, not bothering to ask her leave. When he stepped back from the kiss, he said, "A pirate doesn't stay in port for very long. It's not conducive to remaining free."

"I see. A moving target is harder to hit."

"Indeed."

"Would you care to accompany me on tonight's hunt?"

He bowed. "I would be honored, milady."

As they strolled into the night, a feline shadow trailed behind them along the rooftops.

☠

They spent the first few hours hunting. At first, they haunted the business district. Many locals took advantage of the relative coolness of the tropical evening. The victims they took there were more difficult to take unaware, but they had a better diet.

After the streets started to clear, the vampires moved their hunt to the alleys of the dock district. Prey proved easier, if more inebriated.

During their hunt, the two carefully observed and analyzed each other. Although both did so surreptitiously, both noticed.

"I've been watching you watching me, pet." Viktor chuckled as they tidied up from their final kill for the night.

Thia smiled coyly. "I find you to be a fascinating creature, Captain Brandewyne. I have never met another vampire quite like you. Your scent, your heartbeat, your warmth, they all give the illusion that you are alive. Even your robust color; given how long you've been a vampire, you should be as pale as I am. Is it makeup? Why do you go to such trouble?"

He wondered if she realized her verbal missteps. She'd just confirmed to him that she'd been hunting him for quite some time. He doubted Jeorge had told her about him, given how little she knew about him. Someone had put her on his scent, though. He needed to find out whom.

"My mother was from one of the mountain tribes west of Carolina and Virginia. I've always been dark skinned." He figured that was a harmless bit of information. He knew better than to share too much. He hadn't survived as long as he had as a pirate by being too free with talk of himself. "As for the rest, I really don't give it much thought."

"Intriguing." She remained silent for a while then sighed. "I am afraid I have to cut our night short, Captain."

"Please, call me Viktor." The request earned him a delighted smile from her.

"As you wish, Viktor. You may call me Thia. Carpathia is such a mouthful."

He gave her a lascivious look. "I like a good mouthful, Thia."

"As do I," she said huskily and stepped in close to kiss him. When they broke from the kiss, she continued, "But it will have to wait until tomorrow night. I have business to attend to before the sun rises."

"Then I will leave you to it." He bowed over her hand and kissed it before he launched back into the night sky.

The next evening, Viktor strode up the gangplank of the *Lorelei* just before sunset. As expected, a sailor stopped him at the top.

"State your business, mate."

"I've come to call on the Lady Carpathia."

"Hie, George!" the sentry called. "Fetch the Cap'n!"

Another sailor headed towards the aft of the ship, where the cabins were located. Shortly after that, he returned with a man around Viktor's age.

"What's this all about Coggins?" the man asked.

Viktor recognized him in short order, even though it had been over a decade since he'd last seen him. "Wormy! Well, that explains a few things."

Wormsloe knew the hated nickname right away. "Coggins do not allow that man aboard my ship."

"He said he came to call on m'ladyship, Cap'n. Figured she'd sent for him."

Wormsloe frowned. "Did the Lady invite you aboard?"

"No."

The captain of the *Lorelei* raised an eyebrow and gave a smug smile. "Well then, I don't have to worry about you coming aboard, since you haven't been invited."

"Is that so, Wormy?" He sounded more amused than irritated or insulted.

"I know what you are, Brandee. You have to have an invitation to come aboard. I own this boat; Lady Carpathia is just a passenger."

Viktor found it interesting that the man made a point about the ship's ownership. "So, if she owned it, I would not need to be invited?" He laughed.

In the next second, Wormsloe felt an arm around his shoulder in a companionable way. Viktor gave him a gentle squeeze and grinned. "Wormsloe, you of all people should know that I go where I please and take what I want regardless of who gives me leave or no. I'm a pirate, man! You know that."

The man paled but gave no other indication of fear. His voice remained calm and even. "You are a vampire. You should not have been able to do what you just did."

"I've heard that quite a lot, sir. I've even been told I shouldn't be able to move about freely while the sun still rides the sky. Yet, here I stand."

The realization of that fact caught Wormsloe off guard, and he looked Viktor in the eye. He immediately realized his mistake and looked away. He swallowed hard.

"Tell me, Wormy, do you still hold a grudge over those crabs?"

"You took our crabs, our boat, and left us out in the salt marsh to drown for all you cared." His voice held a quiet fury over the decades old dispute.

"True, but it was your own fault. If you and your brother had just given me the crabs when I told you to, you could have kept your little boat and crab pots."

As they talked, the sun sank below the horizon. In the next second, Carpathia stood facing them, her expression deceptively pleasant. "Viktor, I didn't expect you so early."

"I want to make the most of the evening, milady."

"These men are under my protection."

He smiled. "I thought as much. Wormy and I were just discussing old times." He released the man's shoulder and stepped around him to kiss her hand. "You look Hungry, pet."

"Famished." She chuckled. "Captain Wormsloe, I have arranged for a safe house for the day and will not be returning until tomorrow evening."

"May I caution you, milady?" He stepped forward and touched her arm lightly, which earned him a warning glance from her. "Do not let this one know where it is. Send him back to his ship before daybreak. He is not to be trusted, and he can tolerate sunlight, for a while at least. He arrived here a full quarter hour before the sun set."

She looked up at Viktor. "Is that true?"

Hell's Dodo

"Every word, pet; I am a pirate, and you may trust me at your own peril." He grinned rakishly. "And yes, I can function quite well in full sunlight."

"My, my, my; you are full of surprises." She returned her attention to Wormsloe. "While I am sure Captain Brandewyne's intentions toward me are far from pure...."

"Oh, they are quite wicked, I assure you, pet."

"I do not believe they are malicious," she concluded. "Thank you for your concern, but it is unnecessary."

As they turned to leave, Viktor couldn't resist a parting shot. "Face it, Wormy. Women prefer a man with a bigger — boat."

During their hunt, Carpathia noticed her companion seemed more relaxed than he'd been the previous evening; relaxed and cocky. She found his arrogance amusing. She decided to play with him.

"You were rather rude to Captain Wormsloe."

"He's always been a little prig, even as a lad."

"Still, there was no call to be so rude. The more I think about it, the more inclined I am to follow his advice and send you back to your ship alone."

"No you won't. You want me."

"You presume too much, sir. Your services are no longer required," she huffed. "Begone."

"No."

"I said away with you!"

"Make me." He grinned wickedly.

"You don't think I can?" She arched an eyebrow at him.

"I don't think you will."

On impulse, she shoved him back. It sent him through the wooden wall of the warehouse behind him. He picked himself up and dusted off the splinters. She saw him do a quick survey of the contents of the building and heard him mutter, "I'll have to have Mr. Jon bring some of the lads to empty this place tonight."

Carpathia assumed he meant one of the vampires aboard his ship.

"Is that the best you can do, pet?" He smirked as he climbed back through the hole in the wall.

She rushed him again. Ready for her this time, he sidestepped the attack and caught her about the waist. He held her off the ground with one arm, effectively removing her leverage. With his free hand, he began to fondle her breasts. She twisted in his arms to face him and saw from his expression she had impressed him with the small feat.

"You are good at this," he said.

"I am only getting started." She laughed and kissed him.

"Mmm, so I see," he said when they broke the kiss. "Where is this safe house? I don't think you want to sport here in the alleys like a common whore." He set her back on her feet.

"Follow me." She launched into the air with him right behind her.

They flew to the interior of the island. Thia led him to a plantation manor. A handful of local vampires and their human slaves greeted them at the door. Viktor took particular note of the fear and respect they showed to his companion. She truly was an aristo among her kind.

Their hosts escorted them to a luxurious suite carved into the rock beneath the mansion. Waiting for them were a nubile young pair of humans; one male and one female.

The pair kneeled and bowed their heads. "We are here for your pleasure, milady, and that of your guest," the male said.

"Do with us as you wish," the female added.

Carpathia stepped forward and placed her fingers under each of their chins. She lifted their heads and bared their necks. "Have either of you been with a vampire before?"

"No, milady," the young man responded. "We are both virgins and blood virgins."

The young woman said, "We have been trained in the arts of pleasure through observation, but we have been kept in reserve for special guests and forbidden to partake with others or to experiment on ourselves."

"That seems to be cruel," Viktor commented.

Thia gave him an indulgent smile. "Hardly cruel, Viktor; rather, it heightens the experience for all involved when they are initiated. It has been a common practice among our kind for millennia. These two are willing sacrifices to our pleasure, whether it is sex, food, or both. It is a guest's discretion on whether or not to bring one over, allow them to remain human, or destroy them. They were groomed for this purpose."

He looked at the young pair with a considering eye. He saw them for the trap they were; but he didn't want to reveal that knowledge to her. Even if he didn't outright convert one of them, if he fed on one directly, he would give her a means to spy on him. All she would have to do would be to kill his victim and allow them to rise as a vampire.

"My Hunger is quiet for now. Perhaps some sport instead?"

"Very well. Which do you prefer, or would you like to try both?"

"The wench will suffice. Never really cared for men that way, although some of my crew are so inclined."

"As you wish." She smiled. "I believe I shall indulge in an appetizer." She held her hand out to the young man. He stood and kissed her hand. She directed him to the wall where several manacles were set. She removed the brooch which held his tunic in place and allowed the garment to slide to the floor.

He was well-formed but not overly muscular. Clearly, he had never done laborious work. No marks marred his body, not even a childhood scar.

Hell's Dodo

Viktor had never seen such a healthy, near-perfect human before. That the man had been bred for the vampires' pleasure sickened him on some basic level. He couldn't imagine picking such a specimen for his crew, let alone making him vampire. He was nothing more than food one could play with.

So was the wench, for that matter. He'd found women, even virgins, to be remarkably resilient and able to survive circumstances that could drive all but the strongest of men to despair, though.

Thia chained her snack to the wall spread-eagle facing outward. She began to nibble at his flesh with only her lips. She started at his earlobe, moved along his jawline, and down the curve of his neck. Goose flesh raised along his entire body. He began to grow hard, even though she had not touched him there yet.

"So sensitive." Her voice held a wanton heat. Viktor and the girl both found themselves captivated by the performance. He could almost taste the untapped sexual energy pouring off the two humans. He found it intoxicating.

Thia continued to gently torture her willing victim. She drew her tongue along his collar bones from one shoulder to the other. She reversed direction and blew gently on the moistened skin. The young man moaned in ecstasy, and his eyelids fluttered shut. She lightly traced her fingertips down his ribs in the barest of touches. He shuddered in delight.

She trailed kisses down his chest from sternum to navel. This, she circled with her tongue before quickly darting her tongue in and out of the indentation. He quivered in rhythm with her thrusts; his sac tightened, and his manhood jumped.

Even Viktor emitted an involuntary groan of pleasure as he imagined her touch on his body.

She still avoided the most sensitive and demanding area of her victim's body. Instead, she moved to nibble at his hip bones then down the outside of his thighs to his knees, paying equal attention to each leg. Her breath played over the fine hairs as she moved back up the insides of his thighs. She stopped just short.

Her victim flexed his hands and toes and looked down at her with lust-filled eyes. "Please, mistress!"

In response, she traced her tongue up the underside of his shaft from base to slit and captured the moisture beaded there. His eyes rolled back in his head, and he quivered and groaned.

"I don't think he can hold it much longer, pet," Viktor commented with a chuckle.

"Yes, I can taste that he is ready," she replied. Slowly, she slid her lips around him and let him fill her mouth halfway up his length. Just as slowly, she lid him back out. He whimpered.

Without warning, she took him into her mouth again, this time all the way to the hilt, and drove her fangs into his base. He screamed as he climaxed; a mixture of pain, pleasure, and release.

Hell's Dodo

When she finally released him, Viktor could tell he was nearly dead. He hung limp, unconscious, and noticeably paler.

Thia stood and faced Viktor and the girl. She smiled at the way her display affected him. "Your turn, Captain."

To her credit, the girl seemed a little more nervous than aroused. She glanced at her counterpart with worry.

"Will Calyx be all right?"

"Was that his name?" Thia asked.

"You killed him?" Her voice grew panicky.

Viktor lifted her chin and brought her gaze to his. His eyes emitted a soft emerald green glow. She calmed instantly. "That's better, pet. You shouldn't let yourself get so upset over little things like that. What is your name?"

"Prisca," she replied with a smile.

"Well, Prisca, your friend is dying, but it will be fine. He may rise tomorrow night anew."

"Am I to die tonight, as well?"

"Not by my hand, pet." He caught a minute frown from Thia for that comment. He ignored it. "Now, let's have a look at you." He unpinned her tunic and smiled at the way it slid down her body. He walked around her, inspecting her.

A single fingertip stroked lightly down her spine caused her to gasp. Goose flesh popped all over her, and her nipples stood erect. He leaned down, lifted her hair and drew in a deep breath along the nape of her neck.

213

She smelled of soap, rose oil, sweat, and arousal. He could easily spend all night on her, but she was meant to only whet the appetite. Carpathia was his true desire that evening.

He decided to toy with the girl long enough to prove to Thia he could put on as good of a display as she could.

He stood behind the girl and ran his hands down her arms then lifted them out to the sides. Turning each of her hands over, he kissed her palms, the insides of her wrists, and the creases of her elbows. He brought his hands back up her arms on the underside. She giggled and jumped a bit.

"Oh ho, you are ticklish," he said with a grin. "Let's see what else my hands can learn about you." With that, he lightly traced his fingertips down her sides to her hips. He rested his hands there and began to rub with his thumbs in small circles to either side of the base of her spine. She moaned in delight.

He traced the curves of her butt, kneading gently, before he moved his hands around to the front of her thighs. He pulled her against him so she could feel how he had grown hard. He drew his hands up slowly; his fingers grazed the creases where thighs met hips, but he did not touch her mound. Instead, he splayed his fingers so that they covered her belly from just above her pubic hair. With a feather-light touch, he brought his hands up over her stomach and ribs to cup her breasts. She leaned into his touch with a soft moan, as he kneaded her soft flesh.

Hell's Dodo

After a few moments of this, he turned her around to face him. She started to reach for his waistband, but he stopped her.

"Not so fast, pet. I am ready for you, but I must make sure you are ready for me," he chided.

He lifted her up and laid her back on the edge of the bed with her legs off the edge. He smiled at the way her breasts partially flattened out toward her armpits. They were full enough to not disappear entirely like some he had enjoyed in the past. Since he'd started wenching in his teens with the women at the Black Flag in Savannah, he'd encountered every body type and pretty much enjoyed what each had different to offer.

With a lustful growl, he knelt over her. He captured her mouth at the same time his hand found her inner thigh. Gently, he nudged. She helpfully spread her legs, opening herself to him. He brushed his fingers over the soft curls and opened her folds. She bucked against his touch as he caressed her.

He pulled back from the kiss and concentrated on his exploration. She gasped when he slid a single finger inside her.

"Ooh, you are wet enough, pet, but you are too tight to accept me yet. We shall have to do something about that. This may hurt at first."

"I don't mind," she replied with a shudder.

He proceeded to ply her with his finger. While his hand was busy, he began to pay attention to her breasts with his mouth. Careful not to pierce her flesh with his fangs, he drew a nipple in and sucked hard. She cried out, and he started using two fingers, slowly widening her opening.

He turned his attention to her other breast with the same fervor and added a third finger into play. He kept the pace slow for a few moments. He eased his fingers in held tightly together then spread them out to stretch her as he withdrew. Gradually, he increased the pace. Her breathing quickened.

He added the fourth finger and flicked her clit lightly with his thumb. She began to moan and writhe.

She screamed when he went from shallow thrusts to forceful, deep ones and pierced her hymen. He did not stop. Instead, he grasped her hair at the back of her head, baring her throat, and continued to torture her with his hand.

She clawed at the sheets as he brought her to climax. He held his hand inside her and reveled in the feel of her body convulsing around it. He did not withdraw until the spasms calmed.

With a lusty, dark chuckle, he stood and licked her juices and virginal blood from his fingers. "Damn, but you taste good!"

She lay quivering, re-learning how to breathe, her body limp. He knelt on the floor between her knees, placed her thighs on his shoulders, and pulled her closer to the edge of the bed.

She whimpered as he assaulted her opening with his tongue. He licked, sucked, and probed her, as he tried to capture every drop of blood from her maidenhead.

Hell's Dodo

Once more, she cried out in orgasm.

He stood and started to remove his clothing. Before he could finish, Thia crouched naked on the bed over Prisca. He smelled fresh blood. The girl's body lurched and writhed.

He quickly finished undressing. The scent of the blood threatened to unleash his Hunger. Even after their hunt earlier, it lurked just beneath the surface. He refused to allow it to rule him. He channeled his appetite into lust instead.

He returned to the bedside and grasped Prisca's legs to lift her hips to his. His ministrations were not gentle and his speed surpassed any that a human male could match. Thia continued to feed greedily.

For a while, the girl screamed. Soon, she only gasped. Within minutes, her body relaxed and grew cool. He withdrew.

Thia sat up, blood coating the lower half of her face. "You were right. She was delicious!"

She reached over and pulled a silken cord next to the bed. Almost too fast to see, vampire servants entered and removed the dying humans. She stopped one and instructed them, "Behead the male. Take the female to the nursery and prepare her for rising tomorrow night."

"It will be done, mistress. Thank you for your blessing." The vampire bowed and left.

She turned her attention back to Viktor. With a smiled, she looked him over. "I see you are still at the ready, Captain; impressive for one so young."

"You will find I am full of surprises."

Thia sighed contentedly and laughed.

"I'm glad you enjoyed yourself, pet." Viktor chuckled smugly and traced a fingertip down her arm.

"Mmm; you have amazing staying power and control. No lover, vampire or human, has been able to satisfy me like that in centuries," she admitted. "I know you fed well during our hunt, but I am surprised you could maintain your potency. Most vampires can't last much longer than a living man."

"Really? I've never had a problem with it; even before."

"Amazing."

He propped up on his elbow and smiled at her. "You are beautiful, Thia. I am afraid you have spoiled me for the wenches for a time, as well."

"Oh?" She raised an eyebrow at him.

"Yes, pet. No human woman can match you. The release of magic when you came was intense."

"As was yours, my love." She didn't tell him that his release of power had opened things about him to her. She'd been amazed to learn that he really was alive yet still vampire. Until then, she had thought his warmth and heartbeat were just vain expenditures of energy to appear human.

She'd also been able to sense all the vampires he had made; something she could not do before without being close enough to smell them. She could not sense or touch their presence after sex, but they had been revealed to her during the act.

He had nine existing "children." Six were on his ship, with a seventh that was very difficult to pin down somewhere in the vicinity. There were also two very distant ones being used to spy on him. He seemed unaware of one of them; but he seemed very aware of the other and where it was.

New Orleans.

She determined to check in on Jeorge and his kiss. It had been far too long since he'd come to her or her master's attention.

Viktor brought her attention back to the present when he rolled her over on her stomach. He nudged her knees apart, which let her know what he wanted. She raised herself up onto her elbows and knees to allow him to crouch over her from behind.

"You are ready again?" She laughed.

He growled into her ear as her thrust deep into her. "I am insatiable, pet."

Close to dawn, they finally stopped. Viktor traced a pattern he found just above her left shoulder blade. The tattoo depicted a dragon with wings spread coiled around a scythe.

"I've never seen workmanship of this quality before. Even Jon-Jon doesn't have anything with detail this fine. Where did you get it and why?"

"Hmm?" She stretched. Languor stole over her with the approaching dawn. "I keep a tattooist on retainer to freshen it every decade. I have had it for so many centuries I can't remember when I first had it done. Only a member of my Order may bear this mark."

"Your Order?" he chuckled. "Funny, but you don't strike me as a nun."

"I am a warrior, Viktor Brandewyne. I am the eldest of the Daughters of the Dragon. Our Order dates back millennia. We were charged with policing vampirekind."

He leaned over her with a wicked smile. "So that was why you were hunting me."

She blinked up at him, taken off guard by the comment. "How did you know I was hunting you?"

"I am a pirate, love. I make it my business to know when I am being hunted and by whom."

She reached up and brushed his hair behind his ear, her smile almost sad.

"What is it, pet?"

"Dawn approaches."

He heard the pain in her voice. She died before his eyes, and he knew the sun now rode the sky.

Chapter 24

"Ah, Mr. Grimm! Good; you're already aboard."

The first mate looked up from the desk in the captain's cabin, where he'd been looking over the log books. "Morning, Captain. I take that comment to mean make ready to sail."

"Aye, Hezekiah. We are resupplied?"

"We are."

"Good; the lads are on their way back to the ship, and Belladonna will join us outside the harbor. High tide should be in about two hours."

Grimm closed the book and stood. His back crackled as he stretched. "I'll roust Jon-Jon and have him get the lads started. If you don't mind my saying so, Vik, you seem to be in a pert mood this morning."

"Aye, I am." He grinned and held the crystal vial he'd gotten from Clarissa. In it, Grimm saw a small amount of nearly black blood.

"What is that?"

"The blood of a very special vampire."

"You didn't drink any of it, did you?" he asked sharply.

"No, you old granny woman; I know better than to taste another vampire. Celie was very clear about why that was dangerous."

Grimm visibly relaxed. "You worried me for a moment, Vik; that's all. I know you're not foolish. So, why do you have that blood?"

"It turns out Carpathia is a Daughter of the Dragon; they're some sisterhood of warriors among the vampires."

"Well, that was fortuitous; although it seems too easy. That's usually a bad sign."

Viktor shrugged. "I imagine it was dangerous enough. If she knew, she would be very angry — and she is as powerful as some of the Sisters. The temptations she presented tested my self-control. She is truly amazing, Hezekiah."

Grimm glanced sharply at his friend. Vik had only used that tone of voice in regards to one other female; Belladonna. He knew the vampire was not one to tie himself to any one female. Now that he had his Brianna, he recognized the early signs of infatuation, if not love, in his captain.

He kept his silence about it. "I'll go find Jon-Jon."

Shortly after sunset, Carpathia returned to the *Lorelei*. She seized the first sailor she came to and asked, "Has there been any activity around the *Incubus*?"

The terrified man sputtered incoherently and wet himself. Only Wormsloe's timely arrival saved him from having his throat torn out by the irate vampire.

"Lady Carpathia, welcome back aboard. Carlos is new to the crew and doesn't know much about our business here, yet. I would appreciate it if you didn't eat him."

She snarled at the captain but released the sailor. "Very well, Captain. Perhaps you have some news for me."

He nodded. "A conversation best held in my cabin."

Once safely in Wormsloe's cabin, he told her, "The *Incubus* left port at high tide this morning. We are fully supplied and crewed. The quartermaster should be directing our own cast off to pursue, as we speak."

She frowned. "The local vampires are upset. They believe Brandewyne has compromised their safe house. He was gone when I rose this afternoon. None of Clio's pet humans saw anyone come in and take him, but how else could he have left?"

"He can move about in daylight. You just didn't want to believe it. My scouts saw him board his ship this morning two hours before it left. It was full daylight, and he was by himself."

"I did learn last night that he is truly alive. How, I do not understand; but I intend to learn. This makes me wonder what other unique abilities he possesses. Can we catch him?"

Wormsloe laughed harshly. "Hardly, now; maybe if we'd left port at the same time. His ship outclasses this one several times over. I may know where he's headed, though."

"Oh?"

"There was talk of New Orleans among some of his crewmen who were loading supplies."

Her smile was far from pleasant. "I need to pay Jeorge a visit, anyway."

Belladonna perched on a railing and watched Viktor talk to the helmsman. The ship buzzed with activity. The crew swarmed the deck and rigging to get fully under weigh.

She could smell the female vampire on him. It rankled that he wouldn't heed her warnings about the creature. She feared for him, an emotion she was unaccustomed to.

"Ah, Belle, there you are," Grimm said as he approached her. "Surprised you're not up there with the Captain."

"He reeks of that vampire. I don't care to smell her on him. He should bathe."

He chuckled at her. "A whole ship full of smelly buggers, and you think Vik is the only one who needs a bath." He sobered and added, "I'm worried about him, too, lass. The more we can avoid that wench, the better. She could make him forget his quest."

"He is growing infatuated with her?"

"I fear so."

Hell's Dodo

"She is dangerous to him."

"He got what he needs from her; there's no reason to have further contact," Grimm said.

"What do you mean, 'he got what he needs from her'?"

"She's a Daughter of the Dragon. He stole some of her blood." He held up a hand to forestall her rant. "No, he didn't drink any of it."

She relaxed a bit, but not much. "That's good; but she is hunting him and will come after him. I already knew she was looking for him, but not why. If she truly is one of the Daughters of the Dragon, her reasons are most likely not in his best interests."

"Why do you say that?"

"They are a sisterhood of enforcers among vampirekind. Sometimes they are only sent to investigate anomalies, but more often they are dispatched to eliminate problems."

Viktor strode by them at that moment. "Both of you, my cabin. Now."

"It seems both of you forget I can hear very well." Viktor pinned the siren and his first mate with a meaningful stare.

Belle refused to be intimidated. "And you seem to forget that it is our job to try to protect you."

"She's right, Vik. We're only worried about you," Grimm added.

"I can understand Belle's jealousy, but not yours, Hezekiah. You should have stayed in Savannah with your wife." He managed to make the word sound derisive. "Then you wouldn't begrudge what I feel for Thia."

Grimm got right in his face. "I know where my duty is, Captain. I begrudge you nothing. However, I know how easily feelings for a woman can cloud a man's judgement. If you think this is mere jealousy on Belladonna's part, you don't know her as well as you think you do. She wouldn't be here if she was just jealous. She'd be off somewhere pouting, and you know it."

Belle blinked at the display. She'd never seen Grimm that confrontational with Viktor.

The vampire snarled at his first mate but did not attack. "Damn it, Hezekiah! Why do you always have to be right about these things?"

"It is my job."

Viktor put his hand over his eyes, shook his head, and chuckled. "I can see why old Zeke picked you two to be my nursemaids." He sighed. "I did say Thia offered temptations that were hard to resist. Perhaps you are both right, and I should distance myself from her. I could ask Jeorge about her."

Belle opened her mouth to protest that idea, but he didn't give her a chance to speak. "I won't, however. I don't really want to have to deal with the price he would exact for that kind of information. I really don't like the idea of involving him in any of this; but he has the most extensive library I've ever seen. Surely there will be some sort of information on dodos."

"Well, it is good to know that you are learning the wisdom of avoiding other vampires," she said, when he finished.

"They are extremely time-consuming creatures," he acknowledged. "I guess with eternity ahead of them, they don't feel particularly rushed about anything except feeding. I cannot afford to waste time."

"No, you can't," she agreed. "I will sing up a wind to speed you on your way."

Unexpectedly, he gave her a tender kiss. "Thank you, Belle," he said when he pulled back.

She stood there for a moment, pupils dilated. Grimm took her by the shoulders and steered her toward the cabin door. "Go sing up your wind, lass. You can bed him later; business first. I'll let the lads know to prepare the rigging."

Belladonna climbed onto the railing of the aft castle. She faced out behind the ship and read the winds and currents as only a creature of the sea could. Abruptly, she hopped back to the deck and walked over to Grimm.

"Problem, Belle?"

"Hopefully not. I think the *Lorelei* might be following us. I caught scent of that vampire on the wind."

He frowned. "I don't like that. Can you slow her down?"

"Oh definitely." She gave a very unfriendly smile. "She couldn't catch up to the *Incubus* in that tub, anyway. She might get close enough to fly over to us, though. I'll see to it that she can't."

"Good, but be careful, lass. I don't think it would sit well with the Captain if you harmed her."

"I won't even touch her," she snarled. "I can't guarantee the survival of her crew, however."

The *Lorelei* made good headway beneath the full moon. Some of the newer crewmen hadn't wanted to set sail at night, but Captain Wormsloe did not give way to their argument.

They had made open sea, with land nowhere in sight, when they heard the singing.

Carpathia arrived at the helm with enough speed to make it seem she had materialized there. "That bitch!" she snarled.

Wormsloe managed to recover from her sudden appearance rather quickly. "What are you talking about, m'lady?"

"Don't you hear her, Captain?"

"The singing? I thought it was a mermaid, at first, but none of the men seem inclined to go swimming. Sound carries at night. It may be some wench on a ship over the horizon." He shrugged.

"It is a siren's song, Captain Wormsloe, not some human female."

He thought her a bit daft. "If it's a siren, why isn't any of the crew eager to swim out to her?"

Hell's Dodo

She glared at him as if he were ignorant. "Sirens are not the same as mermaids. Their song is not to lure men. They are weather witches and use their magic to harness the winds and currents. Viktor has a siren as a pet."

He finally noticed a disturbing fact. "Rigger, trim your sails! Any man caught sleeping aloft will be flogged!" he bellowed as the sails grew limp.

"Cap'n, wind's died down!" The call came back from the crow's nest. "Look to the sea! She's like glass all around the ship!"

He saw the truth of it. The ship slowed to a lazy drift. "This is not good."

"Indeed it is not," Thia agreed. "She has becalmed us. Who knows for how long?" She stared at nothing for a moment. "There; I have ordered my slave dormant. He will not need to feed for some time."

Wormsloe had worked for vampires long enough to know the solution for that problem came with a price. "He won't feed, but you still will."

"I cannot afford to lie dormant for long periods of time. Eventually, my reserves would deplete until I could no longer control him. He would rise starved and insane."

He frowned, clearly not happy about the predicament. After a few moments, he noticed a change.

"The singing has stopped."

Thia moved to the railing and cocked her ear. "She is returning to his ship. Her heartbeat grows fainter by the second. You were right, Captain. He is headed in the direction of New Orleans. It should be safe to put out small boats now."

Wormsloe saw what she suggested but did not understand the qualifier. "Why would it not have been safe to tow the ship earlier?"

"Sirens are man-eaters. Viktor feeds his kills to his pet."

"Oh." He thought about it for a moment and remembered something. "Didn't that rogue mermaid you had to put down say a siren was after her? The creature stole aboard and made off with her whelp, too, if I recall."

"Yes. I believe this is the same siren. By all accounts, they are very territorial, and their territories are quite vast. The question, after this action, is how much does she know about my true mission, and what has she told my prey?"

Chapter 25

The *HMS Quicksilver* made a very conspicuous entrance into Savannah's harbor. There was no way it could not. The huge warship dwarfed all but the largest merchant vessels.

One sea captain, in particular, took the ship's arrival as a cue to get piss drunk.

Chadwick Harris took one look and headed straight to his favorite tavern. He'd seen the ship before, or thought he had. It didn't surprise him that Brandee would change the ship's name. What he wondered was why the pirate would think it wise to fly the Union Jack in a colonial port, given the current tension and rebellion.

Still, with a ship like that, few would dare openly challenge him.

Commodore Critchfield looked out on the river port from the deck of the aft castle. Savannah was the tidiest colonial port he'd visited. Unlike many of the much older colonial cities, this one had been planned out before the first structure had been erected.

This wasn't to say it was particularly clean. Just like any other port, odd bits of garbage, omnipresent rats, and the stench of bilge water marked the river district.

He loved it.

"Commander Turlington."

"Aye, sir?"

"We will be spending at least a week in this port. See to it that the crew rotates out on shore leave and watch duty. Once done, join me on an excursion."

His officer grinned. "Aye, sir!"

Later, Critchfield, Turlington, and a cabin boy stepped onto the cobbled surface of River Street dressed in common attire.

"Commodore, I would advise on keeping on the alert," Turlington said. "The rebellion has been gaining favor among the colonists."

"I am aware, Mr. Turlington. Reports place most of the rabble-rousers in the northern colonies, however. Georgia still remains home to many Loyalists."

They walked on in silence for a while, weaving in and out of the bustle on the street. Warehouses and trading offices made up the majority of the buildings along the riverfront. Tucked away between them, the occasional tavern could be found, though.

"I do take your advice to heart, Mr. Turlington, but not for the reasons you stated. Savannah is reported to be Brandee's home port. I am more concerned about those loyal to him than to those fools in Philadelphia and Boston. Ah, this looks like a good place to start."

Hell's Dodo

He stopped at the entrance to a side alley. A grubby two-story building of wood and stone had the only doors opening into the alley. A few men stumbled out the door; the sound of people talking, some low, some loud, plates and cups clattering, and a feminine laugh told him it was a tavern. The sign above the door bore a crude Jolly Roger and proclaimed it to be The Black Flag.

"Seems a little too conspicuous," Turlington opined.

Critchfield chuckled. "That's the beauty of it, man. It is so obvious it makes it the perfect place to find a pirate."

"Hide in plain sight?"

"Exactly."

Conversation in the common room stopped briefly as the trio entered the Black Flag. Once the strangers had been assessed, patrons returned their attention to their own business. Critchfield, Turlington, and the lad found a corner table and waved for a serving wench.

A ginger-haired woman came over to the table. Unlike the other girls working the room, she wore no cap or apron. "Afternoon, sirs. What may I interest you in?" she asked as she leaned over the table. She made sure they all got a good look down her blouse.

Peter, the cabin boy, blushed but did not look away.

"A bottle of your best rum and whatever you've got in the kettle for now, lass," Critchfield said. "We're fresh from sea and hungry for good food." He slid some silver across the table then tossed a gold piece on top. "I'd also like a word with the owner of this establishment."

The coins quickly disappeared into a pocket hidden in the folds of her skirt. She clapped her hands to draw the attention of one of the other girls. "Bess! Fetch a bottle of the good rum, four glasses, and three bowls of stew!"

"I'm busy!" Bess hollered.

The ginger-haired woman put her hands on her hips and shot back, "Well, you best get busier, or you'll find yourself back with the wharf rats. Who is that you're with?" She peered into the gloom. "Cord McVarish? Bess, you get these gentlemen their order right now! Cord hasn't paid in a month, and they gave good coin!"

"Oh, all right." Bess got out of the man's lap and headed to the kitchen.

McVarish piped up, "Oh come on, Maggie. You know I'm good for it."

"Cord, you're lucky I even let you eat here. If I don't see some coin out of you by the end of the week, you can find somewhere else to dip your wick." She turned back to Critchfield's party and pulled up a chair.

"I apologize for the delay, sirs. I'm Maggie Purnell, owner of the Black Flag."

"Nathan Critchfield, Joseph Turlington, and Peter Broward, Madam Purnell," he said.

She peered at him sharply. "Critchfield? Commodore Critchfield, the pirate hunter?"

Hell's Dodo

He smiled grimly and nodded confirmation. "I see my reputation precedes me. How did you know I wasn't some other Critchfield?" He'd already guessed the answer.

She proved him right. "That war horse in the harbor is a dead giveaway, Commodore." She gave him a wry, slightly wicked smile. "Don't get many Navy men in the Flag. I may have to start charging more."

"So," Turlington spoke up, "you support the Crown rather than the rebellion."

She gave him a pitying smile. "Politics and business don't mix well, Mr. Turlington. I tend to my business and whoever has the coin for it. I leave the politics to the politicians."

Critchfield chuckled. "Spoken like someone who knows there will always be a demand for her kind of business regardless of who is in power."

She nodded and smiled. "So, Commodore, what brings you to the Black Flag?"

"I am hunting a pirate."

She laughed. "If it's old Billy Black, you're a few years too late. He left me the Flag when he died. He died on top of me, as a matter of fact."

He raised an eyebrow. "Did he now? Well then, I guess we can finally remove William Blackthorne from the lists; but he isn't the one I'm looking for."

"Who then?" she grew wary.

"Viktor Brandewyne; have you seen him recently? Consider your answer well before making it, Madam Purnell."

She paled a bit but managed to keep her composure. Slowly, she answered, "Yes, but it has been several months."

"How long ago and where was he headed?" Turlington demanded.

"Tut-tut, Mr. Turlington; no need to be so rude and demanding," Critchfield chided. "Madam Purnell may be a whore, but she is still a member of the fairer sex."

Maggie glared at them. "You can have your money back. Look for answers elsewhere."

She reached in her pocket and put the money back on the table then started to stand. Critchfield grasped her wrist and forced her back into the chair. He scooped the coins up and put them back in her hand.

"Even if I don't get the answers out of you I want, I fully intend to get my money's worth out of you upstairs. I've been at sea a very long time."

She smiled warily. "Well now, that I can help you with, but I can't tell you anything about Vik Brandee."

"Can't or won't?" Turlington asked.

"Won't." She gave him an honest answer. "And before you threaten me, keep in mind that the most you can do is have me hanged."

"You fear Brandee more than death," Critchfield noted. "Why is that?"

"She's right to fear Brandee if she knows what kind of monster he's become," a male voice said from the shadows of a nearby table. "But I'm betting she's more afraid of the Thunderbolt Witch."

"And who are you, sir?" Critchfield asked.

"Chad Harris, you are piss drunk!" Maggie tried to distract them. Bess arrived with the rum and the food. "Took you long enough, Bess."

Peter got a mouthful of the stew, too hungry to wait for the others. He immediately made a face and nearly spit it back out.

"Gah! That's almost as bad as burgoo!"

Maggie chuckled. "Should have warned ye. Men don't come to the Flag for the food. You look like a strapping young buck, though. If you can finish that and keep it down, I'll see that one of the lasses takes care of you; no charge."

The lad blushed bright enough to tell even in the dimly lit tavern.

Bess grinned and tousled his hair. "Ooo, he's a virgin! Eat up, luv. I'll take you up and see you're properly trained," she cackled. He blushed even brighter.

Critchfield smiled wryly. "Ah for the favors of youth. Go on, Peter. The experience will do you good." He looked over at the man who had interrupted earlier. "Why don't you join us, Mr. Harris, was it?"

The drunkard stumbled to his feet, grabbed his bottle, and dragged his stool over to their table. He held out a grubby hand and said, "Chadwick Harris, captain of the *Georgia Belle*."

Critchfield recognized the name of his ship and realized the fool just handed him a bargaining chip. The *Georgia Belle* was a known pirate ship.

"Well met, Captain Harris. That will be all for now, Madam Purnell. I'll seek you out when I'm done here."

Maggie stood, gave him a smile, gave Harris a glare, and left the table.

Under guise of checking on other patrons, Maggie made her way over to Cord McVarish's table.

"How would you like to settle your debt now, Cord?" She smiled and sat down.

"Now Maggie, m'dear, y'know I've no coin on me as yet."

"I mean barter, not coin."

He perked up at that. "What did y'have in mind?"

She leaned forward and spoke low. "See to it that Chad Harris never sets foot in here again. Don't hurt him, mind you, at least not too much. His father could cause me trouble. If you can keep him out of here, I'll consider your debt settled. If you can do it without causing trouble, you can hire on here as a head-thumper."

He extended his hand. "Consider it done, Maggie."

She shook it. "I'd suggest you wait until those Navy bla'guards head upstairs."

Hell's Dodo

"Aye. I see your point."

☠

"Captain Harris, you speak as if you have personal experience with Brandee," Critchfield said.

Harris took a swig from his bottle before he nodded. "Aye; it's because of that bastard that I can't get up a crew."

"Oh?"

"Every time we cross paths he commandeers most of my men. Only ever leaves me enough crew and supplies to make it to the closest port; then word gets out, and no one will sign with me for fear of him. The man, no, the monster delights in tormenting me." He took another swig and sulked.

Critchfield found it interesting that Brandee apparently had no desire to kill the man. He already found Harris to be childish, foolish, and rather irritating. Still, information was information.

"You say he's a monster? I know he has a bloody reputation. Is that what you mean?"

"No. He has become an unholy demon; some kind of blood drinker. There's a she-demon that travels with him. I hear she eats men alive. With that mouthful of sharp teeth, I can well believe it, too."

"I see. That is the first we've heard of a female with him." He locked onto something Harris said earlier. "How long ago did he leave you stranded here in Savannah?"

Harris thought for a few minutes as the grog slowed his mind. Finally he said, "Been several months ago, maybe seven or more? He was leaving port just as I was returning."

"Why didn't you turn around and flee, if you knew he would attack?" Turlington asked.

"Bugger's sneaky and tricky; rigged his ship to look derelict. Curiosity got the better of me." His state of drunkenness made him honest. "Wouldn't have been able to outrun him, anyway. Thought he'd changed ship names and returned when I saw your ship."

"Yes," Critchfield confirmed, "I have heard that he'd acquired the sister ship to mine. *Incubus* I believe he calls her, although the original name was *War God*."

"Aye, she's the *Incubus*."

"Tell me, Captain Harris, do you know what Brandee's heading was?" He leaned forward and endured the drunkard's foul breath.

Harris blinked at him, his focus blurred at that distance. "Couldn't say for certain, but I heard talk among his crew about Salem."

"Thank you, sir. Now do you have any suggestions about this horrid stew?" He laughed.

"Rum," Harris said decisively. "Pour some in it or at least drink enough to not taste it anymore." He grew silent for a while. Eventually, he looked as if something crossed his mind. "There's more scuttlebutt about what Brandee was doing in this port. I'll tell you for a price."

Hell's Dodo

"Finally," Critchfield thought. *"I was wondering when he would bring up money."* Aloud, he said, "How much?"

"Thirty silver."

"Judas' price," Turlington commented.

Critchfield smiled a predatory smile. The fool had played right into his hands. "Very well, Captain Harris, I will pay your price. If the information merits it, I will even give you something extra."

Harris might not have recognized the trap even if he'd been sober. He leaned forward in a conspiratorial manner, darted his gaze left and right, and said, "I heard he dropped off a pregnant woman. There was hushed talk about her marrying the Grimm Reaper to save her honor. Rumor has it she's out to Thunderbolt and staying with the old witch."

242

Chapter 26

Critchfield counted out thirty silver coins and placed them in the middle of the table. When Harris reached for them, the Commodore grasped his wrist.

"That is indeed valuable information, if it is true. I will give you the extra I promised." He turned and looked at Turlington. "Commander, Captain Harris seems to have a problem gathering a crew. See to it that he gets one and that his ship is fully provisioned and ready to sail by the morrow's high tide. You will accompany Captain Harris and lay in wait for Brandewyne."

"What? No! No, that won't be necessary! Please, I don't want to see him ever again!" Harris protested.

"Aye, sir," Turlington replied grimly with a nod. He ignored Harris' outburst. "I just hope that tub will hold together long enough to find him."

"Yes, sorry about that, Commander. The *Georgia Belle* is a rather pathetic sight, isn't she?" Critchfield said.

"Now see here! Just because you have that big fancy man-o-war is no reason to besmirch my *Georgia Belle*!" Harris said, stung.

Critchfield fixed him with a cold glare. "Be grateful that you are being conscripted and your ship commandeered, Mr. Harris. I could just have you hanged and sail your ship as a trap without you. The *Georgia Belle* is a known pirate vessel, albeit a pathetic one. You are more a nuisance than anything else, but you've committed enough acts of piracy and mayhem to warrant a trip to the gallows, sir."

Turlington took mercy on him. "Think of it this way, Mr. Harris. You've earned some coin, you will earn a pardon, and you will have revenge on the man you say delights in your torment."

Harris turned a pale face to him. "More likely earned my death by his hand. I've seen what he's become."

"I believe you, Mr. Harris," Critchfield said. "Commander Turlington and I have met and dealt with similar creatures as well as received training from one who hunts them."

Turlington clapped a hand on his shoulder. "Come on, man. There is hope yet. I'll escort you back to your ship. I need to inspect it anyway to see what skills I'll need among my mates."

Harris rose and turned to leave with him, his head hung in deject acceptance of his fate.

A couple of minutes later, McVarish left the Black Flag, as well.

Long shadows and boys making the rounds to light the street lanterns marked the late hour. Turlington and Harris never even noticed the third shadow that joined theirs.

Hell's Dodo

Without warning, the Navy man collapsed. Before he could react, rough hands grasped Harris by the upper arms and dragged him into an alley. "Come on, boyo!"

He turned to see who had accosted them. Blearily, he recognized Cord McVarish. "Are you mad, man? They'll hang me for sure!"

"Not if they don't find you. There's a packet leaving on the tide in half an hour. Be on it. She's bound for the East Indies."

"But what about my ship?"

Cord shook him. "Think about it, man. They already said they don't need you if they have the *Georgia Belle*. You can get another ship, one that Brandee doesn't know."

"That's right!" His thoughts instantly brightened. "Where's the packet?"

"Five berths down from your ship. Oh, and one more thing: never set foot in the Black Flag again. Maggie's mad at ye and doesn't want you around."

He thought about it for a moment. "Fair enough. None of those tarts are good enough to risk her selling me out to Brandee."

"Good man; you're smarter than you look."

A constable woke Turlington several hours after full dark. He found him in the alleyway where McVarish dragged him.

"Are you well, sir? Almost mistook you for one of the local drunks; but you are too well-groomed to be one of them," the constable said as he leaned over him.

A painful throb at the base of his skull let Turlington know what had befallen him. "Someone cudgeled me," he said and gingerly rubbed the back of his head. He didn't feel anything wet, and his hand came away clean, so at least he hadn't been bleeding.

Next, he checked his pockets. He was amazed to still have all his coin and effects. "It's all still here."

"You don't say?" The constable sounded surprised. "That is most peculiar. Wonder why someone this close to the docks would go to the trouble of drubbing you; then just tuck you away unmolested."

"Harris," he hissed. "He must've had a compatriot back at the Flag that helped him escape."

"Chadwick Harris?"

"Yes. Do you know him?"

The constable snorted. "Nearly everyone in Savannah knows Chadwick. It's a wonder his da hasn't died of apoplexy over the mewling, mincing brat. He's a sore disappointment to his da, but his ma protects him. She says he gives the family color. More like a black eye, if you ask me. Fancies himself another Vik Brandee, not that he could ever match Brandee. Heard tell that devil's sent the pup limping back to port every time they cross paths."

Hell's Dodo

Turlington rubbed the back of his head and looked toward the docks. "I guess he's taken the *Georgia Belle* and sailed by now. The Commodore is not going to like this."

"Oh, he'll show up before long," the constable reassured him. "Three ships left with the tide, but the *Georgia Belle* wasn't one of them. After his last run in with Brandee, no one in this port will sail with him."

"Thank you, constable. You've been most helpful." He nodded and turned to the docks. An hour later, he finished moving his gear into the captain's cabin of Harris' ship and chose a modest crew from the sailors aboard the *Quicksilver*.

The next morning, Critchfield sent Peter to check in with Turlington.

The boy showed back up with the Commander shortly after.

"We lost Harris, but we have his ship, sir." Turlington thought it best to get the bad news out of the way first thing.

"And just how did you lose him, Mr. Turlington?"

"Best I can figure, a mate of his followed us last night and drubbed me from behind. A constable found me tucked away in a dark alley otherwise unmolested."

Critchfield frowned then shrugged. "We have the ship, at least. That should be sufficient bait for Brandee."

"Aye, sir. The constable confirmed that Brandee seems to bear Harris some grudge." He thought about it for a while. "If I may speak freely?"

"By all means, man. You are one of my best officers, despite this recent bout of carelessness."

Turlington winced at the reproof. Thankfully, it wasn't as harsh as he'd feared. That madam must have put the Commodore in an exceptional mood. He hoped he would have the time to find a wench for himself.

"Mr. Turlington?"

"Oh, sorry, sir; I must still be a touch addled from that blow to the head. No sir, at first I worried that my mission aboard the *Georgia Belle* might be one of suicide. Given that Brandee seems to allow Harris not only to live but to retain his ship, I am not as fearful of being sunk on sight. With that in mind, I selected not only good sailors but some good marines."

"Good man. I am glad I can count on you to handle the mission. Why don't you find yourself a good wench? It will help clear the cobwebs." The Commodore patted him on the back. "Peter, you can go on back to the ship. That local lad I hired this morning should be along shortly."

"Local boy?" Turlington asked as the cabin boy returned to the *Quicksilver*.

"Aye, I need a guide who knows where this Thunderbolt Witch is. I would like to meet the woman who raised Viktor Brandewyne."

Hell's Dodo

"Sorry sir, but this is as far as I dare take you. That old woman scares me," the boy said as they stopped at the edge of a grove of live oak. "Her hut is in there somewhere."

"Very well, you took me as far as you'd promised. Here's a shilling." Critchfield handed him a coin. The lad turned and ran back the way he'd come.

Critchfield raised an eyebrow, shook his head, and headed into the moss-draped grove. The tangled, gnarled limbs spread wide from the trunks, some of them thick enough to count as tree trunks themselves. Many branches bent low to the ground before they turned upward in search of the sun. The Spanish moss beards hung as thick as curtains and blocked visibility.

He walked up on the witch's tabby shack before he knew there was a structure there. An ancient woman looked up from the cook fire she tended.

"Pardon me, old mother. I am looking for the Thunderbolt Witch."

She tilted her head then returned her attention to the fire.

He wondered if maybe she hadn't heard him clearly. He knew that the very old were prone to hearing loss. "I said I am looking for...," he said louder.

"I heard you the first time, Nathan Critchfield," she replied without looking up.

"You are she, then; the woman who raised Viktor Brandewyne."

"I am. What do you want?"

He frowned. "Are you really a witch? Is that how you know my name?"

She looked at him. "Is that really important?"

"No. I heard a rumor that Brandewyne abandoned a pregnant woman in this port and that she was the Grimm Reaper's bride. Is she here?"

The old woman cackled. "You honestly think Viktor or the Reaper would care a whit about some poor girl with child? And you call yourself a pirate hunter."

He tried to loom over her, stung by her words. It did not have the desired effect. She just shook her head and continued to chuckle. "Tell me, Nathan Critchfield, do you think the woman who raised Bloody Vik Brandee, whom he still calls Mother, is intimidated by a Navy popinjay such as yourself? No. Oh, you might think so, but it is not in your power to bring me any harm."

"I could have you burned for witchcraft." His smile was cruel and sinister.

She placed her hand in the fire, waved it around as if fishing for something, and pulled it back out. She opened her fist and held it out to him palm up. A bright flame danced there. Her skin remained unharmed.

"This is some trick or illusion."

"Then touch the flame," she challenged.

Stubbornly, he reached out for it. He could feel the heat of the flame but thought it part of the illusion. He continued to hold his hand over the flame she held on her open palm, a grimace of pain on his face.

He did not pull away until he felt his skin blister and crack. A faint odor of roasted meat reached his nose. The blood and other juices that dripped from his blistered skin sizzled and popped as it was consumed by the fire.

"Nyyaaaaah!" he cried as he held his damaged hand close to his chest, finally.

She tilted her hand, and the captive flame flowed back into the cook fire as if it were water. She showed him her completely undamaged hand and said, "It is not in your power, Nathan Critchfield. Now give me your hand so I can heal it."

About a half hour later, Celie said, "You can come out now, child. He is safely away, and I don't think he'll be back."

A curtain of moss parted on a nearby tree to reveal another one-room tabby hut. A soft moan and a startled yelp emanated from the open door. The old woman quickly got to her feet. Brianna waddled to the opening and braced against the doorjamb.

"Help me!" she managed to strangle out, her voice full of pain. A second later, a wet spot grew on her skirt until she looked drenched from the hips down.

"Oh child! They are coming early!"

Chapter 27

Jeorge raised an eyebrow as Melanie entered his chambers. "You usually hunt at this time of night. I did not summon you, child. Why are you here?"

The young vampire curtsied and cast her eyes down. "Forgive my intrusion, master. My sire wished for me to let you know he is traveling here."

In a flash, Jeorge stood in front of her and lifted her face to meet her eyes. They showed him fear, lust, and Hunger. "When did he send you this message and how? It has been over a year since you could see or feel his presence."

"He blocks me out, Master. I still try every night when I rise, before I hunt. When I rose tonight, he summoned me before I could try to contact him. It was as if he was waiting for me to rise."

"I see. Did he say why he is coming here?"

"He wishes to use your library. He is hunting for something and hopes to find a clue to where it may be found written in one of your books."

"Hmm. Did he say what it was specifically?"

"No, Master."

"Very well; although it would make it easier to find the right books if I knew what it was," he sighed. "Did he give you an idea of when to expect him?"

Her body stiffened, and she moved like a puppet. "Well, this is interesting," she said, but something about her voice rang deeper, rougher. "I had no idea I could do this. Damn, the female body is even stranger from the inside!"

Jeorge quickly grasped what had happened. "Hello, Captain Brandewyne. I see you have acquired a new ability."

"Indeed." Viktor grinned using Melanie's form. "I knew I could hear and speak to my vampire offspring. I did not know I could inhabit their bodies. I was just trying to speed this conversation up. The relay of question and answer grew tedious."

"Ever impatient." Jeorge laughed. "How may I help you, Captain?"

"I am looking for information about a creature called a dodo. All I know is that it lays eggs. I need to know more precisely what it is, what it looks like, and where it can be found."

He smiled. "Truth be told, I am not sure I have ever heard of it. It shall be an interesting challenge to research. Do you have an idea of when you will make port?"

"Given our current speed, I should reach New Orleans in two days."

"The challenge increases." Jeorge raised an eyebrow. "I look forward to your arrival. Oh, before I forget, you might want to place Melanie in a chair. Possession by one's sire tends to have a draining effect."

Vik nodded from her body. "Duly noted. You have my thanks for your help, Jeorge. What will be the price?"

"In this instance, the challenge is payment enough. You have given me a means to combat the boredom. I thank you."

"I will see you two nights from now, then." Melanie's body moved to the closest chair and sat down. She fell limp with a look of fear and confusion on her face.

Jeorge rang a bell, and Anton, his second, answered the summons. "Bring a meal for Melanie and someone to see she feeds. She is very weak and may need to be force fed at first. Also, have Guillaume found and directed to the garden. I will speak with him there. I want you to be present."

Anton nodded his understanding and left the room.

Jeorge looked at Melanie's mute, limp form. "Do not fear, child. You will recover with a good feeding. It is never a pleasant experience to have your sire take control like that, but the first time is the worst. It does get easier to bear."

He left unsaid the fact that he only knew of three other vampires that could do what Brandewyne had just done to her. One had been his own sire. He had not inherited the ability from his long-gone maker. The other two were the most powerful and feared vampires known.

He hoped Viktor Brandewyne was and remained ignorant of that fact. If the pirate thought all sires had that ability, he would be less likely to use it against him. Until then, Melanie would bear watching.

Viktor withdrew from his vampire daughter, and had to sit down, as well. He didn't feel weakened or drained by the experience. Rather, he felt invigorated. His senses returning fully to just his body felt disorienting, however. It reminded him of the first time he'd used Lazarus to "see" things.

Inhabiting a woman's body had been strange, to say the least. It left him both curious and aroused. Once his senses settled, he rose and left his cabin.

He soon found himself outside the door of Belladonna's cabin. He gave a perfunctory knock before he went in. The siren lay tangled in her blanket, oblivious to the world.

He reached out through his link with her. It worried him a little to find she had no defenses up at all. Vulnerability from her was rare. Still, it made what he wanted to try a little easier.

Cautiously, he probed with his power. He felt his consciousness submerge into her subconscious, to a point. Some invisible barrier or presence prevented him from taking over her form as he had Melanie's. He wasn't sure if it was because she was a siren, the fact that she was still alive, or that she was not a vampire of his making.

Hell's Dodo

Satisfied with that part of the experiment, he "looked" around her dreamscape. Mists swirled around him on an indistinct landscape. He thought it might be an island, given the sound of surf and gulls.

Then he heard the singing. It drew him with its haunting melody; siren song. He smiled and followed the sound over the sand. The mist kept him nearly blind. It struck him as odd that the mist felt warm rather than cool, and that he could feel it all over his body. He looked down at his dream self to discover a complete lack of clothing.

He chuckled lustily. It seemed the siren's mood reflected his.

The singing grew louder as he moved through the mist. Finally, he found himself in a hollow in the mist. Before him, Belladonna laid spread eagle on a rock. He thought it strange until he saw the manacles and chains that held her there.

"Who dares chain you like this?" he demanded as he approached her.

She stopped singing. "Viktor? You came for me? I've been waiting so long."

"Who did this to you, pet?" he asked again.

"Don't you know? You forged these chains," she answered.

"No!" he protested. He moved forward and placed his hands on the chains. They dissolved into the mist at his touch. He had to move fast to catch her before she tumbled off the rock.

She wrapped herself around him and smiled. "You are naked. Why? Were you going to take me while I was helpless?"

"This is your dream, pet, not mine. I am naked because you dreamt me this way. As for taking you while you were chained and helpless, where is the sport in that?"

She kissed him and impaled herself on him. He moaned as she used his shoulders for leverage to work up and down. Out of instinct, he grabbed her hips to give her better leverage and to guide her thrusts.

As good as it felt, though, he wanted more.

"You need to wake up, pet. As nice as this is, I want the real thing."

They both opened their eyes at the same time. Belladonna gasped and looked surprised to find Viktor leaning over her in her bed.

"What are you doing here?"

He chuckled wickedly. "I'm about to make your dream come true, pet."

Grimm approached his captain at the railing of the aft castle. "Afternoon, Captain."

"Mr. Grimm," Vik answered amiably.

Grimm smiled wryly. "Seems you and Belle are on good terms at the present. This is some of the finest weather I've seen in a long time."

"Aye, we've made good time. We should put in at New Orleans tonight."

Hell's Dodo

"Aye." Grimm sighed and leaned on the railing. Somethings wistful in the sound of the sigh drew Vik's attention. He sniffed the air tentatively as he observed his first mate and friend.

"You miss her," he stated.

"Belle?" Grimm asked, puzzled.

"Brianna."

He frowned. "You shouldn't concern yourself with that, Captain. I think I've proven that I won't let my marriage interfere with your search."

"Zeke's meddling makes it my concern, Hezekiah. Her wellbeing and that of your children are vital. I admit I am worried about them."

"Why? I can think of no place safer than under Celie's protection."

"Even Mother Celie has her limits," Vik countered. "For the moment, she has some sort of barrier up. Lazarus cannot get past it to check on things. He is quite frustrated. After we leave New Orleans, we will sail around to Georgia."

"I appreciate the sentiment, Captain, but I would advise against it," he protested. "If Celie is keeping that well hidden, it can only mean someone is there hunting, probably looking for you. This ship isn't exactly inconspicuous."

Vik arched an eyebrow at him. "All facts I am well aware of, Hezekiah. My plan is to sail up the Altamonte far enough to hide her and sail the small ketch up to Thunderbolt by night, just the two of us. We can pass the wards that Lazarus cannot."

"Won't Belle feel left out?"

"I doubt her feelings will be hurt." He laughed. "I plan to give her carte blanche to prey on anyone foolish or unfortunate enough to sail within sight of the ship."

"When is this?" the siren asked as she sashayed over to join them.

"Later, off the coast of Georgia," Vik answered. "Someone has troubled Mother Celie enough for her to put up protective wards."

"That is not good. What about sending Lazarus?"

"He can't get through."

She frowned and started to speak. Grimm stopped her. "He's already countered all my arguments, lass. The Captain's mind is set on the matter."

"Hmph. He is a stubborn thing, isn't he?"

Viktor gave them a humorously disgusted grimace. "What are you doing up on deck anyway, pet? You shouldn't be able to walk right now."

She smiled sweetly if somewhat mischievously. "Remember, lover, I am not a frail human, and I heal very, very quickly." With that, she began disrobing. Neither man made any show of looking away. Once she'd removed her shirt and breeches, she folded them neatly and handed them to Viktor.

Hell's Dodo

She turned and moved to the railing. Nimble as a cat, she hopped up to balance on the edge. Only a slight crouch signaled her backward leap off the rail. She neatly cut into the sea below with barely a splash.

"Hezekiah, have we had any shirkers lately?" Vik asked; his eyes still glued to the spot of the siren's dive.

Grimm seemed equally entranced. "Two of the newer men have been slow to learn seamanship. Holbert tries, but he is completely ham-handed when it comes to knots. Wilkins seems more interested in finding snug spots to nap in than in helping out in the galley."

Silently, Viktor searched the two men out through the blood bond he used to control his crew. They soon headed toward the side of the ship, one from the rigging, one from below decks. They found they had an overwhelming desire to go swimming.

Grimm looked over at Viktor. "The sport must have been exceptional."

"Aye." The vampire leered.

The first mate chuckled, shook his head, and headed for the stairs to the quarter deck. "I don't want to know. Now, where has Mr. Jon gotten off to? He still owes me a bottle of gin for yesterday's game of dice."

Rather than his usual habit of setting anchor out in the harbor, Viktor put the *Incubus* in at the

261

docks. He didn't want to take the time to be subtle. He also didn't give any shore leave.

Mr. Grimm made it clear to the men that they would not be in port long enough for sport. With any luck, they would sail with the morning tide. A portion of the special rum quelled any discontent.

Viktor caught the unmistakable scent of vampire the moment he set foot on the dock. It only took a few seconds to identify the particular one Jeorge had sent to meet him. Shortly after that, he spotted him among the dock traffic.

"Guillaume," he said, strolling over to the other vampire.

"Captain." Guillaume knew not to speak Viktor's name in public unless the pirate had already identified himself. The name Brandewyne could cause panic or riot in the wrong group. As a vampire, Guillaume understood the importance of not drawing attention.

As they shook hands, he said, "The carriage is waiting for you."

"Good to hear it. Lead the way, my friend."

Chapter 28

Viktor wasn't surprised to see very little activity in the reception area of Jeorge's manse. That early in the evening, he imagined most of the vampires had gone to hunt. A servant led him and Guillaume to the library.

Jeorge looked up from the reading desk at the sound of the door. "Ah, Captain Brandewyne! Welcome!" He stood and moved around the desk to shake hands with the pirate.

"Thank you, Jeorge. Have you found out anything about dodos?"

"Only tonight, I'm afraid. It took some time to find the right books." He pulled a gold watch on a jeweled fob from his vest pocket and looked at it. "No wonder I'm famished. It has been twenty hours since I last fed! Guillaume, bring us something up from the cellar. Have you fed yet, Captain? It would be no problem to bring you a meal, as well."

"Thank you. I have not had whole blood for nearly a week and have not had time to hunt." Viktor bowed to his host.

"Guillaume, bring up an extra for our guest."

"*Oui*, Jeorge." The vampire bowed and exited the library.

Jeorge looked at Viktor with some amazement. "For someone who has not had a proper feed for so long, you look incredibly healthy. What have you been subsisting on, may I ask?"

"I keep blood diluted and preserved with spirits, preferably brandy or rum, on board for myself and my cadre. Unlike them, I am also able to get by on solid food for extended periods of time, although if I go too long without blood it takes several men to sate my Hunger."

"I am astonished. I have been unable to eat real food since my first night as a vampire. You truly are not like other vampires."

"As I've told you from the beginning," Vik chuckled.

"True, you have, but given my centuries, you must excuse my initial skepticism."

"I'll grant you that. I've seen how different I am just in comparison to the vampires of my cadre. Of course, with as little experience as I have with our kind, I really don't know how typical or atypical they are, compared to other vampires," he admitted.

Jeorge shrugged. "If their abilities and behavior are anything like Melanie's, I would say they are normal for fledglings. It will take a few decades for special abilities and strengths to develop."

Viktor blinked and nodded. His host had just revealed how very exceptional Viktor was as a vampire. He could see Jeorge's curiosity plainly, but there was the most subtle undertone of fear in the vampire's scent.

Viktor did not fear the older vampire. He did respect him. He knew he would have to make sure not to seem threatening. A war with Jeorge would be unnecessary and would cost time and resources he could ill-afford.

Jeorge consulted his watch again. "What is taking Guillaume so long?"

"It has only been a few minutes." Vik smiled. "Humans do not move as fast as we do, especially if they have been bespelled."

"True. True. My Hunger is getting the better of me, I'm afraid."

"That is an interesting timepiece." Viktor attempted to change the subject. "Where did you come by it? I don't believe I've seen one that compact before."

Jeorge grinned. "Still the pirate, I see. I was wondering when you would say something about this bauble. One of my oldest children is in Switzerland. He took up clock making as a hobby to tide him through the winters. He has been perfecting his craft for nearly two centuries. This is one of the most precise chronometers in existence."

Viktor frowned as he peered at the intricate and delicate workings visible through the crystal on the back of the watch. "How long have you had this?"

"Nearly fifty years. I usually travel to visit some of my children who still reside in the Old World every century or so."

"Why is it I have not seen more of these? I would imagine there would be a great demand for them."

"There would be, if humans knew that such quality and precision existed. The best mortal artisans are still nowhere near this level of craftsmanship. Herbert has no apprentices. Watchmaking is only a hobby, or perhaps an obsession to him. Oh, he tried to pass his expertise on a few times, but he had a nasty habit of eating his apprentices and was nearly discovered by the hunters. So, he keeps to himself, makes his toys, and only comes out to feed," Jeorge explained.

"Seems a bit dreary."

Jeorge shrugged. "Herbert's clockworks keep him happy. Switzerland, at least the area of it he is in, can be quite dull: just the occasional small village and scattered farmers… and the mountains. Have you ever seen mountains, Viktor, I mean real mountains?"

He waggled his hand. "Very few up close. The ones along the Pacific coast seem to be higher than anything around the Caribbean."

"The Alps in central Europe make the mountains in the islands look like ant hills."

"Perhaps I shall go see them someday," Vik said. "For the time being, I prefer to keep close to the sea."

Hell's Dodo

"And your siren," Jeorge added with a chuckle.

Before Vik could respond, Guillaume returned with a small group of humans. Three men and three women stood with confused expressions and stared at the tall man and teen-aged boy who occupied the library.

"This isn't the kitchen or dining room," one woman said as she turned to the vampire who had led them there. "I thought you said there would be food."

"Oh there is, just not for you, *Cherie*," Jeorge gave her a feral grin.

Jeorge watched as Guillaume and Anton removed the bloodless corpses. One had to be carried separate from its head. Out of habit, Viktor beheaded his victim once they were dead.

Jeorge questioned him about it.

"My apologies. I did not want to burden you with a new vampire unbidden. Since we did not play with that lot, I assumed they were merely food, not candidates. It is my custom to behead used food if Belladonna is not with me to dispose of the body," Viktor explained.

"Ah, I see. A wise habit." He accepted his guest's reasoning. Secretly, he was glad not to have another of the pirate's bloodline in his kiss. He didn't want to risk losing his territory.

"I thank you for a most pleasant meal."

Tamara A. Lowery

"Thank you for joining me. I so hate to eat alone."

After the two underlings left with the last corpse, Viktor got right to business. "You said you only found out something about dodos tonight?"

"Ah! Yes, right here, I believe." He shuffled around books on the reading desk until he found the one he wanted. "Can you read Portuguese?"

"No. I haven't had a need to learn it."

"I will translate then." He poured over the text for a moment. "Shall I summarize? There is much that deals with trivialities not related to the dodo."

"I would appreciate it."

"Very well; you are looking for a large, flightless bird. There is a plate with an illustration of the creature."

Viktor looked at the picture. "Hmm; ugly bugger. How large is it?"

"It stands about three feet tall. This says it tastes rather unpleasant, but it is edible. It was discovered on Mauritius. That is all this account says about the creature."

Viktor stroked his beard and smiled. "That is actually to my advantage, for once. It is en route to my next destination. Thank you for your help, Jeorge."

"Thank you for a respite from boredom. Where are you headed to?"

"I am off to the Orient."

"Whatever for, if I may be so bold?"

Hell's Dodo

"To fetch a dragon's egg," Viktor laughed.

After the pirate returned to his ship, Anton approached his master. "Did you smell it?"

"I did. He has encountered Her, most likely within the last month. That is one of the reasons I did not attempt to detain him."

"One of the reasons?"

"Yes. He has demonstrated an ability that my sire shared with Her and her Sire. I know of no other vampire to ever be able to fully possess one of their children, but Captain Brandewyne can. The most I can do is speak through mine. I cannot inhabit their bodies as if it were my own. It seems he stumbled upon the ability by accident. His power troubles me. Now that he has drawn Her attention, I do not feel safe with him around; but he is too powerful to risk making him an enemy."

Anton frowned. "Do you think She will come here seeking him?"

"I do not know."

Chapter 29

Two days out of New Orleans, Jon-Jon brought a problem to Grimm's attention. The first mate verified it and deemed it important enough to bring to the captain's attention.

"Yes, Hezekiah? What is it?"

"Rats. We must have acquired a large number of them recently. At least a third of our stores have been eaten, damaged, or fouled by the vermin," he replied. "Jon-Jon has found two of the ship cats dead and partially eaten."

That got Viktor's attention. "That sounds like wharf rats."

"Aye. My thoughts, as well. I've organized some of the lads for a hunt. We'll have to resupply soon because of this."

"Lazarus, come forth," Vik summoned. Immediately, the cat materialized. "We have a rat problem. You can go in spaces the lads cannot. I want you to help with the hunt."

"Mrrrow, rrrrrrr." Lazarus growled and gave the feline equivalent of a nod.

"Thankye," Grimm replied to the cat.

As an after-thought, Vik said, "If he doesn't eat his kills, I suggest beheading the dead rats. I don't know if vampirism can be transmitted to rats, and I don't wish to find out.

"Agreed, Captain." Grimm frowned and shuddered.

☠

Even with the demon cat's help, it took nearly a week to catch and kill all of the rats. The climax of the hunt came when a large nest was found in the forward magazine.

Three females with large litters hid behind the powder kegs against the bulwark. They'd ruined at least one coil of rope to make the nest.

Lazarus crouched on a keg above the nest and growled down at the vermin. The half-eaten remains of yet another ship cat lay in the middle of the nest. One of the females, which was slightly larger than the demon cat, looked up from her meal and hissed.

Without further warning, she sprang up at him. An unholy din of growls, yowls, hisses, and screams erupted as the two grappled. Fur flew around the enclosed space in bloody clumps.

Mr. Bland and his hunting party set about moving the kegs out of the way. One of the men pulled a blunderbuss and aimed for the tumbling ball of black fur, teeth, and claws. Bland quickly stopped him.

"Are you mad, man? We can't risk a spark in here, unless you want to sink the boat. Blades only; and you better pray you don't skewer the cat."

"It's just a cat," the pirate argued.

Hell's Dodo

"It's the Captain's cat. Hurt that cat and he's liable to send ye swimmin' with Belladonna," Bland warned.

The man gulped and put his firearm away.

"Wise decision, Mr. Reubens," a voice said from behind them. The startled pirates turned to see the captain standing in the doorway. "I am very fond of Lazarus, and he is very useful to me."

A second rat jumped to the top of the kegs and poised to jump into the fray. She never made it. Viktor's sword bisected her in mid-leap. When the third female emerged to defend the nest, he pinned her to the wall with his dagger. The blade buried itself to the hilt in the creature's neck.

"Mr. Bland, get these kegs moved and find and kill all the whelps," Vik ordered. "Lazarus, quit playing with that thing and finish it."

"Aye, Cap'n," Bland said. "You heard the man! Hop to it!"

The remaining rat screamed as Lazarus gutted her with his hind claws. A swift bite to the back of her neck severed her spine. Proudly, he dragged the carcass over and dropped it at Viktor's feet.

He smirked down at the cat. "What are you bragging about? I killed two of them. That's just one."

"Myneaah mow mrrow," Lazarus sassed. He hopped up on a nearby powder keg and began grooming. Viktor laughed at him.

"Bugger me!" Reubens yelped. He'd reached the nest first.

"What is it?" Bland asked.

"There must be fifty of 'em here!"

"Well don't just stand there, man; start bashing heads," Bland replied irritably.

Reubens and two other men began to comply with the order. Mr. Bland moved over to retrieve Viktor's dagger. A second later, his screams mingled with those of the dying baby rats.

The large female was mortally wounded but still alive. When he'd braced his hand against her to pull out the blade, she'd grabbed a finger and bit it. Bland pulled back a bloody stump. The rat clutched the severed finger.

"Reubens, get Mr. Bland to the infirmary. Now!" Viktor ordered.

He strode over, grasped the rat by the throat, and squeezed until her head popped off. He retrieved his knife and used it to behead the rat Lazarus had killed.

The cat leapt to the deck and snagged the severed finger. Vik raised an eyebrow at him. Lazarus gave a meaningful glance at the remaining pirates.

"Put the carcasses in a gunny and chuck it over the side, lads. I think our rat problem has been dealt with for now."

"Aye, Cap'n."

In short order, the dead rats were bagged, and the crewmen out of the powder magazine. Secure in their privacy, Lazarus quickly consumed the finger.

The next moment, Jim Rigger stood where the cat had been. "Where's a wench when you need one?"

Vik noticed a particular part of his friend's anatomy was waving at him. "I'm glad to see you, too, Jim. Now point that thing somewhere else," he laughed.

"Can't help it, Cap'n." Jim grinned and flashed his fangs. "I always get like this after a good fight, and you're just so damn pretty,"

Both men laughed.

"Oh, and for the record, I only had to kill my one rat once. Your second one didn't stay dead," Jim teased.

"Well now, you wouldn't be standing here saying that if I had killed it right off."

"True enough; too bad about Charlie's finger, but I am glad of the chance to stretch my legs again."

"Aye, and I'm glad of the company, Jim." They stood in silence for a few moments before Viktor spoke again. "Damn, but I wish you could stay like this."

Jim shook his head. "Hezekiah is a fine first mate, Vik. I'm more useful to you as Lazarus."

Viktor's face twisted in an almost desperate anger. Pain and loneliness showed in his eyes. Jim was the only person other than Mother Celie he'd ever let see such weakness. "Dammit, Jim! That's not the point! You are my brother! I miss you!" he growled.

Jim's face sobered. He knew how much this display cost his friend. "I miss you, too, Vik. I swear I'll give you whatever help I am able to when the time comes to settle accounts with that bitch who did this to us."

"Thank you, Jim. Rest assured; we will pay her back."

Jim's skin twitched. "The magic is wearing off, Vik. I've got to change back now."

"I know."

Just like that, the cat was back. He leapt to Viktor's shoulder, and they exited the powder magazine together.

The pirates chased a trader from the Florida Strait to Puerto Rico. The prize managed to escape in the night, a fact that surprised Viktor. He'd not had a prize outrun him in longer than he could remember.

The *Incubus* ended up making port in San Juan to take on supplies. While there, several crewmen heard warnings to watch out for pirate hunters. One hunter in particular had been spotted patrolling regularly between Charleston and New Providence. The rumors said the hunter sailed a ship-o-the-line that no pirate stood a chance against.

Viktor and Grimm took the news to heart. Viktor had a plan, however.

Hell's Dodo

"We'll avoid open waters as long as possible on the northward leg," he told his first mate and his chief navigator.

"With a ship of this draft, that will be a risky move," Grimm observed as he looked at the charts.

Zach waved a hand in the direction of the charts as he gave his input. "Those islands are riddled with unmarked reefs and shoals. We're fully loaded and riding deep. I've seen countless merchantmen nowhere near our size run aground in there. These maps and charts will be little or no help."

"Normally, I would agree with the two of you, but we have an advantage our opponent does not," the captain countered.

Grimm grinned. "Now that I think of it, you were always good at losing hunters or trapping prizes there."

"Aye; I know those islands as well as I know the waterways around Savannah. Plus, Belle can help us keep to the channels deep enough for our keel," he confirmed. "You know as well as I do that a couple of good storms can shift those shoals."

Grimm scratched the back of his head and grinned sheepishly. "Trust you to remember that incident."

Zach looked curiously at the two older pirates. Viktor grinned and chuckled. "For a time, Mr. Grimm and I sailed separately, but we remained on friendly terms and often hunted in tandem. One particular time, we both captained small ketches. Our favorite ploy was to herd a prize into the shallows and run her aground. Whoever reached her first got the larger shares."

"So, it was a race?"

"Aye," Grimm answered. "There'd been a hurricane pass through the Turks and Caicos about a month before. We'd run a fat prize loaded with sugar and rum onto a shoal. It was a spot we both knew well, or so I thought."

Vik continued the tale of his friend's embarrassment. "The storm had been strong enough to build a sandbar where there hadn't been one before. Mr. Grimm was ahead of me and found it first."

"At least you let my crew have some of the rum," Grimm laughed.

The *HMS Quicksilver* headed south. Commodore Critchfield decided to make a loop around the west side of the chain of islands and cays that stretched from Florida to the West Indies, pass between Puerto Rico and the Turks and Caicos, then make his way back north to his base of operations at New Providence.

He left Commander Turlington to patrol the southern colonial coasts aboard the *Georgia Belle*. The spiriting away of Harris had been only a minor irritation. He'd a suspicion the man was useless other than as bait for Brandee. He figured he didn't really need Harris as long as he had the *Georgia Belle* to lure the pirate in.

Hell's Dodo

He sat at his desk with a glass of port when the alarm bell broke his reverie. Shortly after, the messenger of the watch knocked at his door.

"What is all the clatter about, Mr. Pugh?" he demanded.

"Ship, sir; a man-o-war flying no colors," Pugh gasped, out of breath.

"Unusual, I grant, but not cause for this much uproar."

"Sir, she is the mirror image of the *Quicksilver*."

That got Critchfield's attention. Only one other ship matched the lines of his flagship.

"Are you sure?"

"Aye, but Commander Bradenton wanted me to request you have a look to confirm it."

A few minutes later, the Commodore was on the fo'c'sle with a spyglass to his eye. "Be damned, that has to be Brandee," he whispered. He collapsed the glass abruptly and handed it to Commander Bradenton. "Commander, have the helmsman set an intercept course. I want that ship."

"Aye, sir."

"That must be the pirate hunter we heard about," Viktor commented when Sniff reported approaching sails from the crow's nest.

"Damn, she's got the same lines as us," Grimm said after looking through the glass. "You don't suppose—?"

"One way to find out," Viktor replied. "Lazarus, come forth."

"Mrrrow?" The large black cat materialized on the railing.

"Investigate that ship."

Lazarus grew amorphous and solidified in his raven form. He launched into the air and flew towards the ship in question.

Something strange in the rigging of his ship caught Critchfield's eye.

"Mr. Bradenton."

"Aye sir?"

"Have you ever seen a raven this far from the mainland?"

"Occasionally, if there has been a bad storm recently, but never at this latitude," he replied, puzzled by the question.

"There is one in our rigging."

"Odd. Do you want it shot?"

"No. There's too much chance of stray shot hitting a sailor. Watch it, though. I have a feeling, unreasonable as it may sound, that it came from our prey."

Hell's Dodo

"A Commodore, no less," Viktor said with a grin. "That is a compliment."

"You don't have time to play, Viktor," Belladonna pointed out.

"Pity, that: but I know I don't, pet. I do want to face him at some point, though. That ship is the twin of this one."

"I am aware of that. It would be a battle of skill and strategy. Please take my advice and do not seek that ship out until all of the Sisters have been dealt with."

He looked at her for a while. She met his gaze steadily. When he caressed her face, it caught her off guard. He leaned down and gave her a gentle kiss.

"Thank you for your concern, pet," he whispered. "But, I know better than to take foolish risks with my ship and my crew just for the sake of braggadocio."

"Good." She smiled, relieved.

"Lazarus, come forth."

"Mrrrrow!" The cat materialized.

"Return to the commodore's ship tonight and blend in with their ship cats. Observe him and his officers. Return to me in two months."

"Mryeh." The cat chirped and evaporated into mist as quickly as he'd appeared.

"Why tonight instead of now?" Belle asked.

"The commodore spotted him in the rigging. Ravens are rare this far from the mainland."

"Oh." As a sea creature, the siren didn't have that much experience with birds.

Viktor's voice drew her thoughts back into focus. "Mr. Jon, Mr. Bland, set full sails! I want us into the islands before that man-o-war catches up!"

"Aye, Cap'n!" both replied and set the riggers to their tasks.

Chapter 30

With Viktor at the helm and Belladonna swimming ahead, the *Incubus* kept three quarters of her sails in use while in the island channels. The siren communicated any necessary course changes along the link she shared with the vampire.

The *Quicksilver* had to furl half her sails to follow safely. Critchfield took the extra precaution and ordered one of the launches to sail ahead of the ship. This served two purposes: it kept the *Incubus* and her course in sight, and it provided soundings to help the man-o-war avoid shoals and reefs.

The *Quicksilver* sat lower in the water than her predecessor. Critchfield surmised that he had a larger crew aboard than the pirate. The extra men would be useful when they caught the pirate, but they could be a liability to safe navigation in the shallow waters. Any sandbar or shoal that the *Incubus* barely cleared would stop the *Quicksilver* short.

A couple of times, the sounding crew were the only ones to keep both ships in sight. The *Incubus* would have vanished through a narrow channel between islands if not for the advance boat. As it was, she'd put quite a bit of sea between them by the time the *Quicksilver* followed her to open water.

As soon as the sounding crew assured him that the ship had reached deep water, Critchfield ordered full sail. He didn't bother to retrieve the launch. It was fast enough to keep pace with the larger vessel. He might need them again, if the pirate reached the next cluster of islands.

A couple of hours later, the distance between the two ships shortened considerably.

Critchfield's navigators estimated they would have the *Incubus* within range of the forward guns within another hour or so at their current speed.

The Commodore issued orders for the *Quicksilver's* contingent of marines to prepare for battle.

Grimm frowned as he looked through the glass at their pursuer. "This makes no sense, Captain."

"What, Mr. Grimm?"

"She's riding lower in the water than us, which should make her slower; but she's gaining. At this rate, she'll have us in range about an hour from now."

"Bugger." Viktor frowned. Grimm was right. It didn't make sense. Both ships had the same lines; running with a lighter load should have given the *Incubus* a speed advantage.

Hell's Dodo

He reached out along the bond he shared with the siren. *"Belle, I need you on board now."* His mental tone let her know not to dally.

A few minutes later, Belladonna stood, nude, next to him. The sight proved almost enough to distract him from the reason for summoning her; almost.

"Thank you for your promptness, pet. I cannot sense any magic connected to our pursuer, but I am not that practiced. Can you sense anything?"

She looked back at the *Quicksilver*, closed her eyes and sniffed the wind. After a few moments, she opened her eyes and shook her head. "No, I don't sense anything. Why?"

"I am trying to figure out how she is gaining on us. In an hour, I'll have to turn and face them."

"That is a battle and a delay you can ill afford, Viktor."

"I am aware of that, pet. She's gaining too quickly and will have us in range before we can make the next islands," he pointed out.

In response, the siren began to sing.

She used no words but wove notes together in a melody too intricate for a human voice to reproduce. As she sang, the pirate crew's spirits buoyed.

The sails of the *Incubus* bellied taut as the wind increased. Viktor saw the sails of their pursuer begin to grow slack. A dense fog sprang up between them.

"Nicely done, pet. Thank you." He smiled at her.

"You are welcome," she replied but did not return the smile. "I suspect I know why they were gaining, but I need to investigate something to be sure. If I am right, it will need to be discussed in private. I will meet you in your cabin in one hour."

Before he could respond, she slipped back over the railing and into the sea.

A little over an hour had passed when Viktor heard a knock at his cabin door. He knew who it was. "Come in, pet."

Mild disappointment settled in when he saw she wore clothes, even though he usually fussed when she didn't. Still, he could easily remedy that.

"I was right," she said.

"Right about what?" He stood and moved closer to her.

"This ship needs to be careened. The barnacle build-up isn't bad enough to weigh it down, but it is wide-spread enough to cause considerable drag. The other ship was in much better shape."

He frowned. "I thought the copper cladding prevented barnacle build-up."

She shook her head. "No, it only slows it and protects the wood from shipworms. A copper clad hull doesn't need to be careened as often as bare wood, but it still needs it." She then gave him an impish grin. "With that in mind, I took the liberty of removing several panels from the belly of the other ship. I also rounded up a few of the more voracious species of shipworms and left them in place of the plates."

He chuckled. "You naughty little fish. Still, careening will have to wait a little longer. It won't be safe to do it anywhere around here for a while."

"Blast and damnation!" Critchfield bellowed as a dense fog enveloped the *Quicksilver*. "Helmsman, stay your course."

"Stay my course, aye," the sailor replied.

"Sir, we're losing wind," the quartermaster reported.

"Chances are, so is Brandee," the Commodore replied.

Chapter 31

The fog troubled Critchfield more than he let on. He'd sailed for decades and encountered innumerable sea fogs, but never one like this. Fog didn't just form that quickly at this density. In his experience, when a fog formed around a ship it was more gradual, and usually overnight.

This fog hadn't so much formed as appeared, as if by magic.

Within only a few minutes, his clothes soaked through to the skin. Visibility no longer existed. He could just make out the helm; the rest of the ship consisted only of shadows.

Sound, however, was greatly magnified and distorted, the effect eerie and mildly disturbing. Sailors' fearful murmurs filtered to him from the rigging above.

"Quartermaster Hobbs," he spoke in a normal tone.

"Aye sir?"

"Relay to the riggers that they are to remain where they are for now and make sure to secure their lifelines. Send one of the powder monkeys around to inspect the capstans and see they are properly knotted."

"Aye, sir," the man replied. "And if the fog does not lift right away?"

Tamara A. Lowery

"In ten minutes you may order the riggers to the deck. They are to return in a slow and careful manner. The shrouds are soaked. I don't want anyone losing their grip and falling," Critchfield said.

"Very well, sir."

About a half hour after the fog arrived, it had yet to dissipate. The only relief from it was that it now formed a bubble around the ship. Sailors could once again safely perform their tasks. They just couldn't see where the ship was or where it was going.

Several of the seamen grew unnerved by the fog. The more seasoned ones had the same misgivings their Commodore kept to himself. They instinctively knew this fog was unnatural.

Then the singing started.

At first, Critchfield thought one of the riggers had started to sing in an effort to calm his nerves. He soon realized the voice was unmistakably female, though. Just as he was about to demand an explanation; the singing stopped.

An eerie silence settled on the ship. No one so much as whispered. The only sounds were the lapping of the waves against the hull and the creak of the rigging.

Finally, the forward lookout broke the silence. "Something ahead in the fog!"

"What is it: land or ship?" the messenger of the watch called back.

Hell's Dodo

"Hard to say," the man replied. A note of fear and panic suddenly tinged his voice. "It's a ship and she's on a collision course!"

"Hard a-port!" Critchfield ordered the helmsman. "Starboard gun crews make ready!" He could see the ship bearing down on them. Its lines matched their own. The pirate had turned to attack.

Critchfield determined that Brandee would not catch them unawares. The gunnery crews scrambled to make ready to fire. The helmsman spun the wheel left.

To everyone's amazement, the approaching ship, still murky in the fog but frighteningly close, mirrored the maneuver precisely. The pirate swung to her starboard even as the *Quicksilver* swung to port. The two now sailed in the same direction at point blank range.

"Fire!"

The *Quicksliver* opened up with all sixty of her starboard cannon. To the crew's horror, so did their prey at the exact same moment, shot for shot.

The enemy's cannonballs and shot collided with theirs and vanished. They watched as their shot continued on to the enemy vessel and through it without damage. Moments later, the multiple splashes of their ammunition hitting the water reached their ears.

A second volley went off before a stunned Critchfield could call cease fire. The thunder of the cannon shook the entire ship.

The faint sound of metal tearing prompted a few of the gunnery officers to order a reload.

"Hold your fire!" Critchfield ordered with a bellow.

The marine battalion commander ordered his men to ready to board the enemy. The Commodore heard the order issued and countered, "Belay that order!"

"With all due respect, Commodore Critchfield, we must prepare for battle," the marine argued.

"Battle with what? Look!" he growled and pointed toward the other ship. Even as he spoke, the fog thinned on that side, and the "ship" faded into nothingness.

"A ghost ship!"

Critchfield frowned at the man. "Don't be a ninny, Commander Parsons. We've been fighting our reflection in the fog — a mirage. That is why it mirrored our every move."

"But sir, you ordered us to fire on it."

"Our opponent is devilishly clever, by all reports, and in possession of the only other ship of this line," Critchfield explained. "I suspected it was a reflection we faced, but I could not take that chance. One volley would have been sufficient. That we were matched shot for shot exactly proved it. We'll have to wait for this fog to clear to continue our pursuit now."

He pinched the bridge of his nose and rubbed. With an irritated sigh, he said, "Have your men stand down but remain on notice, Commander

Hell's Dodo

Parsons. Commander Burris, furl sails and put out the sea anchors. The fog is too thick, and we are too close to the islands now to continue safely. I will be in my cabin if anyone needs me."

He turned and headed off the bridge without waiting for an answer.

The fog lasted for two more days with no change. Critchfield and his officers reasoned that the launch captained by Commander Bradenton hadn't rejoined them because of it.

When the fog cleared, the launch was spotted adrift not a league away. No one answered their hails. The boarding detail discovered a nearly stripped boat with no crew.

They did find a note which they presented to Critchfield.

Commodore Critchfield,

Thank you for the fresh provisions.

Sincerely,

Viktor Brandewyne, Capt.

It was written in blood.

Chapter 32

Bradenton and his small crew continued to pursue the pirate ship after they hit open water. To prevent a collision, they veered to their starboard to make their course parallel with the two dreadnoughts rather than in line with them.

The Commander warned his men not to get too close to the pirate. He knew the *Quicksilver*'s capabilities and that they would apply to the pirate's ship as well.

Still, since the launch was lighter and quicker, they got close enough to hear the eerily beautiful singing just before the cursed fog sprang up.

Confident that they were not in either ship's path, they furled the sails and put out the sea anchor.

Lazarus returned to the navy ship to spy on the Commodore that night. He kept to the shadows and waited for a chance to slip into the man's cabin.

He heard many whispers among the officers about the battle with the ship's reflection in the fog. None declared outright loss of confidence in the Commodore's leadership, but a few hinted at doubts. Others pointed out he had been the first to recognize the mirage for what it was.

After a few hours, Lazarus finally saw his opportunity. A cabin boy made the rounds of all the officers to call them to a meeting. The cat figured he could slip in among the group unnoticed. He'd barely gotten one paw across the threshold when he turned amorphous against his will, and his surroundings changed.

When he solidified again, he found himself on a table inside a tabby shack. It smelled vaguely familiar to him.

"Sh, don't wake them," a voice he recognized said. Mother Celie walked past him with a folded quilt. She quietly opened it up and draped it over a young woman asleep on a cot next to one of the walls.

A sleepy whine caught his attention. He padded over to peer in the large basket at the foot of the cot to investigate. Two infants lay curled together. One kicked at the coverlet, which bared the other one to the air. The baby boy whimpered and squirmed but did not wake.

Very gently, Lazarus caught the edge of the coverlet in his front teeth and pulled it back over the baby. The child sighed and settled into a deeper sleep.

Celie scratched the cat's head and motioned for him to follow her out. Once outside, he realized they'd been in the extra hut built behind the old marsh witch's original shack. He walked over to the fire and hopped up on one of the logs she kept for seats.

"Mrreh?"

Hell's Dodo

The old woman gave him a tired smile. "Yes, those are Mr. Grimm's children. They came early; about a month ago. It has taken me this long to make sure they and their mother survive, but they are fine now."

Lazarus cocked his head at her.

She sighed and stirred her fire. "I want you to go back to Viktor and tell him to stay away from Savannah until he finishes with this Sister. You can give Hezekiah the news about his wife, son and daughter, but make sure he knows that it would be dangerous for them if he came here right now."

"Muh?"

"There was a Navy man sniffing around about a month ago. I hid Brianna from him. Jimbo, I have seen this man in my fire. He is just as ruthless and mean as Viktor. He would not hesitate to use Brianna and the children as bait or leverage. He is gone now, but he has eyes in this port."

"As long as Mr. Grimm's family remain hidden here, they will be safe. Now go on back and tell them."

The second day of fog showed no sign of respite. Bradenton and his small crew began to ration their meager supplies. The launch hadn't been stocked for a prolonged voyage.

Without warning, the boat lurched and dipped the bow dangerously close to the sea's surface.

"What was that?" one of the sailors asked, startled.

"I don't know, Cairns," Bradenton replied. "Maybe a whale or shark bumped the anchor line."

The fog hampered their ability to look for fins or whales breaching. The sea remained silent.

The boat lurched again, sideways this time. It then surged forward, the anchor line stretched tautly ahead of it. The boat picked up speed as they were pulled along.

When the line went slack then ran back beneath the boat, Cairns grabbed his hatchet to cut the line. He feared whatever had towed them was about to capsize them.

None of his crewmates moved to stop him. Their attention was given to the blur that arced from the water to the top of the mast. At first, they thought a large fish or shark had jumped and become caught in the rigging.

The fog started to thin and they saw it was some mermaid-like creature; half shark, half woman. By the time she reached the deck, legs replaced the shark tail.

"Hello boys," the naked redhead said. "The Captain would like a word with you."

Lazarus arrived back at the *Incubus* near sunset. He saw five nude males suspended by their ankles over five large rum kegs. Blood ran down from their slit throats into the barrels.

Hell's Dodo

He remained in his raven form and sought out Mr. Grimm. The first mate took him to the captain's cabin and left Jon-Jon to oversee the blood-letting.

"Captain?" Grimm said as he knocked.

"Enter," Viktor replied. When he saw the raven perched on Grimm's shoulder, he asked, "What is this?"

"I was going to ask you the same thing. He just showed up and landed there."

Lazarus pecked at Grimm's coat and cawed at Viktor. The vampire raised an eyebrow at the behavior and concentrated on his bond with the creature. After a moment, he reached out along his link with Belladonna.

"We'll have some answers we can understand in a few minutes, Hezekiah," he said.

Before long, the puzzled siren entered the cabin. She had one of the drained bodies draped over her shoulder. "I was about to go eat," she said.

"I know, pet. I need part of that body to give to Lazarus."

"Why?" She eyed the bird suspiciously as it finally morphed into a cat.

"He has a message to deliver, but he has to eat first."

"Why not get him something from the galley? Why does he need part of my meal?"

Viktor moved with lightning speed and severed one of the feet from the corpse. "It has to be human flesh," he replied tersely and gave the foot to the cat.

Lazarus made quicker work of eating it than a natural cat could have. Grimm looked a little green around the gills by the time the cat finished. The sight hadn't bothered him so much as the wet crunching sounds had.

"Oh! How…?" Belladonna blurted in surprise as Lazarus transformed into Jim Rigger.

"Uncle Zeke once told me, 'You are what you eat.'" He grinned at her.

Viktor cleared his throat. He knew his friend couldn't maintain his current form long. "I thought I sent you to spy on that Commodore, Mr. Rigger."

"I was on his ship only long enough to pick up scuttlebutt about him. Mother Celie felt her news was more important," he replied.

Both Viktor and Grimm gave him their full attention. "You have news of Brianna?" Grimm asked. "Is that why you wanted me here?"

"I do, but first do you think I could have some of that blood-brandy, Cap'n? It'll help me hold this body long enough to give all the news," Jim said.

"Aye." Viktor nodded and handed him a bottle. He grabbed another for himself while he had the liquor cabinet open. "You want anything, Hezekiah?"

"Something strong; I've a feeling I may need it."

Hell's Dodo

Viktor set a bottle of clear liquid down in front of his first mate. "Brumble took a few of these off one of the ships he got that turquois from. I haven't tried it yet. He said it is called tequila, and it's supposed to be very potent."

Grimm pulled the cork, gave the contents an experimental sniff, and took a swig. He did not move for a few moments after he swallowed.

"Well?" Vik asked after a full minute had passed.

"Smooth," Grimm coughed and took another pull.

"Looks too much like gin to me. I'll reserve judgement until later," Vik said. He saw that Jim had downed a few swallows from his bottle. "What is the news from Celie?"

"Brianna gave birth about a month ago...."

"But that's too early! Is she well? Did the children survive? I kept my vow! This shouldn't have happened!" Grimm said, distraught.

Jim held both hands up at him. "They are all well. Calm down. They were asleep when I saw them, but they all smelled healthy. It's that Navy man's fault she birthed early. He'd been snooping around for news about you and Vik. Old Celie kept her hidden from him."

"We've got to go get them," he declared.

Jim shook his head. "She said to tell you to stay away."

"Brianna said that?"

Tamara A. Lowery

"No, Mother Celie did. She said the Commodore has eyes in Savannah right now. Your wife and children are hidden and safe. If you go there, she fears they'll be discovered." He looked at the captain and continued, "She has seen this man in her fire, Vik. She said he is just as ruthless as you or Grimm."

Viktor looked at his first mate. He knew he was about to say something that could alienate the man. "We need to be about our business. To go to Savannah now would be a needless risk."

Grimm took a long pull on his bottle and grimaced. He remained quiet for a time.

Finally, he spoke. "I know you're right. Hell, I even said we should just go on and make the crossing not a month ago. I don't like it, but I know you're right."

He seemed to realize he sounded dolorous and tried to put a good face on it. "You say Brianna looked well?"

"Aye; like I said, she was asleep but healthy. The babes are healthy, too," Jim replied. "There's no denying the boy is yours."

"Oh?"

Jim grinned mischievously. "They're both tiny things, but he's practically half balls. Shame his worm is so dinky. Made me think of you right away," he taunted.

"I'll measure mine against yours any time, Mr. Rigger. We'll see whose worm is dinky!"

"Ooo, can I be the judge?" Belladonna asked; the picture of innocence.

Hell's Dodo

"Ha! You'd both lose to old Sniff," Viktor barked with laughter. An unspoken tension evaporated from the group.

"Go have your meal now, pet. When you've finished, you can sing up a wind to speed our crossing. The hunting around Africa should be good when we get there," Viktor declared.

Chapter 33

Jeorge came awake with his customary abruptness and immediately wished he hadn't.

An all too familiar power rested in the nearby harbor awaiting the safety of darkness.

"Merde, what is She doing here?" He thought. He could guess the answer to his own question, however. He'd caught Her scent on the pirate vampire the last time he'd been in New Orleans.

"Such formality," Carpathia commented on the kneeling vampires before her. "It is good to see the old ways remembered in such a remote and wild region. You may rise, Jeorge, and speak with me."

"Thank you, my lady. To what do we owe this honor?" All the other vampires remained in their position.

She did not answer right away. Instead, she glided over to one of the females. "She is new, and she is not of your blood line. Who sired her?"

Jeorge knew better than to play games with the Lady. "Melanie was sired by Captain Viktor Brandewyne in repayment for one of my Children he had killed."

"Rise, Melanie, so I may look at you."

Obediently, the young vampire stood. She could not hide a tremble as the ancient vampire circled her.

Carpathia stopped directly behind her and whispered in her ear. "You fear me, child. Why?"

"I have never felt anyone aside from my Sire as powerful as you, my lady."

"Surely your Master is as powerful as your Sire."

"No, my lady. The Captain is more powerful," Melanie answered.

Jeorge kept his expression neutral. He'd suspected as much, and it frightened him.

"And is he more powerful than I?"

"I — I do not know, my lady," she stammered. "You are both extremely potent, but your power feels different. He is alive."

Carpathia smiled at Jeorge, a friendly expression on the surface only. He knew he had to be very careful how he answered her questions now. The existence of his entire kiss depended on it.

"Did you know Viktor was stronger, Jeorge?" she asked sweetly.

"I had my suspicions, my lady."

"And yet, he sired this Child to replace the one he took from you. Why would he do that?"

"He wanted peace with me and a guarantee of protection from me and mine for two human whores and their employees," he answered truthfully.

Hell's Dodo

"If he is more powerful, why would he feel the need to make peace with you?" she asked. "Why not just eliminate you, if you were a danger?"

He shrugged. "He may not have realized his strength at the time. He did feel stronger the last time he was here than during our first encounter. I do know he has learned how to block Melanie out. I can no longer follow his movements."

"Interesting; when was the last time he was here?" she demanded.

"About a month ago; he wanted to consult my library about a creature called a dodo." He decided to make a bold observation. "He carried your scent on him, my lady."

She gave him an unreadable look. After a moment, she said, "I would have arrived more closely behind him had it not been for his pet siren."

"She does not trust our kind and is markedly territorial about him."

Carpathia nodded. "So I have noticed. We will talk more about this later in private." She turned her attention to the other vampires and let her power spread through the room. "You will all forget the particulars of this conversation."

A tremor spread through the group as their memories were clouded. Jeorge knew the Lady Carpathia was one of a select few who could wield that kind of control over other vampires.

"You may rise and go about your business," she declared. "Jeorge, I wish to hunt."

☠

The Lady's appetite nearly proved excessive. Jeorge worried rumors of a plague might be the only way to cover up so many deaths in such a concentrated area. She went where She would and did not have to worry about the repercussions on the local vampire communities.

In fact, he wondered if she might have used her hunt pattern deliberately to punish him for perceived secrecy.

Carpathia took over Jeorge's throne room and called him to a private audience the next night. She kept him on one knee with his head bowed for two hours before she spoke the first word to him.

"How long were you going to wait to send word of such an anomalous vampire?"

"I do not know, my lady. I felt it prudent to wait until I had a better understanding of the creature or if it became necessary to dispose of him."

"I see. The first reason I can understand and forgive. The second makes me wonder why."

"His power exceeds that of what one so young should have. There is also his claim that he was not made but cursed and is still living flesh. My human agents would stand no chance against him, and he is not bound to darkness and shadows, my lady."

"Explain."

Hell's Dodo

"He can function in full daylight and suffer no damage. He personally took Melanie from her mortal home shortly after mid-day."

"That is curious," she admitted. "What other aberrations or anomalies have you observed about him?"

"He has a child, sired since he became vampire. He brought the boy to this port and left him in the care of a powerful witch out in the bayous. I suspect she may have something to do with his rapid growth in power."

"If it is the child I am thinking of, it is half merman and was stolen from my ship by a siren shortly after I destroyed its dam."

Jeorge risked a quick glance at her, surprised she had shared such information. He wondered how long she had been hunting Brandewyne and to what purpose. He knew she had found him at one point, but she had not destroyed him.

She met his gaze. He lowered his eyes again.

"What makes you suspect the witch aids him?"

"A surge of unimaginable magical energy struck this city shortly after he went to deliver the child. It emanated from the bayous, the witch's home. I did not see him before he left port, but he was markedly stronger when he returned last month."

"I shall have to investigate this. Frankly, Jeorge, I am surprised you have not. I would also like to reclaim possession of the child. He could prove valuable."

He did look at her then. "I would advise against that course of action, my lady."

"You — would advise?" Her tone grew dangerous.

He did not flinch. "*Oui*. I have sent two of my most trusted Children to investigate. It was not long after Brandewyne delivered the boy and left port. The witch sensed them coming. She trapped them with her swamp magic. One, she impaled with a cypress knee; the other she held until the sun took her."

"And you were unable to help them?"

"I was. I headed a large rescue party when I felt the trap enclose my Child. A magical barrier prevented us from entering the bayous at all."

"Have you tried recently to investigate?"

"At least once every month or so; no more of my Children have been lost, but the same barrier appears every time."

"Very well; I will take that under advisement."

Chapter 34

Carpathia retired to her chambers for the day and pondered what she'd learned. She needed to determine if there was some power link between the pirate and the witch. She also wanted to find out if the child was the same merman whose dam she had dispatched.

It frustrated her that Viktor Brandewyne seemed to have as little regard for the ancient laws of magic as he did for human property laws. By everything she had always known and studied, a creature like him should not even exist.

Wormsloe looked up from his ale just in time to see Carpathia enter the tavern. His shoulders slumped slightly. He'd hoped to spend some time in port for a change.

The vampire glided over and sat down without invitation, not that she needed it in a public setting. "I've a task for you, Captain."

"I'm sure you do," he thought but wisely did not voice. "What is your bidding?"

"Assemble a small boat crew and send them into the bayous. There is an old witch woman that may have that merchild in her care. There is suspicion she has been magically aiding

Brandewyne, as well. Tell your men to find out what they can and report back here."

"The bayous are vast and treacherous. It would help to have a general idea of what area to search in. I also take it you have a good reason why you want me to risk my men rather than send your lesser vampires."

She frowned. He knew she did not like to have her commands questioned, especially by a mere mortal. "If you must know, the witch has a magical barrier to keep vampires out."

"What makes you think my men might be able to slip through?" He took another swig of his ale. He knew he'd taken a dangerous attitude with her, but he was drunk enough to not care anymore.

Faster than he could see, she slapped the mug out of his hand. It shattered against the far wall. "I think you have had enough to drink, Captain Wormsloe. It has addled your senses."

She seemed satisfied she'd gotten his attention. "Magic is a very precise thing. For this barrier to be as effective as it is against vampires it must be specifically targeted at them. I do not think she expects humans to invade her territory. I would advise you keep the group small to avoid drawing attention."

He rubbed his stubbly chin and glared at her. "Makes sense when put that way, but you still haven't given me enough of an idea on where to send 'em."

She reached into a pocket in the lining of her cloak and pulled out a small roll of parchment. She placed it on the table, and he took it. Once unrolled, it revealed a map of one edge of the city and the bayou country beyond. One area had been circled in tailor's chalk.

"That is the protected area. She is somewhere in there."

He pushed back from the table and stood. "I'll have Mr. Borescue round up a few lads and outfit them like 'gator hunters. Three should be enough to remain inconspicuous."

"That will do nicely, Captain Wormsloe. If the boy is there, he will be in human form. The swamps are fresh water, and he is a salt water creature."

"Do you want the lads to try to fetch him back?"

"I doubt they could manage it, but they are welcome to try."

"We're past the boundary, lads," the boson in charge of the expedition announced. "Looks like the Lady was right about it bein' against vampires only."

"We just need to keep heading this direction to reach the center of the area, Mr. Michaels."

"Thankye, Lawson. Once we get there, we'll spiral out as best we can. Durning, keep a check on our depth. I've heard these cypress swamps can be tricky to navigate."

"Aye, Mr. Michaels."

Two hours later, they came upon a small hammock with a wooden landing. Unlit flambeaux flanked the dock. A ladder led to an elevated catwalk that meandered back into the shadows of the trees.

A young boy with a shock of coal black hair sat on the edge of the dock. He held a cane pole with a line and cork bobber in the water.

He looked up and saw them.

"Granny! Comp'ny!" He stood up and gave them a suspicious look. "Did you bring me a treat? Timón always brings me a treat. Who are you? Where's Timón?"

"He's sick," Michaels answered. "He asked us to bring your treats for him. They're right here in the boat."

The men eased the boat up to the dock. The boy peered into the boat.

"Where? I don't see any treat." He backed away just out of easy reach.

"I've got it under my seat to keep it safe. What's your name, little man?"

"Robert, take those fish back to the house. I'll be along to clean and cook them in a bit. I need to see what these gentlemen want."

"Yes'm." Obediently, the boy picked up a string of fish and scrabbled up the ladder with it.

The three men stared at the woman who seemed to appear out of nowhere. They'd expected some decrepit old hag, not this dark-haired beauty. When she smiled at them, they almost forgot why they had come into the bayous.

Hell's Dodo

"You certainly don't look like a granny to me," Lawson observed.

She laughed. "You caught me on a good day." To their amazement, discomfort, and delight, she slipped the simple shift over her head and dropped it on the dock. "I haven't had a man in months."

Lawson nearly lunged out of the boat. "I'm a man." He leered down at her.

"Yes, I can see you are." She gave a throaty chuckle as she looked down to where his breeches tented outward. She tugged at the waistband, and he quickly shed his clothes for her.

"Now don't you boys go away; I'll be with you as soon as I'm through with this one."

"You'll be too tired after I'm done, lass." He picked her up and laid her back on the dock.

She opened for him and pulled him to her. "Prove it."

He went at it with admirable vigor.

Suddenly, she flipped them over and put herself on top. She rode him mercilessly.

Durning remained enthralled, but a bolt of fear shot through Michaels. He'd only ever seen vampires move that fast.

Lawson climaxed. The witch continued to ride him as his body spasmed under her. As she gave voice to her own ecstasy, they saw their crewmate wither and age before their eyes.

When she rose from her victim, he lay there, a lifeless, mummified husk. She looked at the remaining men with a seductive yet predatory gaze.

"Who is next?"

"Let's get out of here!" Michaels yelled. He grabbed Durning by the collar to keep him in the boat and pushed away from the dock.

She laughed as they poled the boat back into the bayous.

Her voice echoed around them, even though they'd left the dock far behind. "Do not think to escape so easily. You invaded my home and tried to steal the child left in my charge."

Fear finally seeped into Durning. "What is she?"

"A witch, some kind of vampire, I don't know. We need to get back to the Captain and the Lady and tell them what happened."

The boat lurched unexpectedly. Something wrenched the poles from their hands. Michaels reached over the side to retrieve his. He screamed as a 'gator lunged and clamped onto his forearm. The creature pulled him into the murk.

Durning huddled in the center of the boat. He watched as the bubbles dissipated then ceased.

A hand settled on his shoulder. He screamed. The witch leaned forward and whispered in his ear. "You smell of vampires. I will spare your life. I want you to take a message back to your masters."

Hell's Dodo

He turned terror-filled eyes to her. "Who are you? What are you?"

She smiled. "I am Gloribeau. You could not comprehend what I truly am. Tell the ones who sent you not to send any more. I am older and more powerful than any of them. I am more than capable of protecting the boy."

She cupped his chin and drew close to his mouth. When she spoke again, her lips brushed against his. "Before I let you go, you must pay the price for entering my domain unbidden."

She closed the distance between them. His eyes fluttered closed, and he surrendered to the kiss. He'd never experienced anything like it, and it seemed to last forever.

Everything went black.

Durning woke to a bright sky overhead. He felt so very weak. The boat jostled, but he couldn't find the strength to lift his head to see what he'd drifted into.

Shadowy faces appeared above him. He heard voices, but they sounded distant.

"Is he alive?"

"Aye, he's breathing; see?"

"He's sunburnt pretty bad. I don't see any oars or a pole. Wonder how he got out here?"

One of the voices got louder. "Hey, old man, who are you? Can you hear me? Where are you from?"

Durning frowned. He didn't know why they called him an old man. "I'm from the *Lorelei*," he croaked. Even to his own ears, his voice sounded thin and weak.

The effort to speak proved too much. He passed out again.

Carpathia was less than pleased but not entirely surprised.

It did intrigue her that the witch claimed to be older and more powerful than any vampire. Given the effect she had on her victims, Thia had to cede the point of age, at least. Succubi predated vampires by millennia.

"What are your plans, milady?" Wormsloe asked after he'd delivered the report.

"We will remain in this port for now. The hunting is good. The accommodations are satisfactory. There is a strong possibility Brandewyne will return to this port. He apparently does have an interest in the young mer he sired. I see now that it must have been his pet siren who stole the child from us."

"You think he will check on the boy periodically?"

"He cared enough to deposit him with a powerful protector. It stands to reason he would monitor the child's progress. The boy was incredibly powerful even as an infant. Obviously, Brandewyne recognized his potential."

Hell's Dodo

Wormsloe had his doubts, but he kept them silent. He had voiced them in the past and saw no point in repetition.

To his knowledge, Bloody Vik Brandee had never been known to take an interest in any of the bastards he'd sired over the years.

Thia dismissed the porters that delivered her luggage from the *Lorelei*. She looked forward to an extended stay on shore. On board ship, she hadn't had freedom to hunt.

She arranged the trunks to her liking and set to unpacking. In particular, she wanted her collection of knives. The salt air wasn't good for them. She wanted to clean and hone them.

She blinked when she picked up one that had dried blood on the tip. She'd forgotten about it.

A slow smile spread across her face. "Let's see what you are up to, Viktor Brandewyne."

She carefully licked the blood off.

Chapter 35

Viktor gripped the railing hard enough to splinter the wood and leave finger imprints as he felt the new connection form. Instinctively, he shielded his thoughts.

He didn't want her to know he knew. She was trying to be subtle rather than forceful in her invasion.

"Belle, I need to see you in my cabin."

The siren caught the scent the moment she set foot in his cabin.

"How?"

"She must've nicked me with her knife on one of our earlier encounters. She saved that minute drop until a few moments ago."

"What does she know now?"

"Very little; I used the technique you taught me to block Melanie without seeming to block her."

Belle relaxed a minute amount. "She doesn't know you are aware of her, then."

"Hopefully not; I feel her starting to probe deeper. Subtlety will not be an option much longer."

"How about we give her a show — to distract her, of course." She gave him a sultry smile to make sure he understood exactly what kind of show she meant.

He stepped close to her and leered down. "My naughty little fish."

Thia dropped the blade and staggered back. The sheer power of the man nearly overwhelmed her. For a brief moment, she thought he was blocking her, but she got no sense from him of any awareness her mental presence. His natural shields were just that strong.

Of course, it stood to reason. As a pirate, it would be a survival instinct to not let anyone know what he truly thought. Why wouldn't that carry over into his psychic abilities? He probably thought Jeorge was being nosy and trying to use Melanie against him. The girl had said he blocked her out now.

Since all she could pick up from him at the moment were images, she spent the next few minutes trying to get a feel for the scope of his powers.

What she found both amazed and frightened her. The distinct possibility that he could be more powerful than her made her re-think her plans. She still held hope that his wild magic could revitalize her womb, but she realized she needed to use caution with him. She needed to fully bend him to her will before he realized his true potential.

Hell's Dodo

The surface images she got from him drew her attention. Curiosity and jealousy flared as she watched him undress the siren. The jealousy surprised her.

Memories of her tryst with the pirate flooded through her mind. She found she could not pull out of the connection, almost as if he consciously drew her in.

As the passion she watched progressed from tender to violent, she felt energy build like a lightning charge. She found it more bearable to imagine herself as the recipient of his passion.

The power spiked as he brought the siren not once but twice.

Thia felt she couldn't endure much more. The magical charge built a third time. This time the crescendo was beyond intense. Just as she felt him bring the siren for the last time, he "looked" at her through the link and gave vent to his own release. He'd directed the brunt of it straight at her.

She collapsed and writhed somewhere between ecstasy and agony. The magic felt amazing as it coursed through her body, the effect almost painful.

Finally, she recognized it for what it was: raw, primal life.

She got an odd sensation in her belly, something she barely remembered from her human life centuries ago. Reflexively, she rose to her knees and retched.

As the puddle of black, partially digested blood spread beneath her, the connection with Viktor broke.

Belladonna lay on Viktor's bed, limp. Magical aftershocks danced through her, and she felt as if her bones had turned to liquid.

"I don't care how much I beg you to, don't do that again."

In response, he sat up on the edge of the bed with his back to her.

"Viktor?" She sensed the change in his mood.

Still, he remained silent.

She placed a hand on his back. He stood abruptly and stormed over to the bank of windows. That brought her to her feet.

"Viktor, I didn't mean it."

He whirled on her. "You were right about Thia. I hope you're happy."

Belle's temper flared to match his. "We just had some of the most intense sex I've ever experienced, and you throw that undead bitch in my face?"

"Don't worry, I don't intend to give her the opportunity to get that close to me again. I saw her true intentions."

"Wait. What? You got that far past her shields?"

"I did, and I made sure she'll think twice before she tries to pierce mine again."

Hell's Dodo

The siren studied him for a few moments. She sensed his anger had to do with something more than the invasion of privacy. An undercurrent of pain rode just beneath the rage.

"You said I was right about her. What do you mean?"

"She was sent to kill me. I don't know why she didn't try it back on Trinidad. She has some secret plans for me that she's buried too deep to reach. She fears her master would learn of it and destroy her for it."

Belle tilted her head. Was the force of his personality enough to bewitch the ancient vampire, or was it more like the way it had been with Rosalia? Did Carpathia think she could control and use him for her own purposes? Either proposition worried her.

"She will try harder now to get in your head, Viktor…."

"She can't now." He smiled; a grim and cruel expression. "I sent the result of our combined passion into her. For just the briefest moment, life returned to her body, just long enough to make it reject the blood in her stomach. The link with her is broken."

Fear washed over the siren. "Other than Zeke or one of the Sisters, no one has ever had that kind of power." She began to back away from him without realizing it.

He caught the unmistakable scent of her fear. It hadn't been his intention to frighten her. He'd just been momentarily consumed with the rage and pain Carpathia's betrayal caused.

"Belle," he said softly, "I am not angry with you. I am grateful to you. I doubt I could have freed myself without your help."

"You shouldn't have been able to free yourself at all. Do you have any idea how much power you just displayed?" She still remained out of reach.

"Enough to frighten you, obviously." He made no further move toward her, and she began to relax. Instead, he slowly walked back to the bed and sat down, careful not to block her from the door if she felt the need to escape.

She watched him and realized he'd deliberately left her a way out. He didn't even use any of his power over her when he held out his hand in invitation. Silently, she walked over to him. He smiled up at her, and she saw he was at the ready again.

"Shall I show you my gratitude, pet?"

"You are a very bad man."

"Yes, I am," he chuckled wickedly.

Chapter 36

The rest of the voyage to Mauritius remained relatively uneventful. They stuck to the African coast and pirated their way around to the eastern side of Madagascar then east into the Indian Ocean.

Fair weather remained with them without the need for Belladonna's magic. She decided to hunt.

"Why, pet?" Viktor wanted to know. "The cadre and I have supplied you with plenty of fresh meat."

"Yes, you have. Don't think I don't appreciate it; but I need to keep my skills sharp. There are mermaids in these waters. I have scented them. Given the high population of sharks here, it stands to reason that these mers will provide a good challenge."

"Ah, I see; since they are used to avoiding predators, you think they will be good sport." He smiled. "Very well, enjoy yourself, pet. I will call you if I need your help."

"Thank you." She gave him a quick peck on the cheek. "I promise not to block you."

When she turned to go, he held her arm and pulled her back to his side. "That was not a proper kiss." Without further warning, he kissed her passionately and thoroughly.

She chuckled and smirked at him. "You crafty devil, you're just trying to get me to stay here."

"Is it working?"

In answer, she stood on tiptoe and nibbled at his ear. "What do you think?"

Hours later, the siren strode naked to the large windows in the captain's cabin. She opened the casement and climbed onto the sill.

"I am going to hunt before you can stop me again. That pod is still in the area, but it won't be for much longer."

She dove out the window and disappeared beneath the waves.

Viktor moved to the window and leaned out. "You'll be back," he said with a self-satisfied smile.

He turned from the window, got dressed and headed to the helm.

The *Incubus* reached Mauritius a few days later. Belladonna still had not returned, but Viktor didn't worry about it. A brief "peek" through their link showed him she still tracked the mermaid pod she'd sensed earlier.

He took Grimm and Zach with him when he went ashore. Jon-Jon remained with the ship to oversee the crew. How long they would stay depended on how difficult a dodo egg would be to find. Viktor didn't want to tease the men with shore leave if they weren't going to be there long.

Since the island's primary trade commodity was sugar, he reckoned Zach would prove useful with his trading background. The harbor fee the young man settled on did not please him, but he paid without a show of discontent.

He and Grimm stood back far enough that the harbor master assumed Zach was just a lackey and interpreter. The man had no idea the captain and first mate spoke fluent French.

The harbor master spoke with great disrespect and used several slurs. Viktor smiled when he looked over at them.

After they got out of sight of the harbor and headed toward the port town, Grimm voiced his irritation. "That seemed an exorbitant docking fee."

"It was. I'm sorry I couldn't talk him down more. He refused to budge on it; said he had to recoup his losses from fees for nonexistent trade goods," Zach apologized.

"Not to worry, Mr. Brumble." Viktor maintained his pleasant and calm smile. "I intend to have my gold back from him before we leave — with interest to compensate for his insolence."

Grimm chuckled. "Didn't think you'd let that smelly bugger's remarks slide."

"Of course not, Mr. Grimm; I shall take great pleasure in educating him in proper courtesy."

☠

Tamara A. Lowery

The portside taverns proved useless in finding information on a dodo. The pirates headed deeper into Port Louis to try there.

Still, it seemed no one had ever heard of the creature. Finally, someone directed them to a local historian and school teacher.

A rosy-cheeked old man answered the door. *"May I help you gentlemen?"* he asked in French.

Viktor answered in the same language. *"I hope so, sir. I need to find a dodo or more accurately, a dodo's egg. I was told the creature is native to this island, but no one here seems to have heard of it before."*

"Please, come in!" The old man fairly bounced with enthusiasm. The pirates accepted his invitation.

The place smelled of vellum, myrrh, and mint. Golden sunlight streamed in through large bay windows which faced the harbor. Shelves of books lined three walls. A well-worn table with an oil lamp on each end dominated the rest of the room.

He motioned for them to have a seat on the bench along one side of the table. *"I apologize for my lack of more comfortable seating. I usually have my students, planters' and merchants' sons, in here. The hard seat helps keep them awake through their lessons."*

"This brings back memories," Zach muttered.

"Oh! You speak English! Good! I always enjoy any chance to practice mine," the old man chirped. "Oh, where are my manners? I am Jean

Hell's Dodo

Beaujolais. I was just about to have some mint tea. Would you gentlemen care for a cup? I always brew too much."

Grimm started to decline, but Viktor cut him off. "Of course, *m'sieur*. Thank you," he said with a bemused half-smile.

With a happy bounce in his step, Jean trundled off to another room. He could be heard humming and puttering about with what they assumed was crockery.

"Hmph, my tutors were never that pleasant," Zach observed.

"Nor mine, Mr. Brumble," Grimm agreed. "What about you, Captain?"

"Didn't have any. Mother Celie saw to it that I could read and write. I learned to cipher from Captain Black." He rubbed his beard and smiled. "I like this man."

The others nodded their agreement.

Jean bustled back in with a tray laden with a teapot and four cups and saucers. The smell of mint became the predominant scent in the room. He set the tray down on the table and served. He took a sip from his cup, closed his eyes, and sighed. When he opened them again, his gaze was sharp and focused.

"Now then, you said you were looking for a dodo egg. Let me see. The creature's name is vaguely familiar. I have a book of native fauna here somewhere." He carried his cup and saucer over to one of the bookshelves and peered at the spines. Finally, he gave a small cry of triumph. "Ah, there it is."

He set his cup and saucer on the table and fished the book down off the shelf. He set the book down and opened it to an index. "Since it lays eggs, I assume it is either a reptile or a bird."

"It is a bird, a large, ugly, flightless bird. A friend of mine in New Orleans found a citation in his library which had a plate of the creature and a brief description. Unfortunately, the book was rather old and more concerned about the business of the Portuguese explorers who discovered the island than anything else," Viktor said.

"Oh, I would dearly love to get my hands on that book. I've a passion for history. You'd be surprised at what secrets can be found in the recording of the most mundane things."

"I will let Jeorge know the next time I see him. I have a feeling he would like you."

"Aha! Here it is! The dodo. Oh my, that is not good news for you."

"What?"

"While it was native to this island and our neighbor, Reúnion, I am afraid it is extinct."

"Extinct?" Grimm asked. "Are you sure?"

"Well, I suppose it's possible some were bred for menageries abroad, but the Dutch did a lot of damage when they held this island. They cleared whole forests of ebony, and their pigs and dogs destroyed many of the dodo's ground nests." He glanced back at the book.

Hell's Dodo

"The dodo has been gone for over a century. The last known one here died about eighty years after they were discovered."

"Damn," Viktor said.

Zach looked in his bag and found a scrap of vellum. "*M'sieur* Beaujolais, may I use a quill and ink?"

"Of course, of course. May I ask what for?" Jean said and retrieved an inkwell and quill from the small cabinet he stored such supplies in.

"I want to make a copy of the illustration to show the crew. If there have been dodos preserved and bred elsewhere, one of them may have seen it in their travels."

"Good thinking, Mr. Brumble," Vik said. "The idea never occurred to me to check with the lads."

"I asked about it shortly after we left Clarissa's," Grimm pointed out. "None of 'em had ever heard of a dodo."

"Perhaps they know it by another name. It wouldn't be the first creature to be called different things depending on where a man's from," Zach said.

"Good point."

Jean peered over Zach's shoulder to watch him sketch the copy of the illustration plate. "My, what a steady hand and accurate eye you have, young man. You know, I never thought to ask you gentlemen for your names. Did I hear correctly that you are a Brumble? You wouldn't happen to be related to the owner of Brumble and Sons, would you?"

The navigator looked to his captain, the color drained from his face. Viktor took over the conversation.

"*M'sieur* Beaujolais, allow me to introduce my chief navigator, Zachary Brumble, formerly employed by and heir to the aforementioned shipping company."

"Oh my! Really? Why then that would make the two of you Bloody Vik Brandee and the Grimm Reaper. How exciting!" The old man clapped his hands in delight.

"Well, can't say as our names have gotten that reaction before," Grimm laughed in surprise.

"Of course they have, Hezekiah, just not from a man." Viktor's mood went from jovial to alert and slightly irritated. "Bugger."

"What is wrong, Captain Brandee?" Jean asked.

"Are you finished with that drawing, Mr. Brumble?"

"Aye, sir."

"I am afraid we have to cut our visit short *M'sieur* Beaujolais. The local authorities seemed to have figured out we are in this harbor." Vik rose and bowed.

"But how? I mean, how do you know?"

In answer, the sound of cannon fire drifted in from the direction of the harbor.

"Oh. I am sorry to hear that. I was hoping to entice you to tell me some of your adventures." He looked down for a few moments then looked

Hell's Dodo

Viktor straight in the eye. "If it's not too much trouble, you'd best tie me up before you leave. It will protect me from suspicion, and it will give me a better standing with my students."

The three pirates looked at him with bemusement.

"How will it improve your standing?" Grimm had to ask.

The old man winked. "If I know something important enough to draw the attention of the two most notorious pirates of our day, it would be worth their while to pay attention to me. You know how easily bored young lads are. A little adventure and excitement helps hold their attention."

"Clever," Zach chuckled. "I wish my tutors had been more like you. Might have saved me a few beatings at home."

Viktor left the room for a moment and returned with a swathe of fabric in hand.

"Are those my curtains?"

"Aye. Forgive the liberty, but there was no rope to hand, and it will lend credence to your alibi." He moved behind the old man and secured him to the chair."

"What about the tea cups?" Zach asked.

In answer, Viktor fished his coin purse out and slipped five gold coins into the old man's vest pocket. He then swept the entire tea set onto the floor where it shattered. As a finishing touch, he kicked over the bench.

"There, that should make it convincing enough. Thank you for your help and entertainment, *m'sieur*. Let's be on our way, lads."

"*Bon chance* on your escape!" Jean called after them.

They exited out the back shortly before a *gendarme* knocked at the front door. Without prior warning, the vampire grabbed his first mate and his navigator around their waists. "Hold on." He took to the sky.

As they approached the harbor, they saw the *Incubus* headed for open water. Although several ships trailed her, none posed a serious threat.

The shore batteries presented a different problem. The guns were large bore enough and had the range to damage the ship if the local gunners were accurate.

Vik dropped his passengers off on deck and launched back into flight. Unencumbered, he flew faster than the eye could follow.

The two gunnery crews had the range on the fleeing pirate now. They had used their test shots to gauge the proper angle and trajectory. Loaded with chain shot to take out the masts, they prepared to fire again.

A dark clad man with raven black hair and flashing green eyes dropped from the sky to stand next to the northern gun. Before the crew could grasp the sudden change of events, he flung them aside as if they were rag dolls. He then hefted the cannon from its mounting and aimed it at the wall just below the southern gun and crew.

The chain shot hit strategically and collapsed the masonry which supported the southern gun. Its shot splashed harmlessly into the harbor as the gun and crew tumbled down the battlement.

The strange dark man tossed the cannon he held out into the harbor and disappeared back into the sky.

The harbor master jumped when a heavy hand fell on his shoulder. He turned to find the pirate captain he had overcharged and reported to the *gendarmerie* standing there.

Viktor smiled and bared his fangs. *"It is time to settle my account with you, m'sieur,"* he said in perfect French.

Chapter 37

That night, Thomas Brumble paid his brother a visit. He found the navigator well into a bottle of rum.

"It's not like you to drink like this, Zach. What's wrong?"

He turned bloodshot eyes to the young vampire. "Did you know he could fly?"

"Yes."

"Can you?"

Thomas shrugged. "I've never tried."

"Why not?"

"Never felt the need to."

Zach shuddered and took another pull from the bottle then offered it to his brother.

"I can't drink that anymore, remember."

"Oh, right. I had to fight not to piss myself. Mr. Grimm didn't seem bothered by it, though."

Thom snorted. "He wouldn't even if he was. The Reaper has a reputation to maintain. Can't say that I would have been comfortable with flight when I was alive, though." He looked at his brother and blinked, sudden realization hitting him. "I'd forgotten about your problem with heights."

Aye. I'm just grateful I trained with George rather than Father. It was over a month before I could comfortably climb the rigging."

"Good thing you concentrated on navigation. That doesn't require going aloft so much."

"No it doesn't," Zach slurred and blinked bleary eyes.

"Turn in, brother. I need to go get my ration anyway."

"Mmm, g'night then."

The currents and winds remained favorable as the *Incubus* skirted the Indian Ocean headed east. Viktor felt no need to recall Belladonna from her hunt.

None of the crew could say they'd ever seen a dodo before when shown the illustration. Grimm carried the drawing with him and showed it at every port they stopped in, as well as to any prisoners they took. He either got the same result or was told the bird no longer existed.

Still, Viktor refused to give up hope. He knew the Sisters would make their tasks as difficult and discouraging as possible, but he doubted they would make them impossible.

They made good time to the islands that played home to dragons. True to the account Mr. Stoud gave, the dragons turned out to be merely very large lizards.

Hell's Dodo

"Damn, bugger's as big as a gator," Jon-Jon observed when they spotted one.

"A regular gator, maybe, although they don't look much like a gator or croc," Grimm agreed.

"I wouldn't get too close, lads," Stoud cautioned. "They're big, but they're fast. Sh, watch that." He pointed in the direction the dragon was headed. In the brush, barely visible, a small variety of deer grazed.

They watch in silence as the dragon climbed a nearby tree. Some slight sound alerted the deer, and it raised its head. Its large ears twitched and turned. The dragon dropped to the ground nearly on it. It sprang away, and the giant lizard gave pursuit.

In a matter of only a few minutes, the reptile took its prey down and dragged it away.

"Impressive," Viktor stated. "We follow it. It may lead us to its nest."

They found it a bit tricky to follow the creature without drawing its ire. At least once, they got too close. The dragon dropped its prey and turned to face the intrusive pirates. It gave a hissing growl and rushed them.

Viktor remembered Stoud's warning about the septic nature of creature's bite and waved his men back. Satisfied that they retreated, the dragon returned to the deer carcass and began to drag it again.

"Lazarus, come forth."

The large black cat materialized beside the vampire.

"I need your eyes, old friend," Vik said. "We need to find out if that dragon is a female with a nest or if we need to keep hunting."

"Mrrreh." The cat's body dissolved into smoke and rematerialized as a raven. The bird launched into the air and hovered above the dragon.

Grimm had the hunting party fan out and keep lookout. He didn't want to risk an attack from another dragon while they waited.

Viktor stood with his eyes closed. He concentrated on the images sent to him by Lazarus.

"What is that Lazarus creature?" Stoud whispered to Jon-Jon.

"Not sure what he is now. He used to be Jim Rigger, the Cap'n's first mate."

Viktor opened his eyes abruptly and grinned. "We're in luck, lads. It's a she-dragon, and she's got a clutch of eggs not far from here. The tricky part will be getting her away from the nest long enough to rob it."

Grimm edged over to the captain to avoid any of the pirates overhearing. "Wouldn't it just be easier to kill it and take an egg?"

"Of course it would, Hezekiah." He kept his voice low, as well. "But you know as surely as I do that the easy way is usually the wrong way when dealing with any of the Sisters."

"True, that; what do you propose?"

Hell's Dodo

"First, we need to get closer to the nest, but not close enough to alarm the creature."

The trail left by the dragon proved easy to follow. Blood, bits of fur, and broken twigs marked where it dragged the deer carcass through the brush. After a few hundred yards, Viktor motioned for them to stop.

About thirty feet ahead of them a small clearing lay at the base of a low bluff. A low mound of disturbed earth covered in plant litter marked the dragon's nest. The creature perched part way up the jagged bluff. Its prey had been wedged into a shallow crevice for future consumption.

A rustle in the brush off to the left drew their attention. A smaller dragon emerged in the clearing and eased toward the carcass. Just as it got close enough to touch it, the larger dragon scrambled down the bluff and chased it off.

"I have an idea," Viktor whispered. "Did anyone bring a grapple?"

"Aye, Cap'n," Jon-Jon confirmed. "Didn't know if we'd need to climb or not."

"Good man." He held his hand out for the grapple and line. "Sutton, you're the fastest of this lot. I plan to lure the beast away. Once it's out of sight, count to twenty then run in and dig an egg out of that mound. We only need one, so don't dawdle. I don't know how long I'll be able to hold her attention."

"Aye, Cap'n," the lanky pirate replied.

Silently, Viktor eased around to the left side of the clearing. A whirr filled the air as he twirled the grapple. He flung it and it landed just the other side of the carcass.

The dragon hissed and growled at the sound of metal hitting stone. Carefully, Vik drew the line in. The hook caught on the deer's leg but soon slid off it.

He retrieved the grapple and tried again. The hook landed slightly higher. Just as he had it nearly to the carcass, the dragon scrambled forward to attack it.

Once again, the grapple skittered to the base of the bluff empty.

Viktor waited for the dragon to retreat to its sunning spot. He then took careful aim. Rather than twirl and toss, he threw the hook overhand.

The meaty thunk of one of the tines sinking into the deer's ribs brought a tight, satisfied grin to his face. He gave the line a quick little jerk. The carcass popped out of the crevice and tumbled to the ground.

The dragon gave a grunt as it jumped to the ground near its suddenly reanimated prey.

Viktor pulled the animal toward him. The dragon gave chase. He found he had to use vampiric speed to keep her from catching it.

He led the creature into the brush.

Ken Sutton followed his captain's instructions to the letter. He counted to twenty after the beast disappeared and dashed to the mound. He began to dig.

It took him a couple of minutes to find any of the leathery eggs. They looked much like turtle eggs, only bigger. He grabbed one and hesitated. The thought of egg soup made him want to take as much of the clutch as he could carry.

As the tallest, Jon-Jon caught the rapid movement in the brush first. Whatever it was wasn't the Captain, and it was headed toward the clearing fast.

"Sutton, get the damn egg and get out of there!"

Sutton looked up at the second mate's shout. He heard the brush rustle ahead of him. The smaller dragon burst from cover and ran at him.

He started to run but stumbled over some of the loose debris he'd dug through earlier. He landed on his rear and almost lost the egg he held. He tried to scramble back from the giant lizard that bore down on him.

The creature proved too fast for him. He screamed as sharp claws tore into his flesh. He kicked at the dragon, and it snapped inch-long teeth at him.

Jon-Jon Dodo Grimm reached him at the same time. The second mate grabbed him under the arms and dragged him back. Grimm shot the dragon in the head with both pistols. For good measure, he severed its head.

Stoud came over to where Sutton lay bleeding. He looked him over and walked over to Grimm. "We need to take his leg now, Mr. Grimm. The beast got a bite in."

Grimm glanced over at the man. "Doesn't look to be more than a scratch, Mr. Stoud; in fact, the scratches look worse than the bite."

"They are deeper; but if we don't take that leg now, he'll be dead in a week. A dragon bite poisons the blood and rots the flesh."

"I see. Let's do this, then." He raised his voice. "Mr. Jon, get a good dose of that gin to Sutton and find him a stick to bite down on."

"Aye, Mr. Grimm. Mind if I ask why?"

In answer, he squatted next to the wounded man and placed a hand on his shoulder. "Sutton, that leg has to come off. I know the bite is small, but it's poisoned."

A look of anguish crossed the pirate's face. "Can't you just bleed me?"

Stoud looked at Grimm and shook his head. "I've seen first-hand what a dragon bite can do. Bleedin' him won't save him."

"No! Please! Not me leg!" Sutton's voice rose in panic.

Jon-Jon struck him in the back of the head with the hilt of his sword. Sutton crumpled into unconsciousness. "Sorry, Mr. Grimm, but it's better this way."

Hell's Dodo

"Aye; I know. Would've taken too long to get him drunk, anyway." He sighed and drew his own sword. "Turn him on his stomach and get a tourniquet on that leg up high. Make it good and tight. Mr. Stoud, have ye any rum?"

"Aye; good idea, Mr. Grimm. Rum'll burn better'n that swill you and Mr. Jon drink."

The men got Sutton prepared according to Grimm's instructions. The first mate took aim at the hollow behind the knee. Plainly, he'd had to do this before. He raised the blade and brought it down in one swift, powerful stroke.

Sutton's lower leg separated from his body with a clean cut.

Stoud showed his previous experience with amputations. He opened his rum flask and dowsed the stump thoroughly.

Grimm stuck his sword in the dirt and fished the steel and flint striker from his tinderbox. Within moments, he'd set spark to the rum-soaked stump.

Sutton woke with a scream and passed out again. Jon-Jon smothered the remaining flames with his huge hands. The charred stump oozed but did not bleed.

"There, that should hold him until Stitches has a chance to work on him." Grimm wiped his blade and sheathed it. "Let's get him and the egg back to the ship before Mummy comes back to check on the ruckus."

Chapter 38

Viktor rejoined them at the shore. He took Sutton's unconscious form from his second mate. Free of his burden, Jon-Jon stretched his back.

"For a skinny man, he's not very light," he complained.

"I've already notified Mr. Coffin to be ready for him. You got the egg?"

"Aye, Captain," Grimm responded.

"I'll meet you back aboard." Viktor launched into the air with his injured crewman.

Grimm found them in the infirmary. Matthew Coffin, the ship's surgeon and affectionately known as "Stitches," worked feverishly on Sutton's leg.

"Ah, Mr. Grimm, there you are," he said. "Thank you for making my job easier. That was a good clean cut. I've barely found any bone splinters."

"Not the first time I've had to do that for a man."

"I can imagine." He cut a bit of burnt flesh away and began to stitch the skin shut. "Captain, if I may be so bold, I'd like to hang on to several spools of this silk thread. For surgical sutures, it is far superior to cotton. The wounds aren't as likely to get infected and feverish."

"Very well; that is a reasonable request."

"Thank you, sir. There; that has the leg sewn up. Now I need to check those claw wounds." He set to work cutting away the patient's clothing.

Dr. Coffin was one of the most fastidious men the pirates had ever encountered. When asked about this particular practice in the past, he'd explained that he didn't want dirty fabric pulled across open wounds. Since his patients seemed to fare better than those of ship's surgeons they'd had in the past, Viktor and Grimm tolerated his peculiarities.

The captain and first mate moved to the other side of the cabin to talk.

"We have two of the items Clarissa asked for. What do you want to do about the third?"

Viktor frowned and stroked his beard. "I doubt we'd stand a chance of finding a dodo egg by heading further east. We already know there are none to be found this side of Africa. We may head north toward England and France after we round the cape. I've called Belle to help us out with the winds."

"Good idea. So, we turn west."

"Aye, Mr. Grimm; straight west. We aren't following the coast this time, hence the need for Belladonna's aide. I don't want to waste any more time in these waters than we have to. We'll go back to coastal raiding when we get to Africa's western shore."

"I'll have the lads make ready."

Belladonna knocked perfunctorily on the cabin door as she entered and shut it behind her. She flounced over to Viktor's bed and plopped down on it. She smiled and leaned back on the mattress.

"Hello, Viktor."

He raised an eyebrow. "You are in a good mood, pet."

She nodded and stretched. "I am well-fed, and if I can get your cooperation, I will be well-fucked before this day is over."

"Hmm, that might just be the distraction I need."

Belle detected a slightly sour note in his tone. "What's wrong?"

"I still haven't found a dodo's egg."

"I thought you put in at Mauritius to get one."

"Seems the damn bird is extinct there and has been for over a century. Every port we stopped at between there and here yielded no hope. I plan to try England, France, or Spain. Maybe some noble in the past took a fancy to one and added a breeding pair to their menagerie."

"That sounds like a slim hope."

"Aye; even had Brumble sketch a copy of an illustration of one to show around, just in case it was known by a different name."

She perked up at that. "That was clever. May I see the drawing?"

He shrugged and fished it out of the pouch he kept it in. She smoothed out the roll of vellum and studied the drawing.

"So that is what those foul creatures are."

"You've seen one? Why do you say they're foul?"

"They stink, they taste nasty, they're ugly, they're loud, they bite, and they have a mean kick, too."

He smirked at her little tirade. Her ire brought a color to her cheeks and a fire to her eyes that he found irresistible.

"You say 'are,' pet. Do you mean to tell me that they are not extinct?"

"Oh, they are very much alive. I swear, Zeke keeps some strange pets."

He blinked and smiled broadly. "Hell's Breath; I should have guessed. Hopefully we'll encounter it before we get back to Clarissa." He stood and started to strip.

Belle watched, mesmerized for the moment. Soon, she began to shimmy out of her own garments.

Hell's Dodo

The next day, the siren sang up a strong wind to push them westward.

Grimm found her later, perched on the railing. "Thank ye, lass."

"You're welcome. For what?"

"For having information about the dodo's whereabouts. I was dreading the idea of sailing to England."

"Ah yes, those waters are a bit dangerous for pirates."

"Aye; that they are. Too many navies with too many ships for my comfort."

She nodded. "Even the biggest predator can be brought down if enough smaller ones attack at the same time."

She stood suddenly and scented the air. "I smell rot and poison — and sickness."

Grimm frowned. "The only injury lately has been Sutton. Dragon bit him, and I took his leg to save his life."

"Why did a dragon bite him?"

"It was hungry, I imagine, pet," Viktor said. He approached the two of them. "It had to be the one the mother tried to run off earlier." He sighed and leaned against the railing. "You might as well have left him his leg, Mr. Grimm. Dr. Coffin said some of his belly wounds were from a grazing bite. The poison has set in and will probably kill him before the day is out."

"So he was attacked while you got the egg?" Belle's tone betrayed an anger that puzzled the men.

"No. I drew the mother dragon off after she supposedly drove a smaller dragon away from her fresh kill. I figured Sutton would be quick enough to retrieve an egg before she caught onto the ruse. I didn't count on the other one sticking around to take advantage of the distraction, as well."

"Is he still in the infirmary?" she snapped.

"He is. Why are you so upset about this?"

"This is the second time one of the Sisters has cost or nearly cost you crewmen. I won't stand for it. You are required to fulfill the task each one sets you. You are not required to sacrifice your men to them."

"I sacrifice them to you to find the Sisters," he pointed out.

"And by that token, they belong to me, not to any of those creatures." She extended her talons and retracted them. Grimm stepped back a couple of steps, which put Viktor closer to the irate siren.

Belle got a determined look on her face. "I won't let her have this one. I need a large cask filled with seawater. Do you still have a link with him, or have you cut him loose?"

"I still have a link. I'm dulling his pain. He's served me well. I see no need to let him suffer before the end. Do you need me to release him?"

"No." She shook her head. "Keep his pain dulled, but also make him hold on to his will to live. All my healing magic will do no good if he gives up the fight."

"You heard her, Mr. Grimm. Get a tun filled with seawater."

They decided it would be easiest to do the procedure on deck. Viktor brought Sutton up from the infirmary.

Dr. Coffin followed to check on his patient. His frown displayed his displeasure at what he deemed an unnecessary disturbance of a dying man.

Several of the crew, not otherwise occupied, gathered around to watch.

"Remove the blanket and the bandage," the siren directed.

"Miss Belladonna, he is nude," Coffin objected.

"I seriously doubt anyone here has never seen a naked man before, doctor. Now, lower him into the water, but keep his head above the surface. Purging the blood poisoning will do no good if he drowns."

Viktor and Grimm lifted Sutton into the barrel of seawater and supported him on either side. Angry red lines crept up the man's thigh from the sutured stump, evidence that some of the dragon's taint had failed to be cut away. His torso glowed nearly scarlet from the virulence in his veins which spread from the swollen and puckered wounds stitched neatly on his stomach.

Belladonna sang.

Her song, in an ancient language no human ever knew, bore very little resemblance to any of her weather spells. It mesmerized all who heard it. Every man aboard the pirate vessel felt a sense of peace and well-being.

She hit a low note and held it then plunged both of her hands into the water. The seawater began to ripple with the thrum of the note. It began to glow.

The note ended, and Sutton began to spasm and writhe. The captain and first mate had all they could do to keep him from braining himself against the barrel's edge.

Belle removed her hands from the water and said, "Come look, doctor, and see if you still doubt."

He moved forward to peer into the water. "Is the glow magic?"

"No," she laughed, "it is natural. Surely you've seen sea foam glow. The same minute animals which cause that are in this water."

He returned his attention to Sutton. Before his eyes, the redness receded and vanished. The man's skin took on a more healthy hue. Then Coffin noticed something odd about the stump.

A translucent, jelly-like pod pulsed and extended. A cloudy core appeared in it and began to solidify.

"Is that—?" Grimm said.

Hell's Dodo

"Aye, Mr. Grimm; bones," Dr. Coffin confirmed. "He's growing a new leg." Disbelief and awe filled his voice.

Only Viktor looked at the siren. He caught the glimmer of surprise and hint of fear in her eyes.

A smelly spider of a man lowered from the rigging to dangle nearby. Sniff made quite the sight: hairless, toothless, one-eyed, an open cavity where his nose had been bitten off years ago, and both legs gone from just above the knee.

"Can ye fix me next, lass?" he asked with a leer.

"As old as your injuries are, I doubt it, troll. I shouldn't have been able to do this. My power was targeted at the blood poison only." Her tone made it obvious that she meant what she said and wasn't being capricious.

"It's all right, lass. I know you love me just the way I am."

"Sniff, back aloft," Grimm ordered with a laugh. "You know she's faster than you."

"Point taken, Mr. Grimm."

He scrambled back into the rigging.

Chapter 39

The voyage to the Cape of Good Hope passed swiftly and uneventfully. Not only did the siren's weather magic provide good winds, she also guided them to a westward current. It added about five knots to their speed.

They had to backtrack northeast to reach the African shore when they left the current. The move puzzled the siren.

"Why didn't you stay to the current and let it carry us on to Tierra del Fuego?"

"We need to hunt. Even at those speeds, rations would run out before we'd reach our destination. While you've fed well, my feedings have been sporadic. I think we both know the danger inherent in continuing that pattern."

She blinked at him as comprehension sank in. "How strong has your Hunger grown?"

"I've been wearing the emerald cross to keep it down for the past two days."

"I'll scout out a prize for you."

Two days later, he heard from the siren through the mental link they shared.

"You'll like this one."

"And why is that, pet?"

He smiled at her mental chuckle. *"She carries a heavy cargo, judging by how low she's riding in the water,"* Belle told him. *"She's not Navy, but she carries a larger crew than most merchantmen this size. You might want to have Lazarus check it out. He won't draw as much attention as I would."*

"We are headed north with the coast just in sight off the starboard. Do I need to change heading to intercept?"

"No. She may try to run, but the Incubus can outpace her easily."

Viktor grinned like a madman at what he saw through Lazarus' eyes. He sent the cabin boy to fetch his mates.

"Our Belle has found us a fat prize, lads; one we should reach by tomorrow afternoon."

"The lads will be glad of that," Grimm said. "What are we looking at?"

"Forty guns, all told, which is a lot for a merchantman; one hundred crewmen; and she's about half our size."

"Pirate hunter, maybe?" Jon-Jon opined.

"If she is, she's carrying the right bait. She's a treasure ship bound for Lisbon."

"Treasure ship? I didn't know any still sailed," Zach said.

Hell's Dodo

"Aye, lad." Jon-Jon laughed and clapped the man on the shoulder. "They be rare, but they're still out there. If they're making for Lisbon, they'll be worried about Spaniards intercepting them."

"Lazarus showed me they're worried about the French, too." Vik stroked his beard as if in thought. With a mock look of concern, he said, "We should really relieve them of such worries."

"Aye," Grimm agreed with a grin. "It would be criminal of us not to."

They all laughed in agreement.

"Make sure we approach at dusk. The cadre needs a fresh feed, and we've no need for extra crew at this time."

Apparently, the captain of their prey spooked easily. Not long after the *Incubus* came in sight, the merchantman changed course and put on extra sails.

The result was that Grimm didn't have to order the riggers to reef any sails in order to achieve a dusk attack.

Even though the *Incubus* was a larger, heavier ship, she rode higher and sleeker than her gold-laden prey. The sun dipped below the horizon just as the pirates reached the merchantman.

"Heave to and prepare to be boarded!" Grimm called to them from the quarterdeck.

"Shove off, or we'll shoot you to ribbons!"

"Ballsy bastard." Grimm smirked.

"Aye," Vik agreed. "Show him what we've got, lads!" He had purposely ordered the crew to mask the majority of the guns to lend the illusion that they were a merchant ship, as well. All along the side facing their prey, the crew opened the gun ports. The *Incubus* outgunned them three to one.

The captain of the treasure ship might have been ballsy, but he wasn't suicidal. He surrendered unconditionally.

Viktor and Grimm stood on the deck of their prize while Jon-Jon oversaw the sacking of the ship and round-up of her crew.

"I am glad you chose to surrender, sir," Vik told the captain. "It would have been such a waste to kill you or your men."

"You are looking to recruit?" The man looked worried. "I need my crew."

The vampire laughed. He didn't bother to hide his fangs. "Alas, no; I am not in need of new crewmen. I am, however, in need of something they and you carry. The blood in your veins is a greater treasure to me than the gold in your hold."

Silently, he called his cadre to come feed.

After they finished with the treasure ship, Viktor decided to make a course west. He reasoned he could at least deliver the dragon egg and the blood vial to Clarissa. The dodo egg would just have to wait until Hell's Breath deigned to intercept them.

Hell's Dodo

Belladonna helped once again with the wind and guided them back to the westward current.

Four days out, an ice fog built around them. At first the siren succeeded in dispersing it. Soon, though, it proved too much for her weather magic. The seas turned slushy and slowed the ship to a near stop.

Grimm ordered the riggers to reef all sails. Despite the fog, the wind blew at near gale force. He didn't want to snap the masts.

Only then did the island appear.

Viktor and Belladonna went ashore to find Zeke.

"Glad to see you, old man." Viktor took a seat on one of the rocks around Zeke's ever-present fire. Belle took the other one.

"Imagine you are, boy, seein' as how I have something you need."

"Aye; Belle told me you had dodos. I need one of their eggs to give to Clarissa; then I'll have all she asked for."

"So you will, since I do; but this egg ain't free."

The vampire nodded. "I expected as much. What is your price?"

"That drop of vampire blood you're carrying."

He frowned. "I thought you wanted to help me. You know I need that blood."

Zeke looked at him and shook his head. "No you don't, boy. The last thing you need to give that bird-brain Clarissa is that blood."

"But she specifically requested blood from the dragon's daughter," Belle argued. "After what has transpired with that vampire, I doubt he could get another from her before the eggs go bad."

"The fact that it is Her blood is precisely why Clarissa should not have it. Lady Carpathia is a very real danger to your quest, boy. I've been watching her."

"I thought you said she was cloaked from you," Viktor said.

"She was. Thanks to you, my magic has seen her. She cannot hide from me anymore."

Viktor leaned forward with an expectant look on his face. "Carpathia said she is the head of her order, the Daughters of the Dragon. Are you implying that I should find a different one for the required blood?"

Zeke gave the siren a pointed but silent look.

"You don't have to find one, Viktor," she said. Viktor didn't understand her look of shame as she pulled off her shirt and turned her back. She pulled her hair to the side. "Reveal the mark, Elder."

Zeke sighed. "You know it can never be hidden again. Take the crystal Mother Celie gave you, boy, and wave it slowly over her left shoulder."

Puzzled but curious, the vampire complied. As the white crystal passed above her skin, the siren cried out in anguish and dropped to her knees. The crystal flared with light.

Before his eyes, her skin bubbled and blistered. A pattern formed as the burn healed to a shiny, raised scar. He recognized it immediately.

"You are one of the Daughters of the Dragon?"

"Not exactly," she answered, her voice still filled with pain. "I was captured and branded by them. They meant it as both punishment for my role in the deaths of two powerful vampires and as a warning to other vampires not to feed on me."

"The assassination of your sister; I remember you'd contracted vampires to carry it out without knowing the effect siren's blood would have on them." Oddly, Viktor found he wasn't upset that she'd kept the mark a secret. Just a scant few years earlier, he would have been.

He tucked the crystal away and turned his attention to Zeke. "She bears the brand, but she is not a member of the order. Also, her blood is toxic to me. I don't see how this will help."

"She may not be a member of that order of assassins, but she is a daughter of the dragon. She is the firstborn of the oldest of the siren sires. The males of her species have three forms, whereas the females only have two. A siren sire's natural form is not the half-human half-shark, nor is it the human guise. They are sea dragons or serpents, and they can swallow a ship whole."

"Damn."

"I know," Zeke laughed. "You don't have to worry about your problem with siren blood. You won't be consuming it. Clarissa will." He shook his head and continued, "That girl always was too ambitious for her own good. She thinks the blood will give her control over vampires. She forgets the spell only works one way, regardless of what kind of egg she uses."

Realization of the true danger came quickly to Viktor. "If I give her Carpathia's blood, it will give that bitch control over a Sister of Power."

Zeke nodded. "Exactly why you need to give me that vial."

Chapter 40

Later, they knew Hell's Breath had vanished when the weather cleared. Once again, the *Incubus* could ride the westward current.

Grimm and Zach checked the instruments and the charts. They determined that they were half a day east of a group of islands off the southeastern shore of South America. They made the appropriate course changes to head them towards Tierra del Fuego.

Viktor ordered portage made at the same cove they'd used before. He, Grimm, Zach, and Belladonna went ashore, but they did not trek inland.

"Lazarus, come forth."

The black cat immediately answered his master's summons.

"Find the Sister. Do. Not. Harm. Her. But, make her aware we are here."

Lazarus transformed to his raven form and launched into the air.

The raven flew in ever-widening arcs from the pirate's landing point. After about half an hour, he spotted Clarissa. The petite woman stood next to a structure that hadn't been there during their last visit.

He landed and cawed at her.

"Where did you come from? Ravens are not native to this land," she said.

He felt her power over birds reach out to him. He instinctively reverted to his feline form.

Clarissa shrieked and leaned back against the crude brick structure. "Get away from me!"

In an effort to calm her, he took raven form again, chirped once, and took to the sky. When she sent her magic toward him again, he kept his form and tried to let her "see" what his message was.

It must have worked. She withdrew her power and said, "Tell Captain Brandewyne to bring what he has found to me here."

Lazarus cawed once and returned to the pirates.

Viktor charged Zach with the task of transporting the small crate that held the dodo and dragon eggs. It took less time to walk to the Sister's location than it had for Lazarus to find it. The brick structure turned out to be an oven. It had been difficult to recognize from Lazarus' perspective. In just the time it took to walk there, some of the natives set up a rough wooden trestle table.

Hell's Dodo

Clarissa stood next to the table. She wore a cloak of feathers.

"Have you brought what I require, Viktor Brandewyne?" He motioned for Zach to place the crate on the table. The navigator opened it and gently lifted the contents out.

"Here are the dragon egg and the dodo egg."

She moved closer to examine the eggs. "Impressive. These are genuine and viable." She looked up at him. "Were you able to obtain the third ingredient?"

"I did." He handed her the crystal vial.

She tilted it and watched the blood in it move freely. She frowned. "This looks fresh. Surely you did not just take it from the dragon's daughter."

"No, I obtained it well before I found the eggs. The crystal holds some sort of magic that keeps the blood fresh. It has been a sore temptation to me the entire time I've carried it. I didn't realize until almost too late just how dangerous she is."

"Yet you appear unscathed."

"Let's just say I left her satisfied," he leered.

She sighed and gave him a look that was hard to read. He left it alone. She turned to face north and whistled an elaborate bird song.

Within minutes, the northern sky grew dark, and a faint raucous call filled the air. It didn't take long to realize the darkness was birds, hundreds of birds.

They swarmed around Clarissa, the oven, and the trestle. Just as abruptly as they came, they flew away again. Various cooking utensils and ingredients now rested on the trestle table.

The Sister set about her preparations without a word. Instead, she hummed, whistled, and trilled.

Viktor and his companions watched her fire up the oven. She turned her attention to the items on the table, once she seemed satisfied with the state of the fire. She mixed up and rolled out the dough for her pie crust with a speed that showed she'd done it many times. She cut the dough and pressed it into a baking dish. She then turned her attention to the filling.

She poured flour, sugar, nutmeg, and cloves into a large wooden bowl and loosely stirred them. She took the dodo egg and held it over another bowl with one hand. She took a wooden spoon in her other hand and gave the eggshell a solid rap. The contents of the egg nearly filled the bowl.

A bent reed whisk came into play next. Once she'd blended the egg with the dry ingredients, she picked up the dragon egg and a knife. Carefully, she slit the leathery egg open lengthwise and let only the white pour into the bowl. Once again, she used the whisk.

Finally, she added the drop of blood and whisked the contents of the bowl to a frothy consistency. Once she poured the filling into the crust, she picked up the dragon egg again. She pulled the shell open to reveal a partially formed dragon.

Hell's Dodo

Clarissa emitted a distinctive trill and threw the shell and embryo into the fire. She also put the dodo eggshell into the flames. With a wooden paddle, she placed the pie into the baking chamber.

The pirates fought boredom as they waited for the pie to bake. Grimm and Zach used a nearby large flat rock to strike up a game of dice. Viktor didn't join them. Although he knew his first mate did not cheat, he also knew the man had the devil's own luck at games of chance. Zach would just have to learn the hard way. Chances were he'd owe his share from the next five prizes to the old pirate before that pie was ready.

The vampire contented himself with sitting on the ground while he patiently waited for the Sister to complete her ritual. Belladonna stood close to him and glared at Clarissa. The siren's body language clearly said *mine*.

The Sister of Power spared her one nervous glance but ignored her for the most part.

"Oh, that smells delicious!" Zach said when Clarissa finally removed the pie from the oven.

"I cannot share it with any of you," she said. "If I do, the spell will not work."

Silently, Viktor used his power to suppress the navigator's appetite.

Clarissa quickly devoured the still-molten pie. The men were impressed that such a tiny woman could eat that much in one sitting and that she could eat something that hot without any sign of pain.

Belladonna hid a small smile as she felt the spell take effect. It was not time to reveal her role yet.

Clarissa looked at the living vampire before her. Only the One could have completed the quest she'd set, and now, thanks to the blood of the Dragon's Daughter, he was in her thrall. She reveled in the sensation of the new magic she now had access to. Soon, she would have access to the Elder's power, too.

"Give me this man to be my consort." She pointed at Grimm.

"That was not part of our agreement, Clarissa. Besides, he is not mine to control," Viktor stated simply.

Grimm spoke up. "Nor would I consent to that. You seem to forget that I have a wife and children. I will not break my oath to her nor betray them."

She seemed stunned, as if she truly had forgotten that fact about him. "But you are a pirate."

"Your point?" He arched an eyebrow at her. "Did you think that meant I would not honor my oath to be faithful to my wife?"

"I… well… hum; truth be told, I had forgotten about them." She pointed at Zach next. "Give him to me, then."

Hell's Dodo

"No."

"What do you mean, 'no'? I command it!"

"I mean no. Giving you any consort was not part of our agreement." Viktor gave her a cold stare. "No woman commands me, nor does any man."

"This isn't right!"

"I agree. It is not right. I have honored my part of the agreement and brought you the items you requested. You, however, have yet to fulfill your part of the bargain."

"But, the blood of the Dragon's Daughter should have given me sway over all vampires."

Belladonna finally spoke. "Did you think that Carpathia was the only one?" She slid her shirt off her shoulder and revealed her brand.

"You aren't a vampire."

"No. I am a siren. More importantly, my sire is Theonikos, the Great Sea Dragon."

Clarissa's eyes shone with renewed hope and ambition. "Power over the sea folk is almost as good. Command your thrall to give me what I want."

"What thrall?"

Viktor chuckled. "Zeke said you were too ambitious for your own good. Belladonna belongs to me, not the other way around."

"She belongs to me now. My spell ensured that."

"No it didn't," the siren smiled. "How can you forget that your spell gives the power to the source of the blood?"

The implication sank in quickly. "What have I done?"

Chapter 41

The siren stepped close to the Sister of Power. "You have gotten very lucky. I am not obsessed with power, save for my power over my prey. You almost enslaved yourself to one of the oldest and most powerful vampires I have ever encountered. The disruption of the order of things that would have caused would have far outweighed any change brought about by the One."

"Now, as my captain pointed out, he has fulfilled his part of the bargain. It is time you fulfilled yours."

Clarissa sighed. "Very well."

Without further warning, she shed the cloak of feathers. She stood, nude and petite, before the pirates for a few moments before she transformed into a dull green hummingbird.

The tiny bird flitted about in a sort of aerial dance. Finally, it lit on the trestle table in a small divot. It seemed to spasm for about a minute then launched back into flight.

A tiny egg lay in the divot.

Clarissa returned to her human form. None of the men moved to pick up her cloak. Some instinct told them it was a trap of some sort.

Viktor sensed a strong flux in her magic. He knew not to make contact with her until the transaction was complete. However, there was the matter of making the transition. None of the crewmen he'd brought with him was magically null.

"Mr. Brumble, return to the ship and send Mr. Jon."

"Aye, Captain."

Jon-Jon arrived a bit winded. "Got here as fast as I could, Cap'n."

"You did well, Mr. Jon." Viktor slipped one of the two silver chains he always wore over his head. It suspended a small, capped silver vial. The other chain held a milky white crystal. He handed the chain and vial to his second mate.

Jon-Jon knew this routine. This wasn't the first time he'd acted as go-between for his captain and one of the Sisters of Power.

He took the vial and carried it to Clarissa. Without a word, she took and opened it. She picked up the egg she'd laid and deftly cracked it on the rim of the vial's mouth. Once it drained into the container, she crushed the shell between her fingers and sprinkled that in, as well.

She capped the vial just as a flash of light emanated from it and handed it back to the tall pirate.

As Viktor took the vial and slipped the chain back on, he asked, "Aren't you going to ask me to give Jon-Jon to you as a consort?"

"He is too large for me."

Hell's Dodo

Jon-Jon put his hand to his chest in mock wounded pride. "You should give me a try, lass. You might be able to handle more of me than you think."

"So you finally admit your shortcomings," Grimm teased.

Jon-Jon made a rude gesture.

"Enough, both of you," Vik laughed. "I'm sorry I got you started."

A vaguely familiar scent made itself known. He glanced at the siren, but she seemed calm, even bored by the masculine banter. He then looked at the Sister and found the source.

Clarissa seemed visibly agitated. He also noticed that she had not put her cloak back on.

"Your pardon, Clarissa; I cannot help but notice your distress and need. I fear you have acquired Belladonna's lustful appetites. I may have a solution to your dilemma."

She turned wary but hungry eyes to him. He held up his hands and took a step back.

"Not me, nor any of my men." He shook his head. "I have someone of yours that I borrowed for a time."

"Nathan Trundle," she said.

"Aye; I am going to miss his cooking, but it is a sacrifice I am willing to make."

His face didn't register that the siren jabbed him through their bond. *Of course you are. You made sure at least three of the younger crew members apprenticed to him once you saw how prone he was to seasickness."*

"She doesn't need to know that, pet."

"I have no intention of telling her. I just don't understand why you are being so generous to her."

"You already pointed it out, pet. Trundle isn't suited to life at sea."

Trundle arrived on the scene in much the same state as Jon-Jon had. He stopped short and gaped at the scene before him.

Without a word, he scooped up the feathered cloak and wrapped it around Clarissa.

"It is cold out here, my dear, and these are very dangerous men!"

Viktor bowed to the Sister. "I fully release him from my thrall back to you, Clarissa. Now, we have business elsewhere."

She barely acknowledged him with a slight nod. Her attention focused on the man before her. She felt it was time to experiment with the new magic gained from the siren.

The pirates headed back toward their ship. Viktor did spare a glance back out of curiosity. He saw that the pair had cleared the table and Trundle had begun to shed his clothes.

"Didn't take her long to get the hang of that," he commented.

"Of course not," Belle replied. "Every woman has the instinct for it."

"Let's find the next Sister.

Hell's Dodo

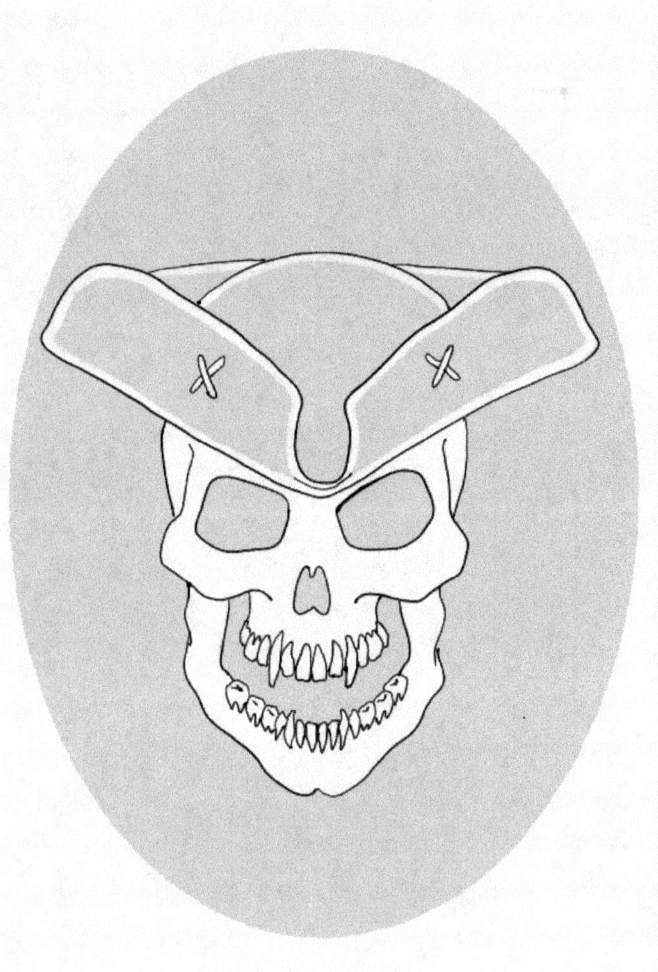

Here Be Spoilers

Blood Curse

After being shipwrecked by a British Navy ship and a killer hurricane, Bloody Vik Brandee and the survivors of his crew make shore in the fishing village of Terra Beau on the north coast of Hispañola. While waiting for a suitable ship to steal, he kills a local boy over a tavern wench, incurring the wrath of Mamaan Juma.

Juma sends her zombies to fetch the pirate. She curses him to become a living vampire. The tavern wench, Carmella, becomes his first victim.

Vik returns to his home port, Savannah, and learns from his foster mother Celie, aka the Thunderbolt Witch, just what has happened to him and how to break the curse before it destroys him. While there, Jim Rigger, his first mate, becomes his second victim. Celie resurrects Jim as a black cat which can take the form of a raven.

Celie sets Vik to find the seven Sisters of Power and sends hum to Hell's Breath Island to Uncle Zeke, an ancient wizard of sorts. Zeke sends the siren/sea witch Belladonna with him to locate the Sisters using her visions.

She pinpoints Madre Dorada on the Isle of Youth. En route, Vik learns an old friend, Hezekiah Grimm aka the Grimm Reaper, has been taken by pirate hunters in Havana. He detours to rescue Grimm despite warnings from Zeke and Belladonna not to stray from his course.

Manages to find and rescue Grimm but arrives at the Isle of Youth only to find Dorada fled. With the aid of Paella, a local girl, he manages to track the Sister down and brokers a deal with her: one of her golden tears in exchange for an opal pendant called the Mermaid's Tear.

After some misunderstanding of what the Tear actually is, he finds it, helps Dorada regain her magic, and makes the exchange.

Demon Bayou

Viktor tracks the next Sister, Granny Glory, to the bayous north of New Orleans. When he finds her, she sets him to capture the demon Tulimanchulo, who possesses the body of a white alligator. He finds and captures the beast with a magic cast-net but is wounded in the process.

Glory slaughters the demon gator, collects its blood in a cauldron, and has Viktor remove all its teeth. She throws them in the blood and pulls them out as a necklace. Viktor must take it to Zeke. She warns him not to wear it at any time. She then has him toss her into the boiling blood. The hag emerges as a beautiful woman.

On Hell's Breath, Zeke burns the alligator teeth, releasing the demon's spirit. He fishes out a coal from his fire and puts it in a conch shell for Vik to return it to Glory with instructions no one else is to touch it and not to let it extinguish.

Hell's Dodo

Vik returns to New Orleans and discovers a storm has altered the paths through the bayous.

While waiting for a guide back to Glory, he encounters true vampires for the first time. He ends up tangled in the local vampire politics because of attacks on two of his favorite brothels, one by agents of the Church, and the other by vampires curious about him. To get out of this predicament, he must kidnap the daughter of the Lord Mayor and make her vampire. This gives Jeorge, king of the local vampires, a means to spy on him.

On his final return to Glory, Belladonna begins to grow weak as the Sister's black water magic wars with the siren's salt water magic. She falls unconscious into the swamp but does not change into her true form. Vik must remove the coal and place it in his mouth to protect it before he can dive in after Belladonna. He knows she'll drown if she remains in human form. When he surfaces with her, the boat with his other companions is no longer in the area. He climbs out onto a hammock of land and Glory appears to him. He passes the coal to her via a kiss, returning the powers the demon stole from her ages earlier. She adds her spit to the golden tear of Dorada in the silver vial Vik carries for that purpose.

He returns Belladonna to the sea and sacrifices several of his crew to her appetite to restore her. He then abducts a couple of unwary sailors from port to swap for Grimm and Jon-Jon, rescuing them from Glory's amorous clutches, as he's learned she now has the nature of a succubus.

Tamara A. Lowery
Silent Fathoms

The search for the third Sister, Tia Rosalia, takes Viktor to Mexico. He lands on the Gulf coast and must travel over the central mountains to the Pacific coast to reach her. She first tries to deceive and enslave him. Her spell manages to control his crewmen traveling with him, but his power proves stronger at the cost of one pirate's life. The Elder's Stone proves to her he is the One, and she gives him the quest of procuring Devil's Hoof, a key ingredient in her spells. She deliberately doesn't tell him where to look or what it actually is.

He follows rumors of a cave in the mountains where the Devil is said to live. Instead, he finds an old brujo (male witch) who was once Rosalia's lover. He tells him Devil's Hoof is an extremely hot pepper said to cause hallucinations with its spiciness. The pirates return to the ship. Navigator Zach Brumble tells Vik about such a pepper his father once dabbled in trading found in the northern part of the Bay of Bengal.

When he tries to contact Belladonna to sing up favorable winds to speed the voyage halfway around the world, he cannot reach her or even sense her presence. Unbeknownst to him, Zeke and Hell's Breath Island have sent her to hunt down the mermaid Alyssa, whom Viktor impregnated while seeking for the Mermaid's Tear. He'd also fed on the creature, and she began to turn while still alive. Belle must kill the mermaid but return the child to the island and Zeke's care. To prevent Viktor's interference, Zeke blocks them from any mental contact until her task is done.

Hell's Dodo

The siren is finally able to rejoin Viktor as the ship is caught in the doldrums near the middle of the Indian Ocean. They make their way to a Bengali village near the Sundarbans, a salt swamp jungle. After warnings from a local elder not to anger the jungle goddess, Bonobibi, or the tiger god, Daskin Rey, they enter the swamps to find the pepper (known locally as the naga pepper). They must also harvest honey to safely transport the peppers in. One of their guides harvests more honey than they need, hoping to profit enough to laze away the wet season. This leads to an encounter with the local deities and the man's death.

With Devil's Hoof acquired, Viktor opts to cross the Pacific directly to Rosalia's home port.

Once back in Mexico, she tries her best to enslave him using fresh ingredients for her spell. He proves his power is stronger than hers, and she begrudgingly agrees to give him the portion of her magic he requires for his quest to break his curse.

After he returns to his ship, Hell's Breath manifests. Zeke introduces him to his son by Alyssa and orders him to get the child off the island. When the island vanishes again, Viktor finds the ship has been transported back to the Caribbean.

Black Venom

Viktor and his crew find themselves deposited close to Havana by the disappearance of Hell's Breath Island. Grateful for not having to sail around South America, they make for New Orleans. He must find a home and guardian for his merchild son, Robert, and wants to see if Gloribeau will take the boy on.

Glory agrees in exchange for Viktor in her bed for one night. The sheer magnitude of magic released by their climax alerts Jeorge, king of the New Orlean vampires, to the child's presence. He also becomes aware of Viktor's increasing powers, growing far faster than those of a truly undead vampire.

Jeorge "summons" Viktor to join him in a hunt. Because he needs to arrange protection of his son from the vampires, he agrees. They attend a reception at the Lord Mayor's for the new governor. Jeorge uses it as a fishing expedition to learn more about the boy and to put the new governor in his pocket.

Samantha Brumble and Captain Bainbridge arrive at the Islas de los Roques and encounter Madre Dorada. They learn that the lead which led them there is nearly three years old but gain valuable information about the nature of what Viktor now is and who sails with him.

After dealing with a small British blockade of the entrance to Lake Pontchartrain, Viktor heads for the Florida Strait. Belladonna rejoins the ship there and is given a victim to induce one of her visions to locate the next Sister of Power. Mere Venoma Noir directs a psychic attack back at the siren, revealing her power over all things venomous, even over Belladonna.

Jeorge's curiosity gets the better of him, and he sends a couple of his vampires to investigate

Viktor's son. Gloribeau's dealing with this invasion of her bayou costs him both his minions and convinces him to leave it alone.

As the pirates near Venoma's territory, she uses her power to attack through the siren. Only the Elder's Stone and Viktor's blood can override the sister's magic. After landfall, she actively tries to kill him and the crew remaining aboard the *Incubus* with hoards of venomous creatures. Once he succeeds in reaching her, she relents and instructs him to retrieve an amulet imbued with her power which was stolen by a notorious slave trader, Quentin LaForte. They make for the west coast of Africa to search for him.

Commodore Critchfield encounters Lady Carpathia and Captain Wormsloe when they return Commander Turlington to the HMS Quicksilver. He has a dalliance with the vampire, never realizing what she truly is. They exchange information about Viktor, and she directs him to sail to Amherst in search of a vampire expert and hunter.

Venoma warns LaForte in a dream that Viktor is hunting him. He doesn't trust the old witch, but makes plans to protect himself nonetheless, especially since she alerted him to the possibility of using Belladonna against Viktor.

Close to the Azores, Viktor pirates a pirate which just took a packet ship. In a bid to thwart Viktor getting ransom for a promised bride taken prisoner, the other pirate kills the woman he believes to be her. The victim was actually the handmaid who'd changed places with her. The true bride, Brianna Belmont, stabs the pirate at the same time Viktor does. Grimm claims her as his share of the spoils and lets her know her intended husband was actually a pimp who specialized in well-bred virgins.

Samantha and Bainbridge arrive in Havana looking for fresher news of Viktor and Grimm. At the Crescent Inn, Luz passes a message to Sam from her brother Zach to abandon the hunt for her own safety. They learned the likely next port Viktor went to was New Orleans.

Lady Carpathia and Captain Wormsloe follow an old lead to the slaver, Delacroix. She learns about Samantha's hunt but nothing else of value. She kills the slaver and a priest looking to buy some new altar boys. The remaining children there, she takes for blood stock.

Viktor gets a lead on LaForte in Tenerife which heads him to Abidjan. They arrive in port and find the man in the process of exchanging a trader's hobbles for his own on a young female slave. She gets loose and provides enough distraction for LaForte to use his black magic to teleport away. They take the woman back to the *Incubus*.

Viktor learns she is called Nahila, and she is LaForte's daughter. She agrees to lead him to the slaver in exchange for her freedom. She leads them to a nearby river. As Viktor takes a small group upriver, LaForte teleports back to his shore camp. He uses the power of Venoma's amulet to ensnare Belladonna and sends her to kill the crew still on the ship.

Grimm's portion of the Elder's magic frees her from the spell. They stage the ship for the

Hell's Dodo

slaver and his crew. Viktor gets word from the siren and flies back to the ship. LaForte falls for the trap. Nahila is brought back and kept captive for her part in helping her father try to trap Viktor.

Viktor nearly kills Grimm for keeping the Elder's magic a secret. Brianna's intervention saves the 1st mate.

They learn Nahila serves as a familiar for her father's black magic when the ship is mired midway across the Atlantic in a mass of jellyfish. Viktor has her drugged, and Belladonna creates a current to clear the obstacle and speed them back to South America.

Venoma requires Viktor and LaForte to fight to the death. Only the slaver's death can release the amulet's magic back to her. When Viktor is victorious but the magic doesn't return, they tell her Nahila holds part of it. She makes the dead man's blood flow onto the slave and turns her into a scorpion. She gives Viktor a drop of the venom as her portion of magic.

The scorpion stings itself, turns back into Nahila, and dies, leaving Venoma forever magically crippled. For good measure and a bit of payback, Belladonna calls a lightning bolt and fuses the sand around Venoma's feet into glass, trapping the witch.

Tamara A. Lowery

About the Author

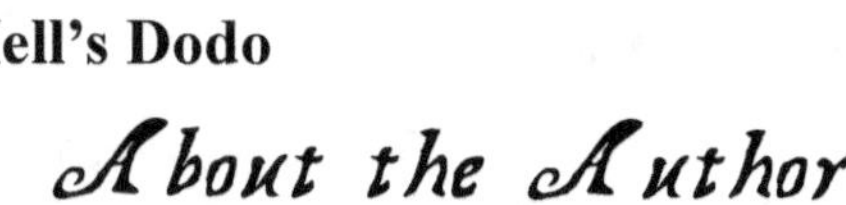

Tamara A. Lowery, who once considered herself close to becoming a Crazy Cat Lady is now down to three cats. She lives with them and her husband in Tennessee and builds cars to pay the bills when not writing. She's been writing since the early 1980s but only published since 2011.

In addition to the Waves of Darkness series, she is the author of a steampunk episodic serial, The Adventures of Pigg & Woolfe.

She hopes to release a short story collection sometime in the near future, as well.

Website: talowery.wordpress.com

Facebook: facebook.com/Waves.of.Darkness

Instagram: Instagram.com/talowery_author

Plurk: plurk.com/Viksbelle

Smashwords author Page: smashwords.com/profile/view/Viksbelle

YouTube: youtube.com/user/Viksbelle

Waves of Darkness

Tamara A. Lowery

Sisters of Power arc

Blood Curse

Demon Bayou

Silent Fathoms

Black Venom

Hell's Dodo

The Daedalus Enigma *May 2024*

Maelstrom of Fate *November 2024*

Daughters of the Dragon arc

Hunting the Dragon *May 2025*

The Adventures of Pigg & Woolfe

Season 1

The Girl Who Fell from the Sky (S.1 omnibus)

Episodes

A Chance Encounter

The Truce

In the Woolfe's Den

Chase the Lightning

Peril in the Philippines

Rendezvous in Hong Kong

Double Jeopardy

Chance and Fortune

Hell's Dodo

The Italian Connection Redux *September 2024*

Peace Talks *October 2024*

Forces Reunited *November 2024*

The Canary's Eye Conundrum *December 2024*

***Season 5** (TBD)*

Tamara A. Lowery